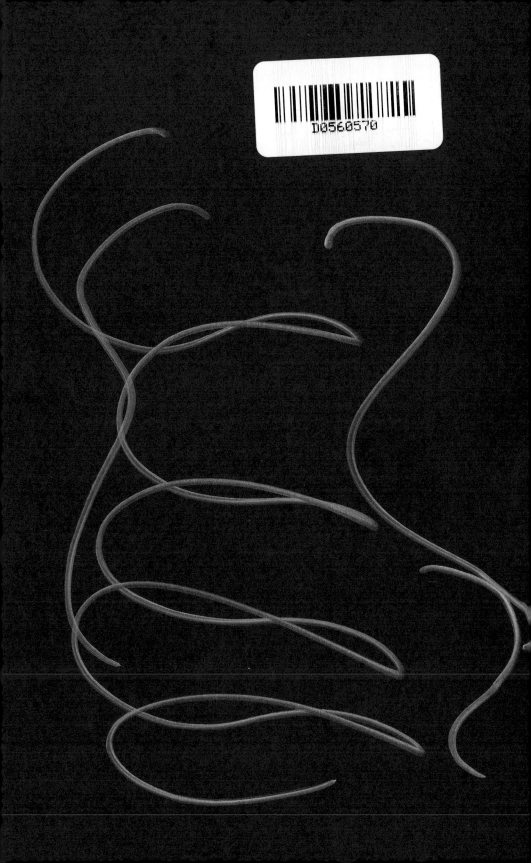

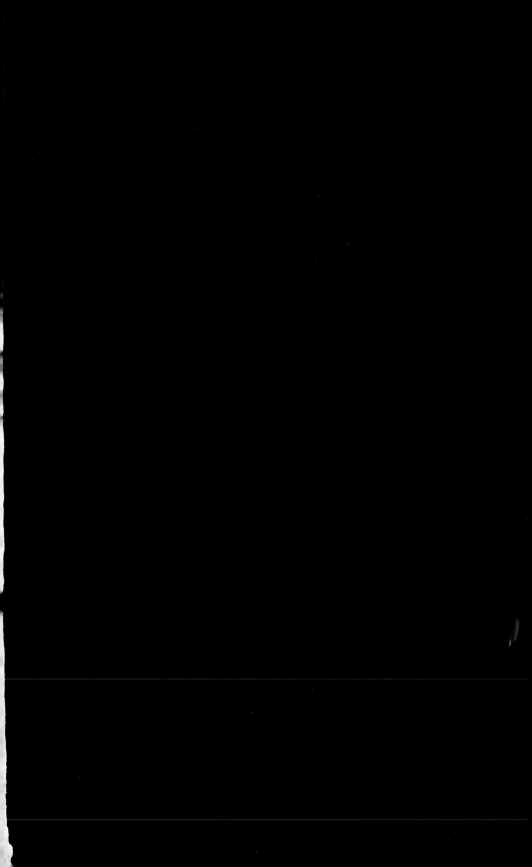

THE NIGHTCRAWLERS

THE BOY WHO CRIED WOLF

Writer: Marco Lopez
Artist/Cover: Rachel Distler
Colorist: Francesco Montalbano
Letterer: DC HopkinS

ABLAZE

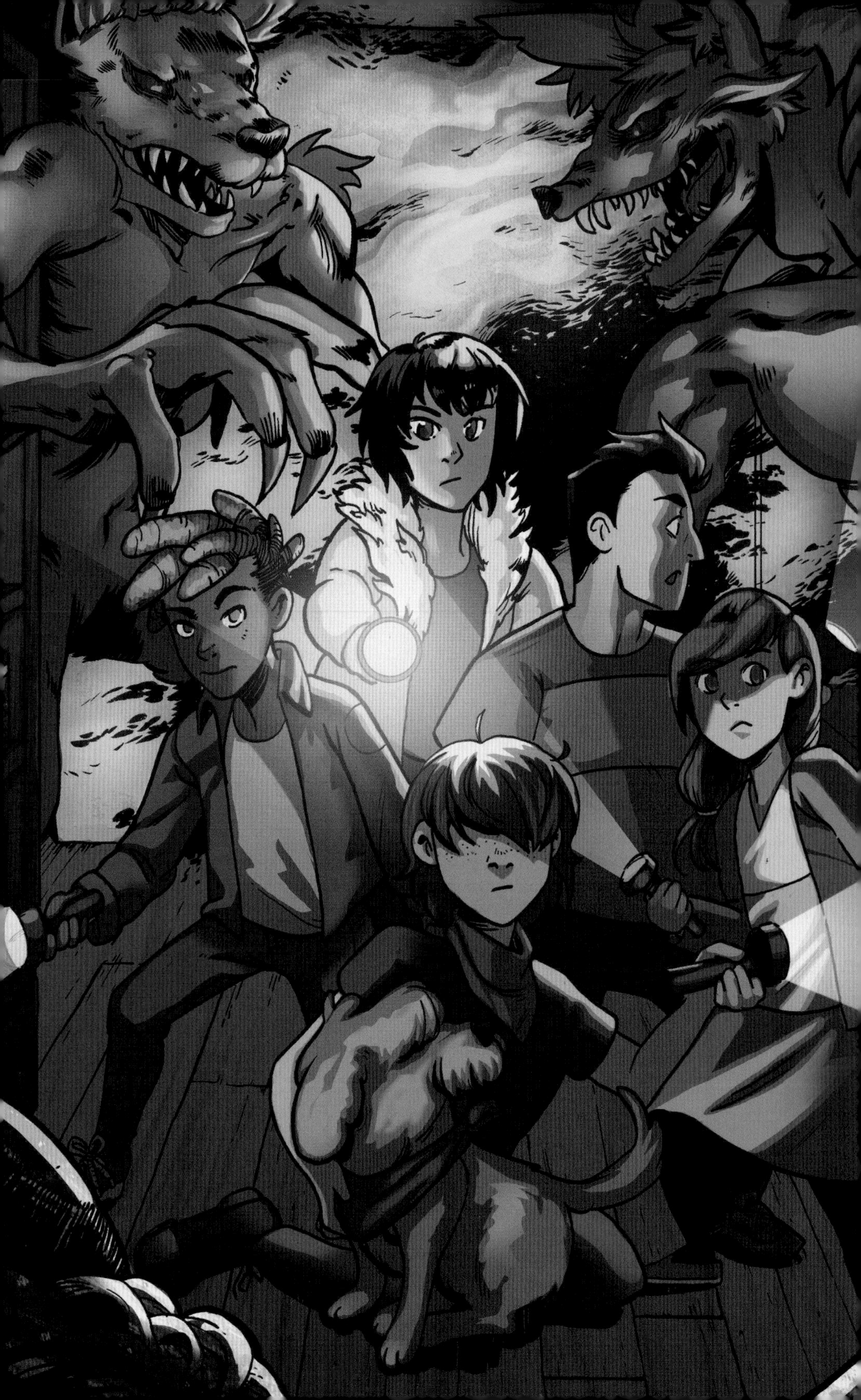

CONTENTS

Chapter One: Your Parents Were Replaced by WHAT?!.................9

Chapter Two: The Past Will Come Back to Haunt You.................32

Chapter Three: Truth Can Be a Painful Reminder.................55

Chapter Four: The Nightcrawlers to the Rescue!.................78

Biographies.................103

Sketches.................108

Dedications

To Molly, the newest Nightcrawler. To Owen, never stop believing you can have it all. And to Shannon, who believes I can do anything.

To my Mom for giving me my love of horror and to my Dad for all the great action films we watched together. You two never let me stop being a nerd.

- Marco

For H, G, and J, who I hope keeps a love of art.
For Alexis, who's kept the dream of a book alive.
And for the Poos, the cat who kept me going while I learned how to draw.

- Rachel

Introduction

Oh, the conundrum. What to write about for this Nightcrawlers introduction? I guess you could say it's crazy that we even got to this point. You always hope that every idea you come up with makes it to publication, but the reality is that of everything you dream up, maybe ten percent makes it out into the world. I guess that's one of the reasons that makes The Nightcrawlers so special.

Now, the second reason this book is special: I'm an eighties kid. I was born in November of 1980, and as a child, I enjoyed one of the best decades of film, television, and music. From movies like my favorite of all time, E.T., to Monster Squad, Little Monsters, Goonies, and the amazing early flicks of Don Bluth. The stories weren't talking down to children. They let kids everywhere know the world can be scary. But when you have family and friends that love you, anything can be accomplished.

Even during the difficult times that life may sometimes bring. And that's probably where the creative DNA of The Nightcrawlers came from: wanting to give the children of the 21st century their own classic stories like I had growing up that had adventure, thrills, excitement, and true friendship, something that they could call their own.

There's a history with The Nightcrawlers and a future, and I hope we get the chance to tell you both for as long as we can or until you get tired of us. And who knows, maybe one day, like I have with my kids with the movies I love, maybe all you fellow Nightcrawlers, when you're adults, will share your love of The Nightcrawlers with your kids.

Just don't ever let go of your inner child. It's important to keep that with you. It helps you be aware of those supernatural monsters outside the corner of your eye that go bump in the night. Or if you got a pair of those cool glasses that William has. Then you will always be aware of the dark.

What am I talking about? You'll find out soon enough. ENJOY!

-Marco Lopez

Chapter One
Your Parents
Were Replaced by
WHAT?!

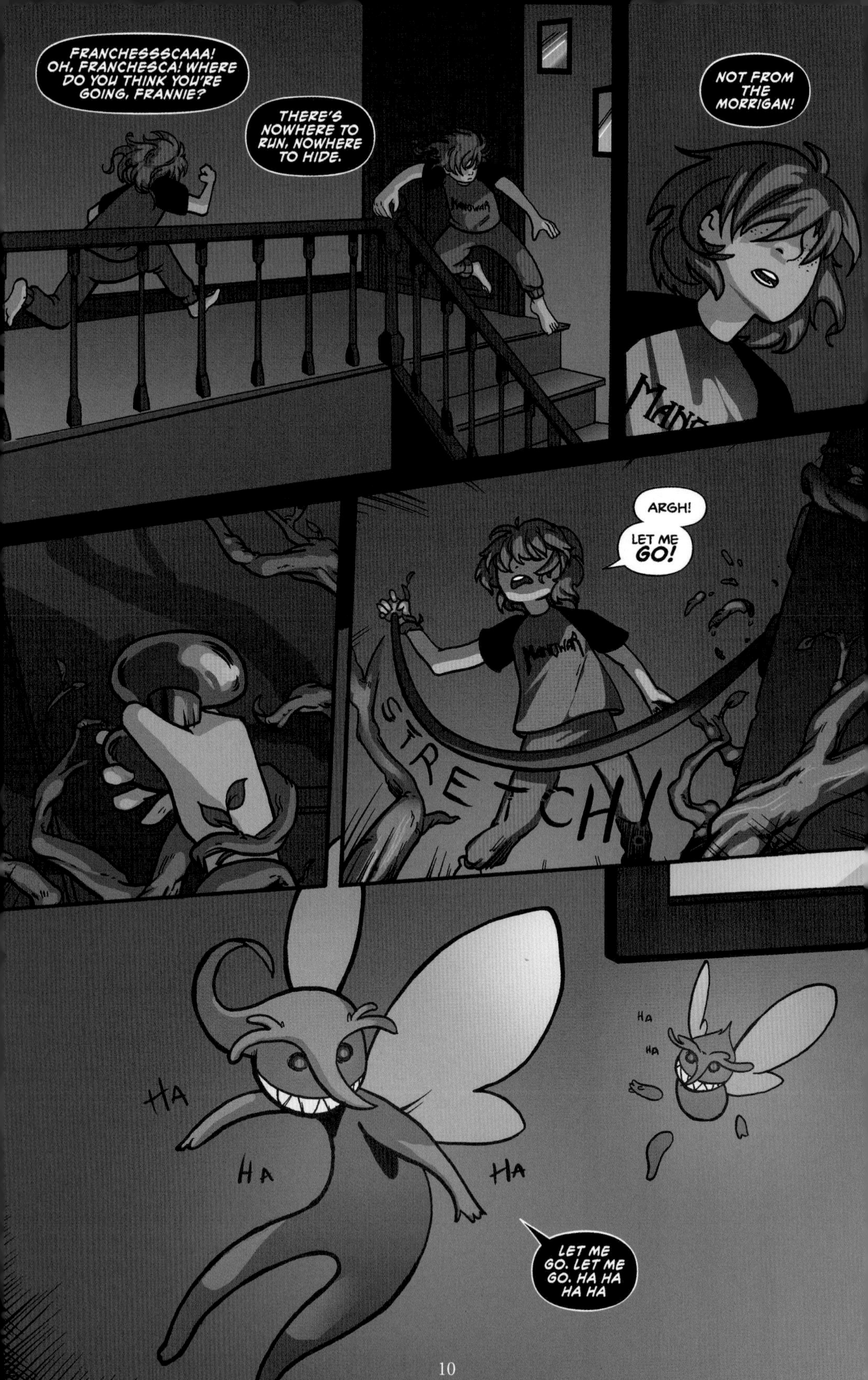
FRANCHESSSCAAA! OH, FRANCHESCA! WHERE DO YOU THINK YOU'RE GOING, FRANNIE?
THERE'S NOWHERE TO RUN, NOWHERE TO HIDE.
MANOWAR
NOT FROM THE MORRIGAN!
ARGH!
LET ME GO!
MANOWAR
STRETCH
HA
HA
HA
HA
HA
LET ME GO. LET ME GO. HA HA HA HA

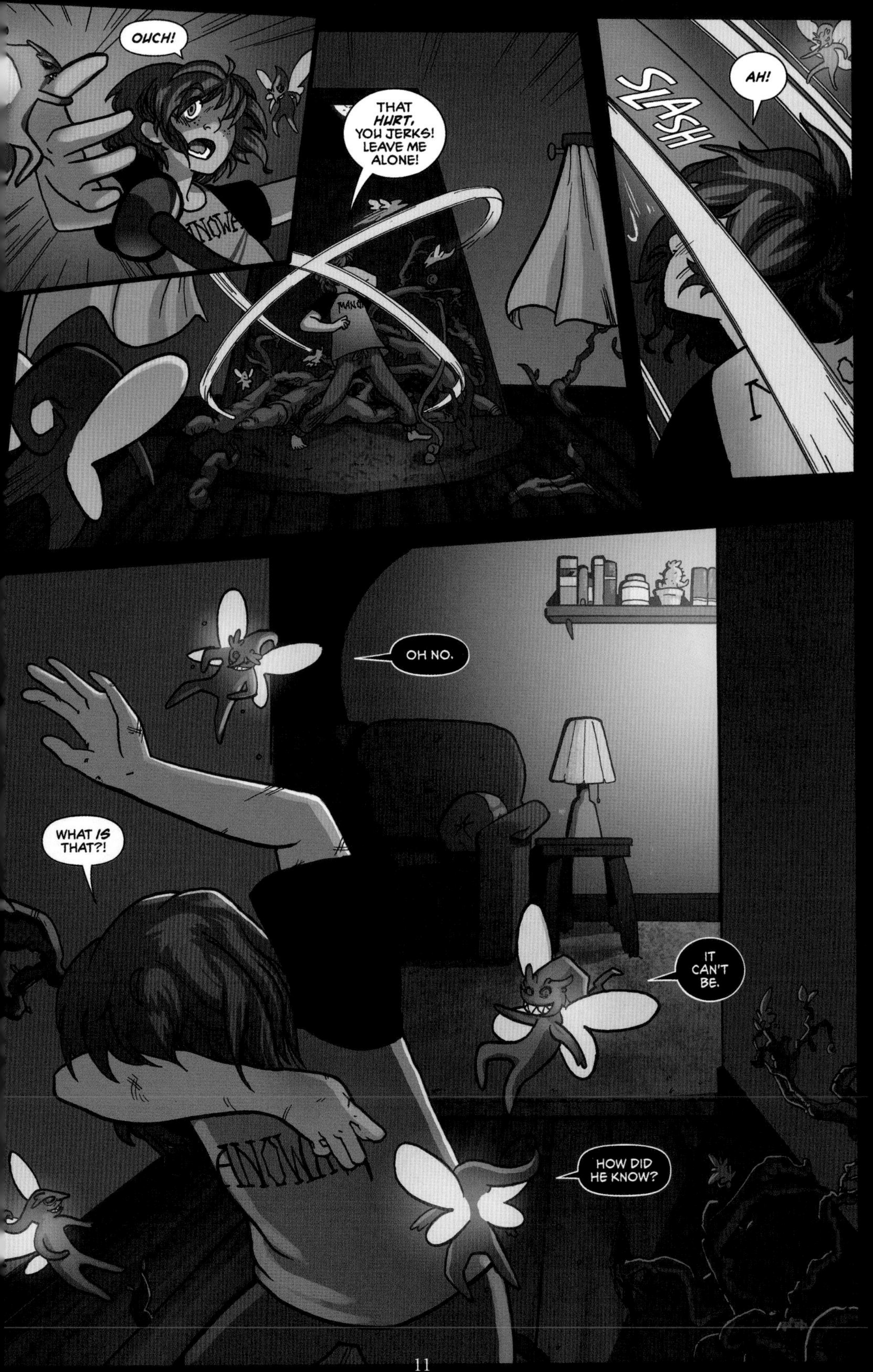
OUCH!
THAT HURT, YOU JERKS! LEAVE ME ALONE!
SLASH
AH!
OH NO.
WHAT IS THAT?!
IT CAN'T BE.
HOW DID HE KNOW?

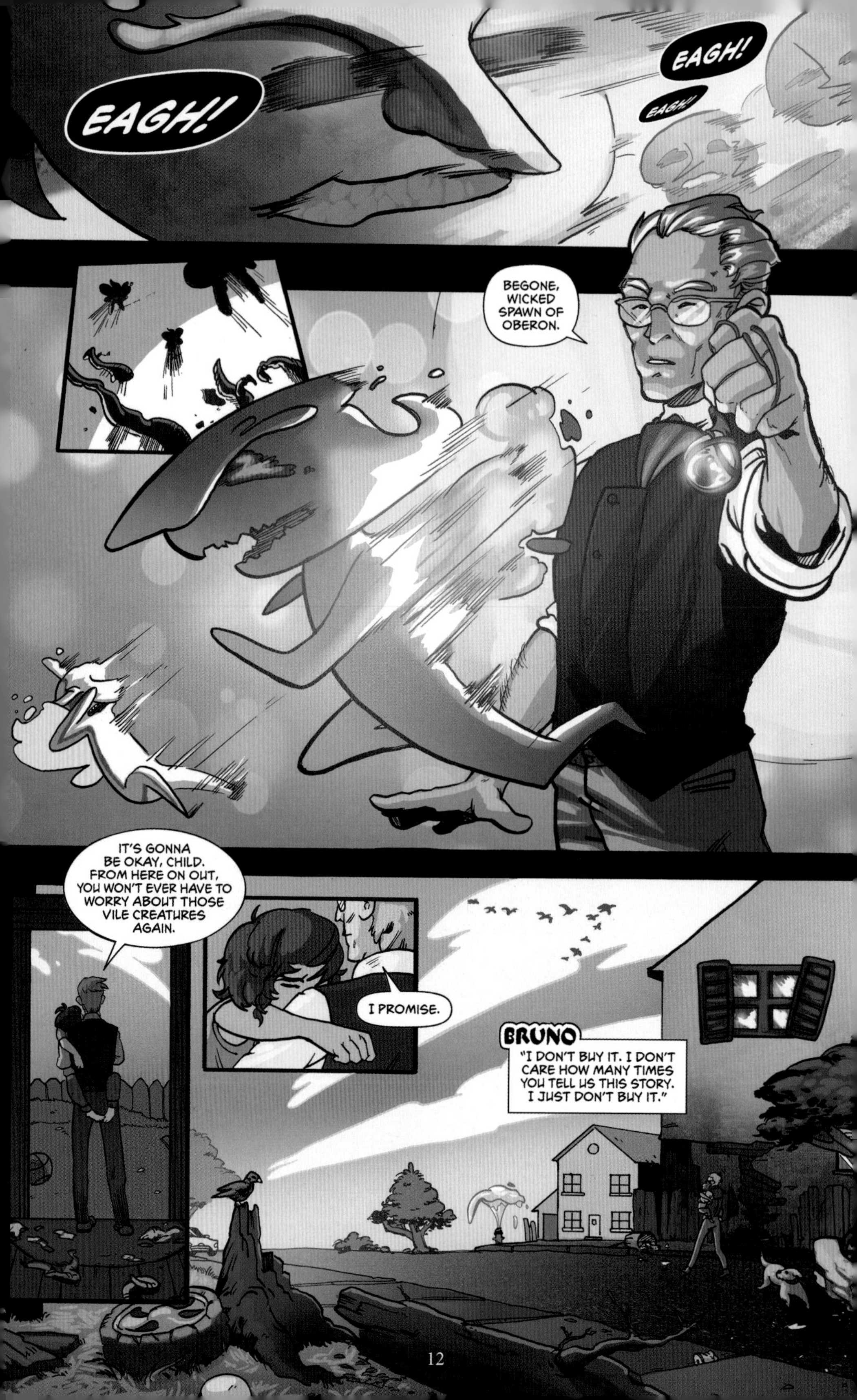
EAGH!
EAGH!
EAGH!
BEGONE, WICKED SPAWN OF OBERON.
IT'S GONNA BE OKAY, CHILD. FROM HERE ON OUT, YOU WON'T EVER HAVE TO WORRY ABOUT THOSE VILE CREATURES AGAIN.
I PROMISE.
BRUNO
"I DON'T BUY IT. I DON'T CARE HOW MANY TIMES YOU TELL US THIS STORY. I JUST DON'T BUY IT."

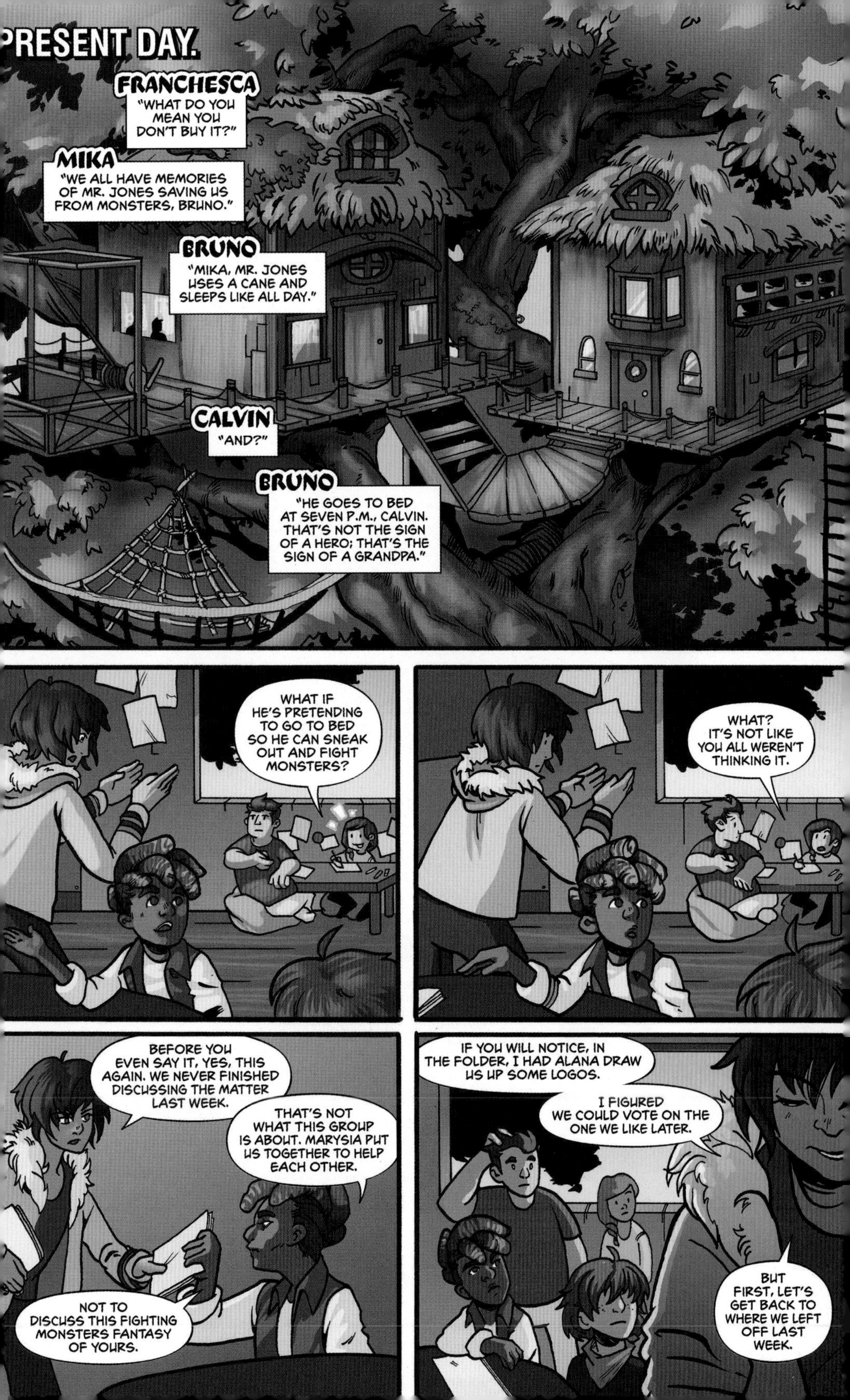
PRESENT DAY.
FRANCHESCA
"WHAT DO YOU MEAN YOU DON'T BUY IT?"
MIKA
"WE ALL HAVE MEMORIES OF MR. JONES SAVING US FROM MONSTERS, BRUNO."
BRUNO
"MIKA, MR. JONES USES A CANE AND SLEEPS LIKE ALL DAY."
CALVIN
"AND?"
BRUNO
"HE GOES TO BED AT SEVEN P.M., CALVIN. THAT'S NOT THE SIGN OF A HERO; THAT'S THE SIGN OF A GRANDPA."
WHAT IF HE'S PRETENDING TO GO TO BED SO HE CAN SNEAK OUT AND FIGHT MONSTERS?
WHAT? IT'S NOT LIKE YOU ALL WEREN'T THINKING IT.
BEFORE YOU EVEN SAY IT, YES, THIS AGAIN. WE NEVER FINISHED DISCUSSING THE MATTER LAST WEEK.
THAT'S NOT WHAT THIS GROUP IS ABOUT. MARYSIA PUT US TOGETHER TO HELP EACH OTHER.
NOT TO DISCUSS THIS FIGHTING MONSTERS FANTASY OF YOURS.
IF YOU WILL NOTICE, IN THE FOLDER, I HAD ALANA DRAW US UP SOME LOGOS.
I FIGURED WE COULD VOTE ON THE ONE WE LIKE LATER.
BUT FIRST, LET'S GET BACK TO WHERE WE LEFT OFF LAST WEEK.

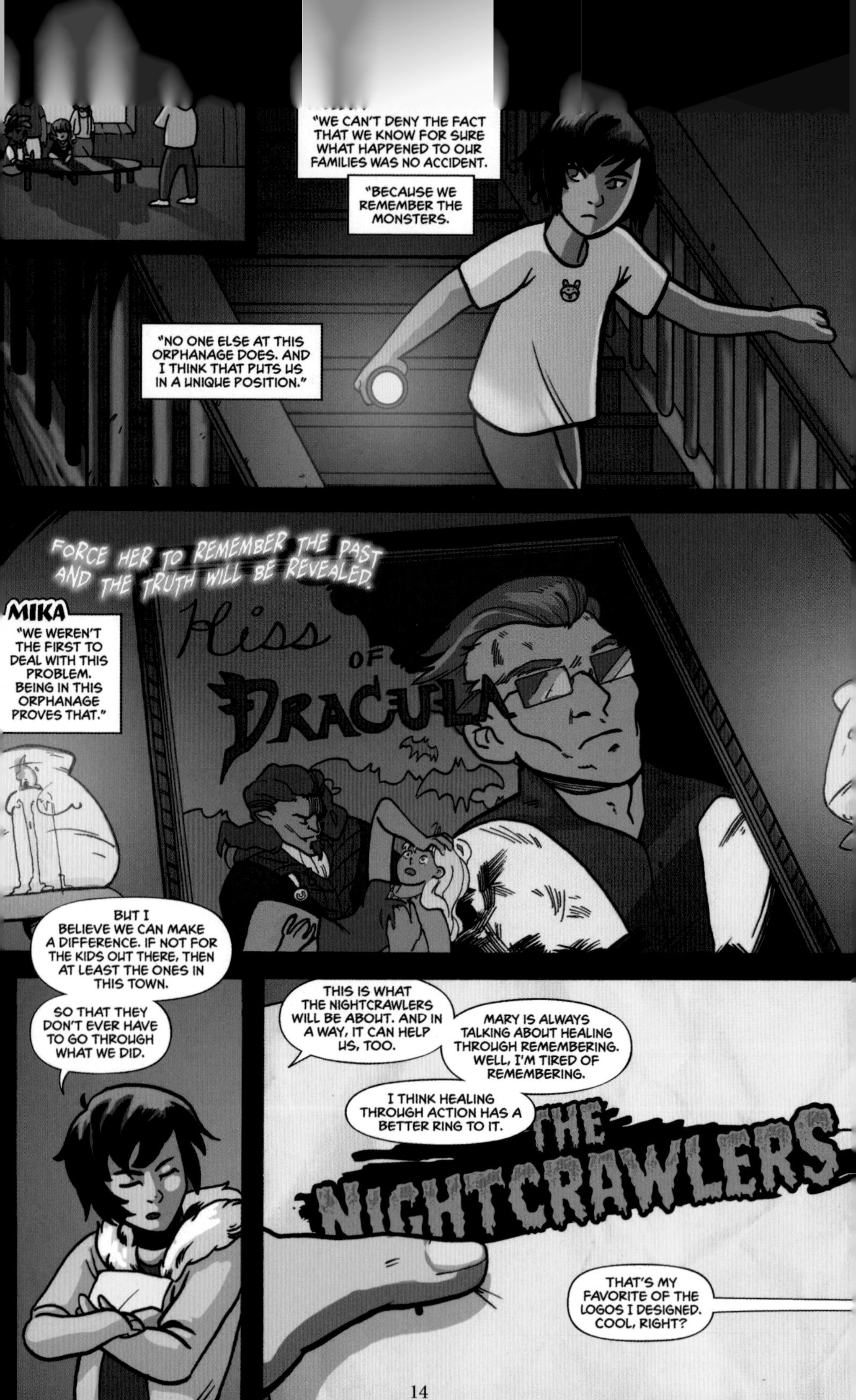
"WE CAN'T DENY THE FACT THAT WE KNOW FOR SURE WHAT HAPPENED TO OUR FAMILIES WAS NO ACCIDENT.
"BECAUSE WE REMEMBER THE MONSTERS.
"NO ONE ELSE AT THIS ORPHANAGE DOES. AND I THINK THAT PUTS US IN A UNIQUE POSITION."
FORCE HER TO REMEMBER THE PAST AND THE TRUTH WILL BE REVEALED!
Kiss OF DRACULA
MIKA
"WE WEREN'T THE FIRST TO DEAL WITH THIS PROBLEM. BEING IN THIS ORPHANAGE PROVES THAT."
BUT I BELIEVE WE CAN MAKE A DIFFERENCE. IF NOT FOR THE KIDS OUT THERE, THEN AT LEAST THE ONES IN THIS TOWN.
SO THAT THEY DON'T EVER HAVE TO GO THROUGH WHAT WE DID.
THIS IS WHAT THE NIGHTCRAWLERS WILL BE ABOUT. AND IN A WAY, IT CAN HELP US, TOO.
MARY IS ALWAYS TALKING ABOUT HEALING THROUGH REMEMBERING. WELL, I'M TIRED OF REMEMBERING.
I THINK HEALING THROUGH ACTION HAS A BETTER RING TO IT.
THE NIGHTCRAWLERS
THAT'S MY FAVORITE OF THE LOGOS I DESIGNED. COOL, RIGHT?

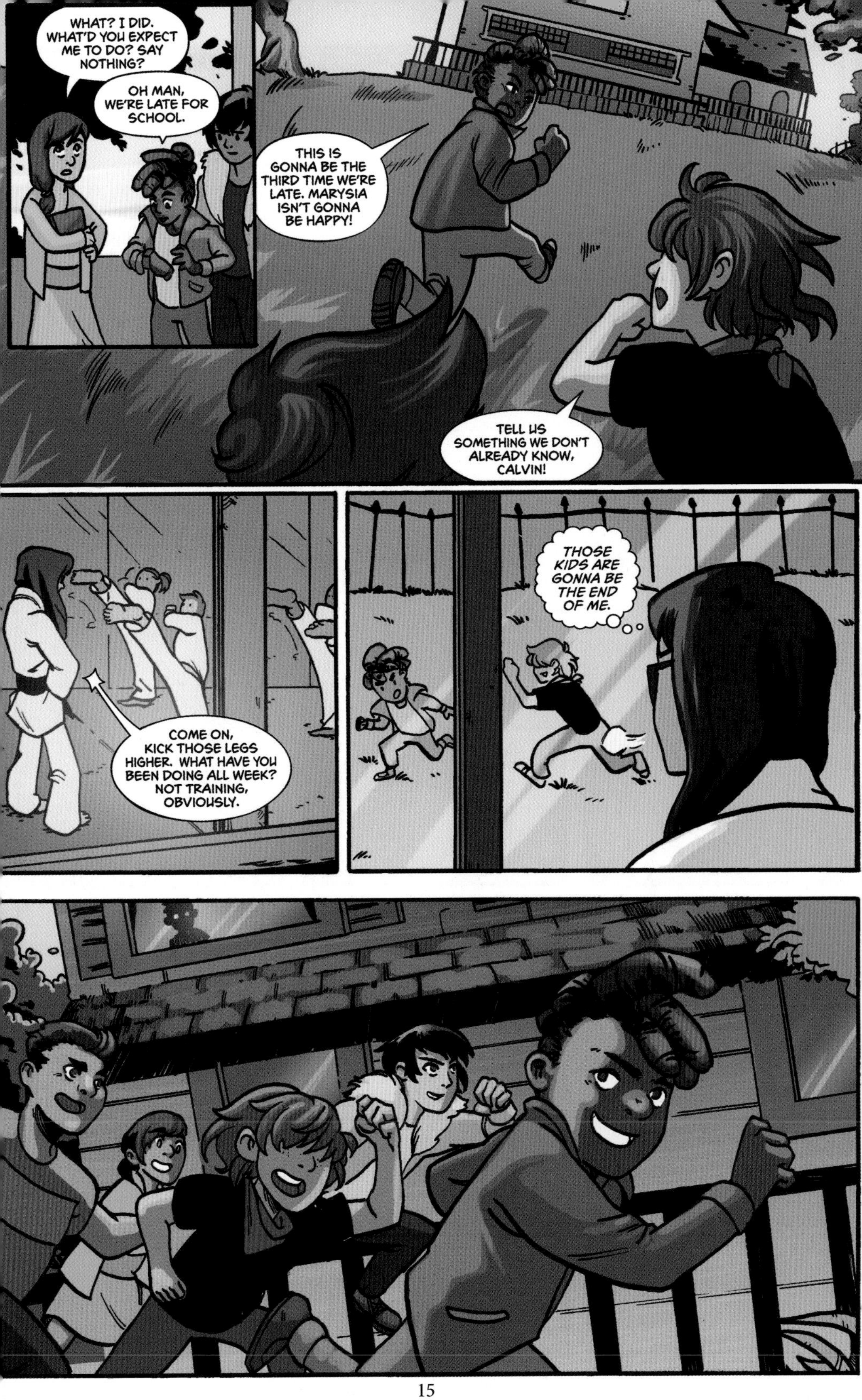
WHAT? I DID. WHAT'D YOU EXPECT ME TO DO? SAY NOTHING?
OH MAN, WE'RE LATE FOR SCHOOL.
THIS IS GONNA BE THE THIRD TIME WE'RE LATE. MARYSIA ISN'T GONNA BE HAPPY!
TELL US SOMETHING WE DON'T ALREADY KNOW, CALVIN!
COME ON, KICK THOSE LEGS HIGHER. WHAT HAVE YOU BEEN DOING ALL WEEK? NOT TRAINING, OBVIOUSLY.
THOSE KIDS ARE GONNA BE THE END OF ME.

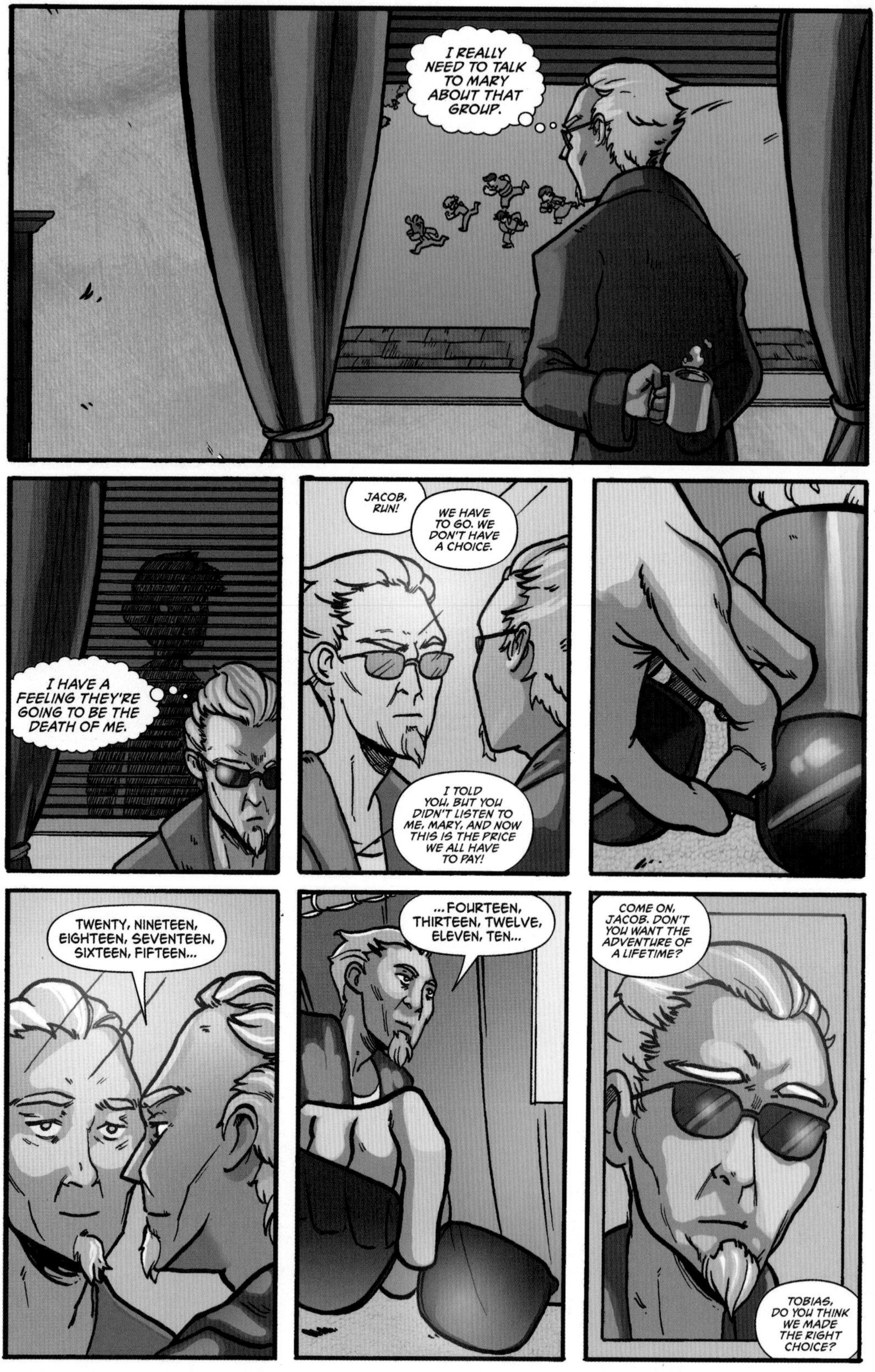
I REALLY NEED TO TALK TO MARY ABOUT THAT GROUP.
I HAVE A FEELING THEY'RE GOING TO BE THE DEATH OF ME.
JACOB, RUN!
WE HAVE TO GO. WE DON'T HAVE A CHOICE.
I TOLD YOU, BUT YOU DIDN'T LISTEN TO ME, MARY, AND NOW THIS IS THE PRICE WE ALL HAVE TO PAY!
TWENTY, NINETEEN, EIGHTEEN, SEVENTEEN, SIXTEEN, FIFTEEN...
...FOURTEEN, THIRTEEN, TWELVE, ELEVEN, TEN...
COME ON, JACOB. DON'T YOU WANT THE ADVENTURE OF A LIFETIME?
TOBIAS, DO YOU THINK WE MADE THE RIGHT CHOICE?

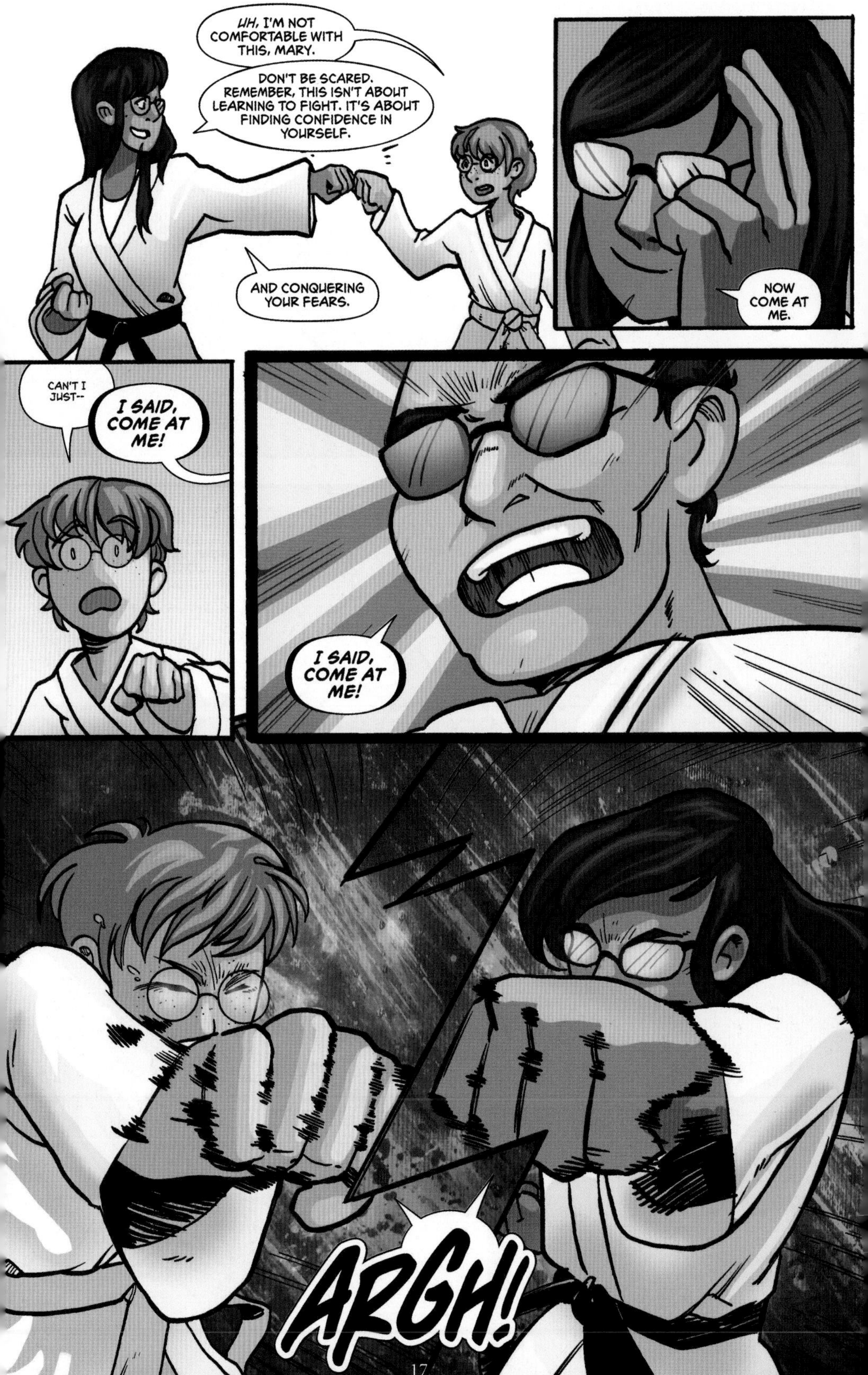
UH, I'M NOT COMFORTABLE WITH THIS, MARY.
DON'T BE SCARED. REMEMBER, THIS ISN'T ABOUT LEARNING TO FIGHT. IT'S ABOUT FINDING CONFIDENCE IN YOURSELF.
AND CONQUERING YOUR FEARS.
NOW COME AT ME.
CAN'T I JUST--
I SAID, COME AT ME!
I SAID, COME AT ME!
ARGH!

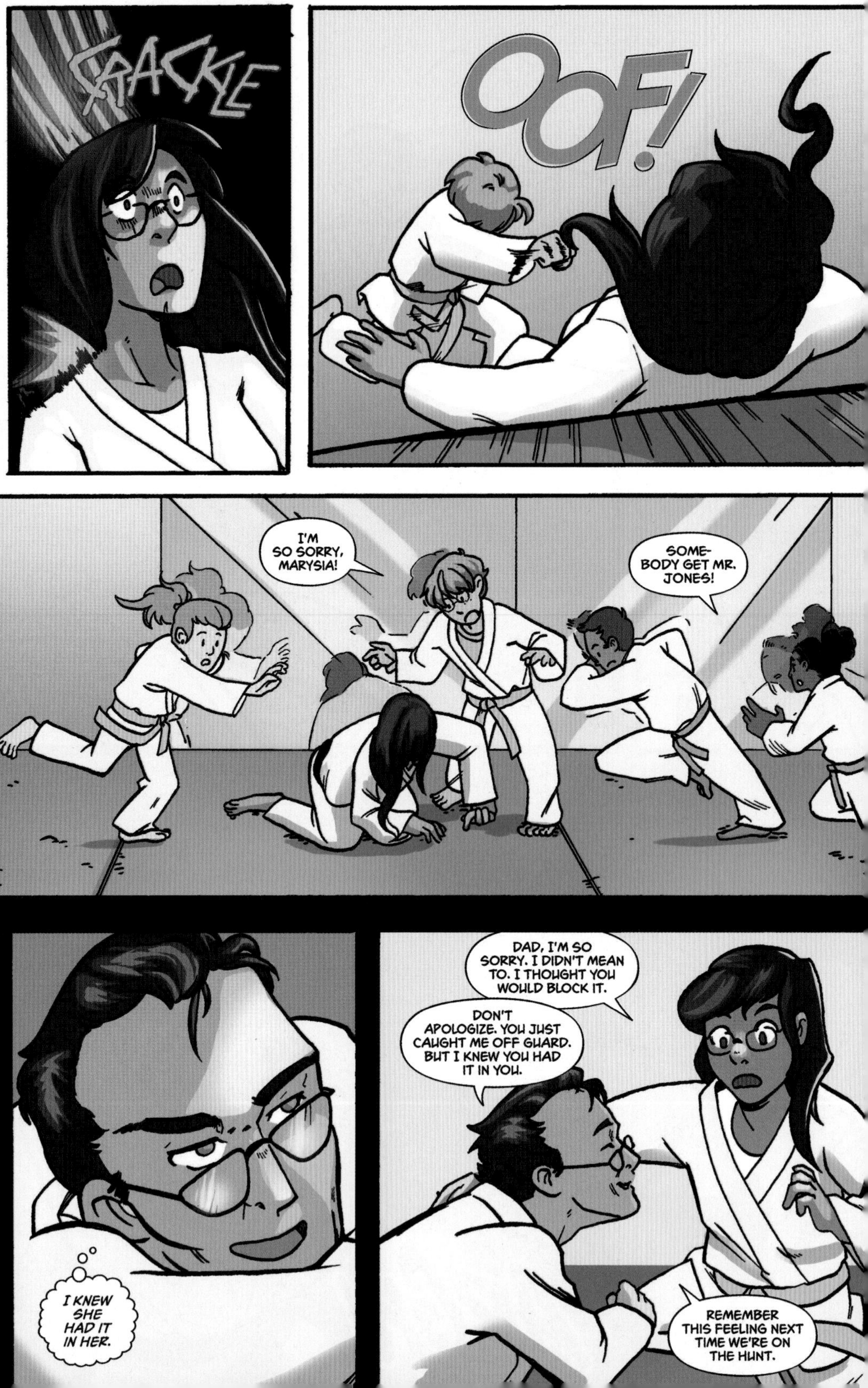
CRACKLE
OOF!
I'M SO SORRY, MARYSIA!
SOME-BODY GET MR. JONES!
I KNEW SHE HAD IT IN HER.
DAD, I'M SO SORRY. I DIDN'T MEAN TO. I THOUGHT YOU WOULD BLOCK IT.
DON'T APOLOGIZE. YOU JUST CAUGHT ME OFF GUARD. BUT I KNEW YOU HAD IT IN YOU.
REMEMBER THIS FEELING NEXT TIME WE'RE ON THE HUNT.

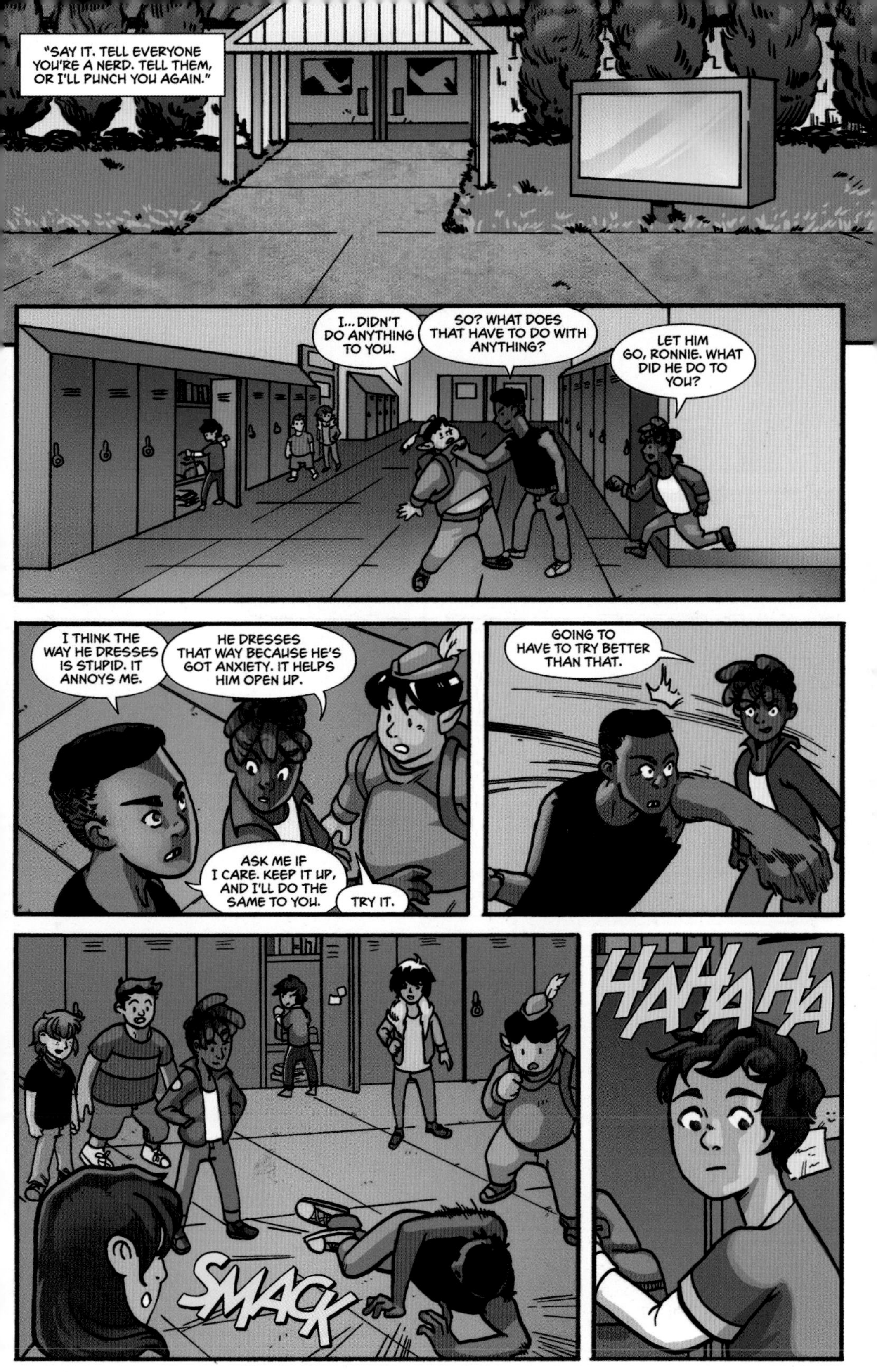
"SAY IT. TELL EVERYONE YOU'RE A NERD. TELL THEM, OR I'LL PUNCH YOU AGAIN."
I... DIDN'T DO ANYTHING TO YOU.
SO? WHAT DOES THAT HAVE TO DO WITH ANYTHING?
LET HIM GO, RONNIE. WHAT DID HE DO TO YOU?
I THINK THE WAY HE DRESSES IS STUPID. IT ANNOYS ME.
HE DRESSES THAT WAY BECAUSE HE'S GOT ANXIETY. IT HELPS HIM OPEN UP.
ASK ME IF I CARE. KEEP IT UP, AND I'LL DO THE SAME TO YOU.
TRY IT.
GOING TO HAVE TO TRY BETTER THAN THAT.
SMACK
HAHAHA

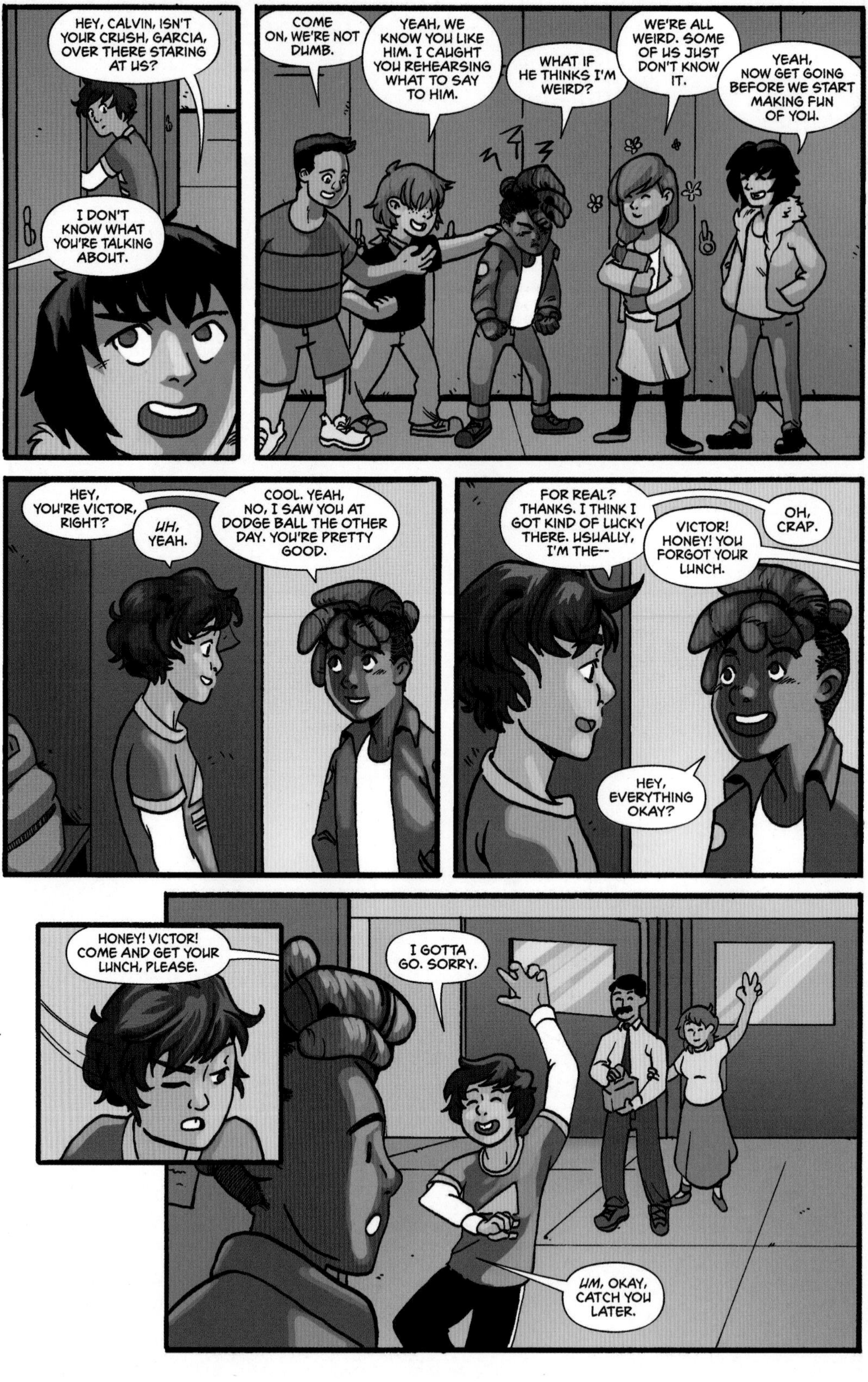
HEY, CALVIN, ISN'T YOUR CRUSH, GARCIA, OVER THERE STARING AT US?
I DON'T KNOW WHAT YOU'RE TALKING ABOUT.
COME ON, WE'RE NOT DUMB.
YEAH, WE KNOW YOU LIKE HIM. I CAUGHT YOU REHEARSING WHAT TO SAY TO HIM.
WHAT IF HE THINKS I'M WEIRD?
WE'RE ALL WEIRD. SOME OF US JUST DON'T KNOW IT.
YEAH, NOW GET GOING BEFORE WE START MAKING FUN OF YOU.
HEY, YOU'RE VICTOR, RIGHT?
UH, YEAH.
COOL. YEAH, NO, I SAW YOU AT DODGE BALL THE OTHER DAY. YOU'RE PRETTY GOOD.
FOR REAL? THANKS. I THINK I GOT KIND OF LUCKY THERE. USUALLY, I'M THE--
OH, CRAP.
VICTOR! HONEY! YOU FORGOT YOUR LUNCH.
HEY, EVERYTHING OKAY?
HONEY! VICTOR! COME AND GET YOUR LUNCH, PLEASE.
I GOTTA GO. SORRY.
UM, OKAY, CATCH YOU LATER.

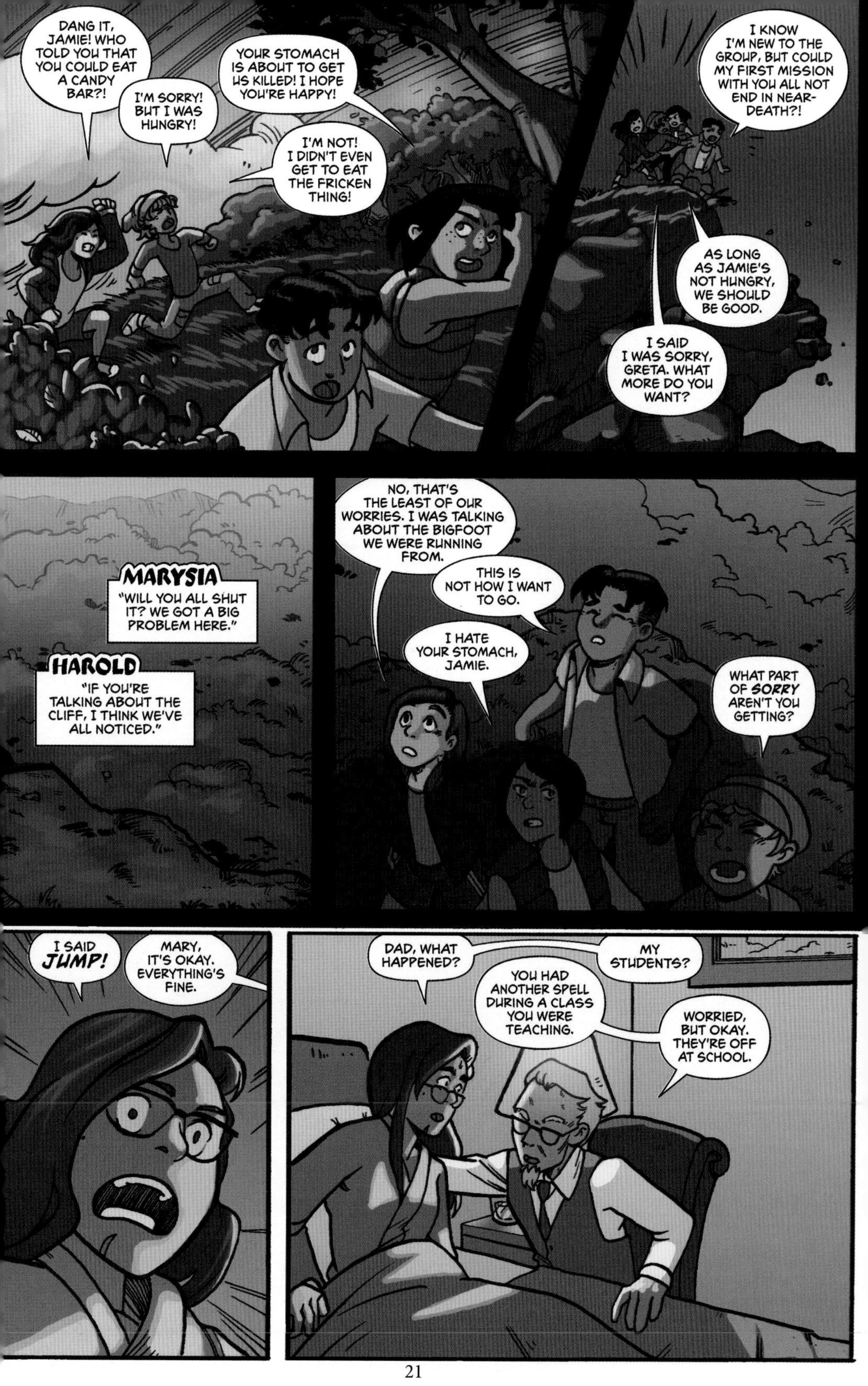
DANG IT, JAMIE! WHO TOLD YOU THAT YOU COULD EAT A CANDY BAR?!
I'M SORRY! BUT I WAS HUNGRY!
YOUR STOMACH IS ABOUT TO GET US KILLED! I HOPE YOU'RE HAPPY!
I'M NOT! I DIDN'T EVEN GET TO EAT THE FRICKEN THING!
I KNOW I'M NEW TO THE GROUP, BUT COULD MY FIRST MISSION WITH YOU ALL NOT END IN NEAR-DEATH?!
AS LONG AS JAMIE'S NOT HUNGRY, WE SHOULD BE GOOD.
I SAID I WAS SORRY, GRETA. WHAT MORE DO YOU WANT?
MARYSIA
"WILL YOU ALL SHUT IT? WE GOT A BIG PROBLEM HERE."
HAROLD
"IF YOU'RE TALKING ABOUT THE CLIFF, I THINK WE'VE ALL NOTICED."
NO, THAT'S THE LEAST OF OUR WORRIES. I WAS TALKING ABOUT THE BIGFOOT WE WERE RUNNING FROM.
THIS IS NOT HOW I WANT TO GO.
I HATE YOUR STOMACH, JAMIE.
WHAT PART OF SORRY AREN'T YOU GETTING?
I SAID JUMP!
MARY, IT'S OKAY. EVERYTHING'S FINE.
DAD, WHAT HAPPENED?
YOU HAD ANOTHER SPELL DURING A CLASS YOU WERE TEACHING.
MY STUDENTS?
WORRIED, BUT OKAY. THEY'RE OFF AT SCHOOL.

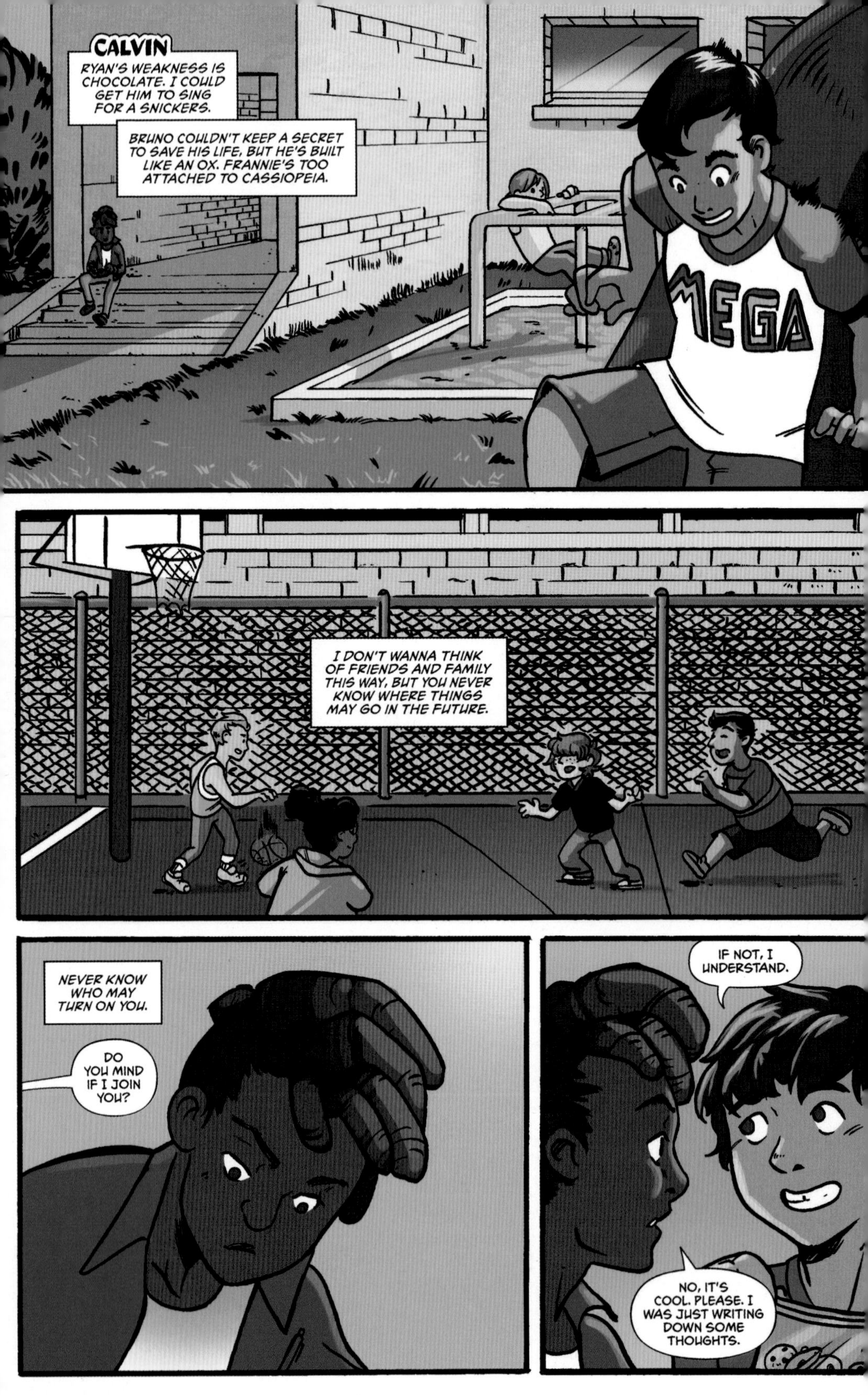
CALVIN
RYAN'S WEAKNESS IS CHOCOLATE. I COULD GET HIM TO SING FOR A SNICKERS.
BRUNO COULDN'T KEEP A SECRET TO SAVE HIS LIFE, BUT HE'S BUILT LIKE AN OX. FRANNIE'S TOO ATTACHED TO CASSIOPEIA.
MEGA
I DON'T WANNA THINK OF FRIENDS AND FAMILY THIS WAY, BUT YOU NEVER KNOW WHERE THINGS MAY GO IN THE FUTURE.
NEVER KNOW WHO MAY TURN ON YOU.
DO YOU MIND IF I JOIN YOU?
IF NOT, I UNDERSTAND.
NO, IT'S COOL. PLEASE. I WAS JUST WRITING DOWN SOME THOUGHTS.

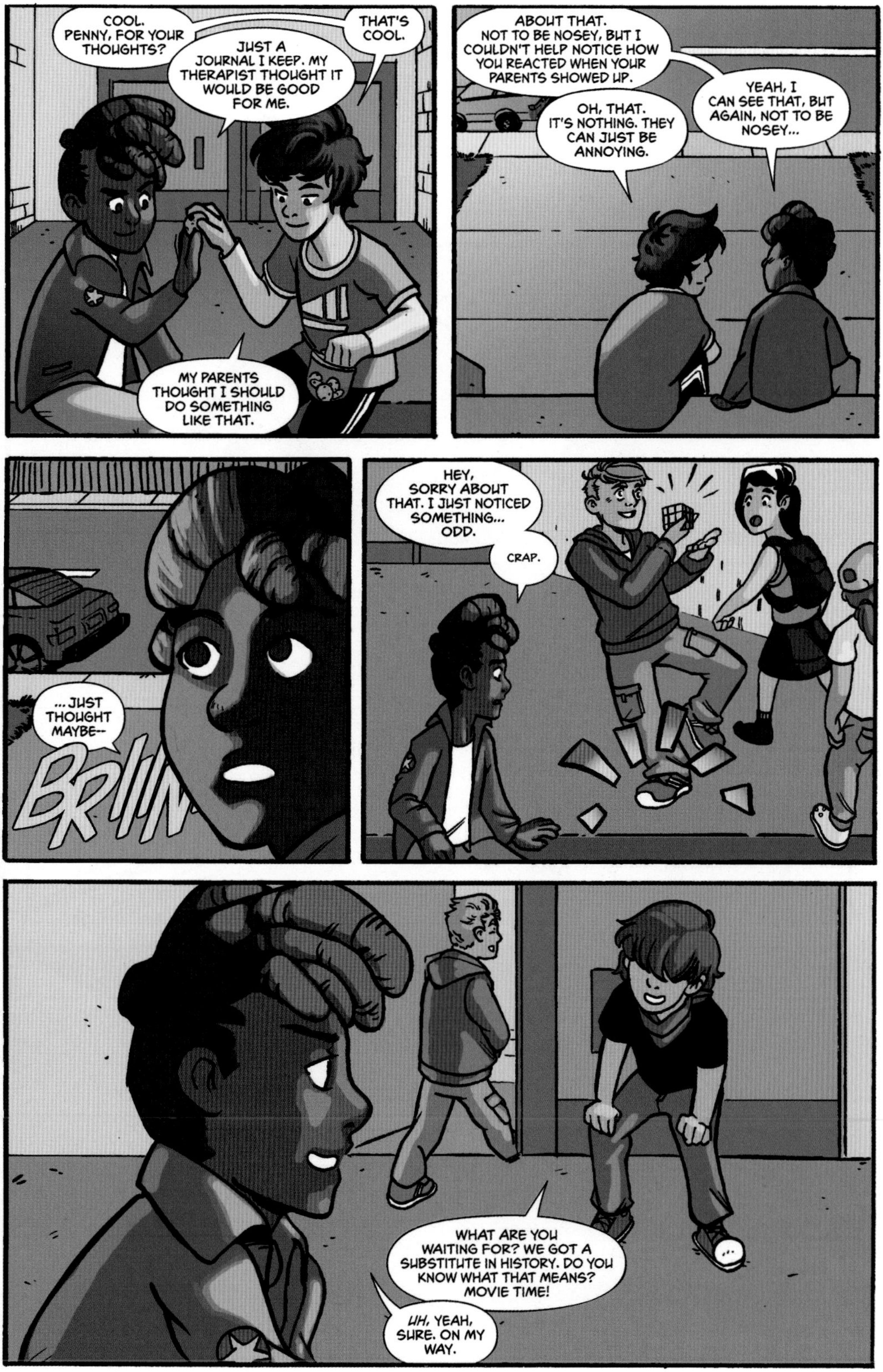
COOL. PENNY, FOR YOUR THOUGHTS?
JUST A JOURNAL I KEEP. MY THERAPIST THOUGHT IT WOULD BE GOOD FOR ME.
THAT'S COOL.
MY PARENTS THOUGHT I SHOULD DO SOMETHING LIKE THAT.
ABOUT THAT. NOT TO BE NOSEY, BUT I COULDN'T HELP NOTICE HOW YOU REACTED WHEN YOUR PARENTS SHOWED UP.
OH, THAT. IT'S NOTHING. THEY CAN JUST BE ANNOYING.
YEAH, I CAN SEE THAT, BUT AGAIN, NOT TO BE NOSEY...
...JUST THOUGHT MAYBE--
BRIIN
HEY, SORRY ABOUT THAT. I JUST NOTICED SOMETHING... ODD.
CRAP.
WHAT ARE YOU WAITING FOR? WE GOT A SUBSTITUTE IN HISTORY. DO YOU KNOW WHAT THAT MEANS? MOVIE TIME!
UH, YEAH, SURE. ON MY WAY.

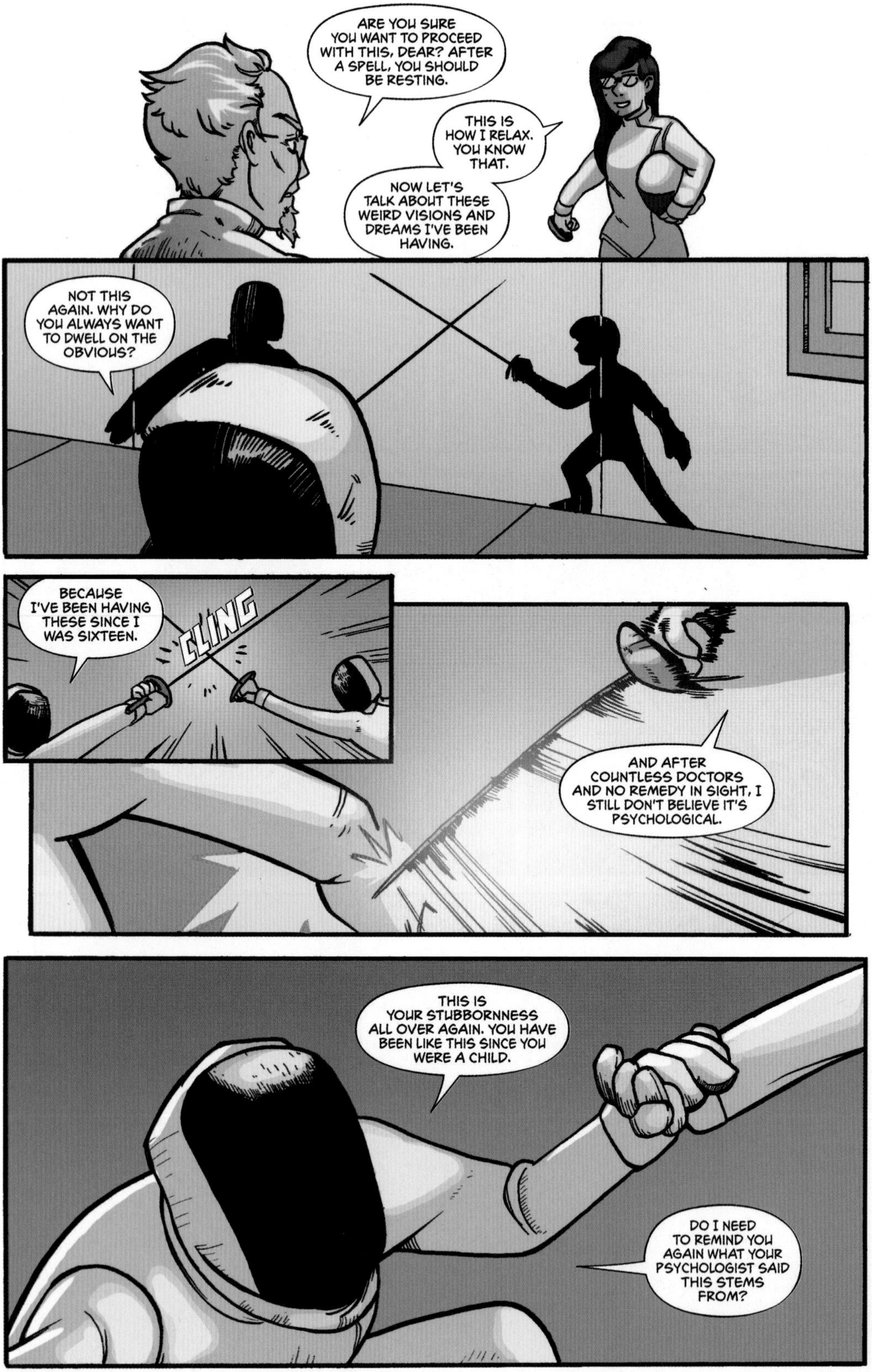
ARE YOU SURE YOU WANT TO PROCEED WITH THIS, DEAR? AFTER A SPELL, YOU SHOULD BE RESTING.
THIS IS HOW I RELAX. YOU KNOW THAT.
NOW LET'S TALK ABOUT THESE WEIRD VISIONS AND DREAMS I'VE BEEN HAVING.
NOT THIS AGAIN. WHY DO YOU ALWAYS WANT TO DWELL ON THE OBVIOUS?
BECAUSE I'VE BEEN HAVING THESE SINCE I WAS SIXTEEN.
CLING
AND AFTER COUNTLESS DOCTORS AND NO REMEDY IN SIGHT, I STILL DON'T BELIEVE IT'S PSYCHOLOGICAL.
THIS IS YOUR STUBBORNNESS ALL OVER AGAIN. YOU HAVE BEEN LIKE THIS SINCE YOU WERE A CHILD.
DO I NEED TO REMIND YOU AGAIN WHAT YOUR PSYCHOLOGIST SAID THIS STEMS FROM?

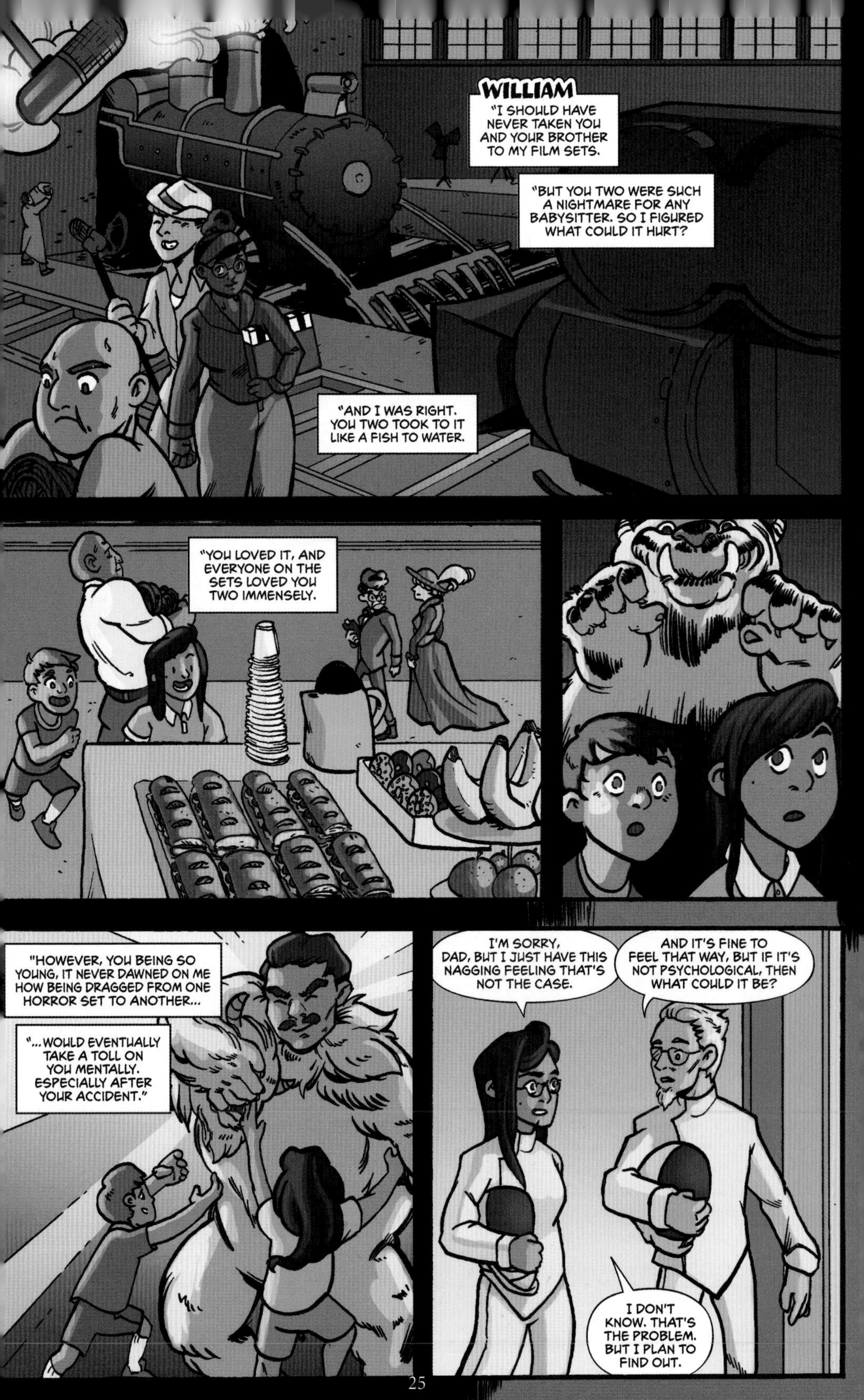
WILLIAM
"I SHOULD HAVE NEVER TAKEN YOU AND YOUR BROTHER TO MY FILM SETS.
"BUT YOU TWO WERE SUCH A NIGHTMARE FOR ANY BABYSITTER. SO I FIGURED WHAT COULD IT HURT?
"AND I WAS RIGHT. YOU TWO TOOK TO IT LIKE A FISH TO WATER.
"YOU LOVED IT, AND EVERYONE ON THE SETS LOVED YOU TWO IMMENSELY.
"HOWEVER, YOU BEING SO YOUNG, IT NEVER DAWNED ON ME HOW BEING DRAGGED FROM ONE HORROR SET TO ANOTHER...
"...WOULD EVENTUALLY TAKE A TOLL ON YOU MENTALLY. ESPECIALLY AFTER YOUR ACCIDENT."
I'M SORRY, DAD, BUT I JUST HAVE THIS NAGGING FEELING THAT'S NOT THE CASE.
AND IT'S FINE TO FEEL THAT WAY, BUT IF IT'S NOT PSYCHOLOGICAL, THEN WHAT COULD IT BE?
I DON'T KNOW. THAT'S THE PROBLEM. BUT I PLAN TO FIND OUT.

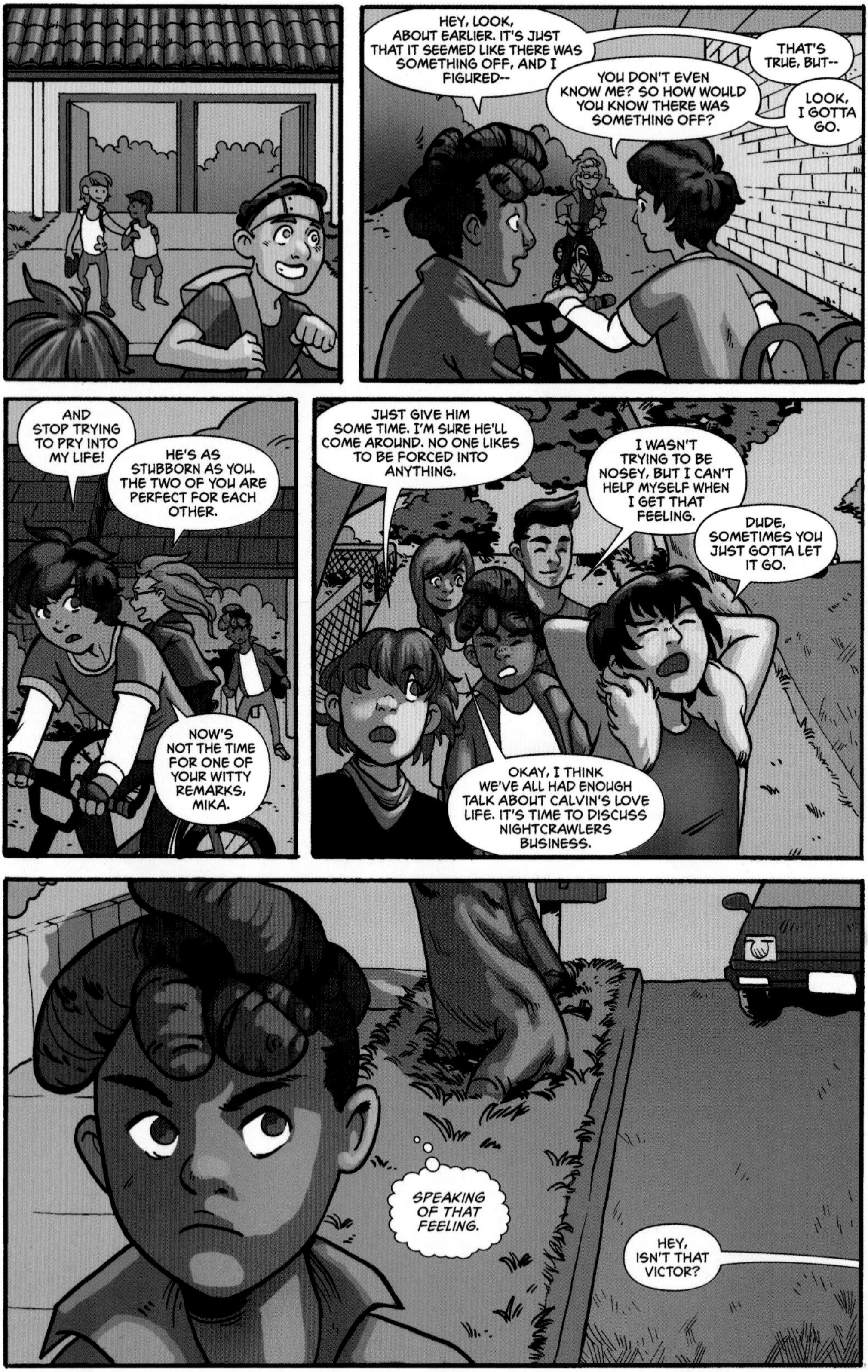
HEY, LOOK, ABOUT EARLIER. IT'S JUST THAT IT SEEMED LIKE THERE WAS SOMETHING OFF, AND I FIGURED--
YOU DON'T EVEN KNOW ME? SO HOW WOULD YOU KNOW THERE WAS SOMETHING OFF?
THAT'S TRUE, BUT--
LOOK, I GOTTA GO.
AND STOP TRYING TO PRY INTO MY LIFE!
HE'S AS STUBBORN AS YOU. THE TWO OF YOU ARE PERFECT FOR EACH OTHER.
NOW'S NOT THE TIME FOR ONE OF YOUR WITTY REMARKS, MIKA.
JUST GIVE HIM SOME TIME. I'M SURE HE'LL COME AROUND. NO ONE LIKES TO BE FORCED INTO ANYTHING.
I WASN'T TRYING TO BE NOSEY, BUT I CAN'T HELP MYSELF WHEN I GET THAT FEELING.
DUDE, SOMETIMES YOU JUST GOTTA LET IT GO.
OKAY, I THINK WE'VE ALL HAD ENOUGH TALK ABOUT CALVIN'S LOVE LIFE. IT'S TIME TO DISCUSS NIGHTCRAWLERS BUSINESS.
SPEAKING OF THAT FEELING.
HEY, ISN'T THAT VICTOR?

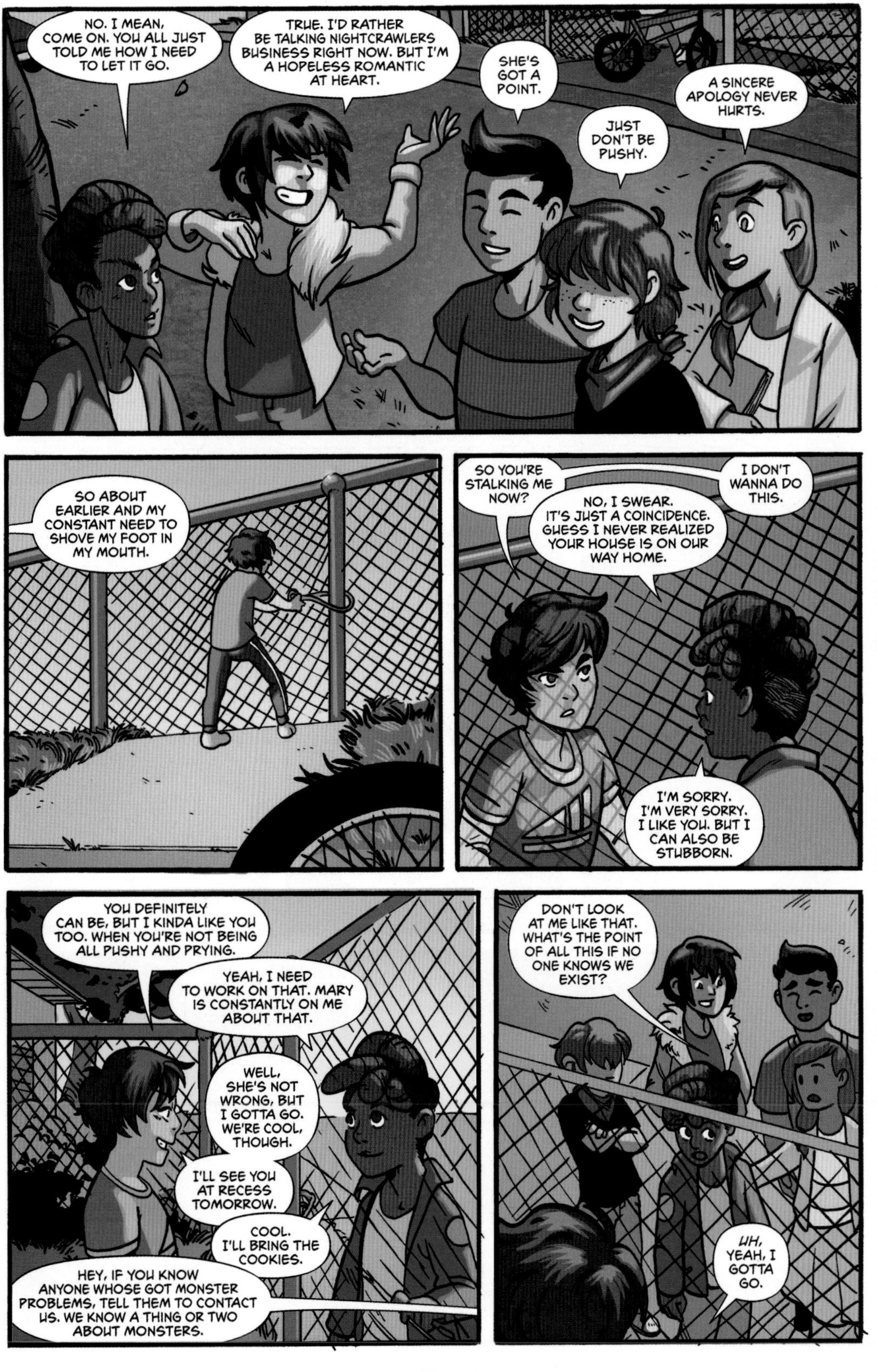
NO. I MEAN, COME ON. YOU ALL JUST TOLD ME HOW I NEED TO LET IT GO.
TRUE. I'D RATHER BE TALKING NIGHTCRAWLERS BUSINESS RIGHT NOW. BUT I'M A HOPELESS ROMANTIC AT HEART.
SHE'S GOT A POINT.
JUST DON'T BE PUSHY.
A SINCERE APOLOGY NEVER HURTS.
SO ABOUT EARLIER AND MY CONSTANT NEED TO SHOVE MY FOOT IN MY MOUTH.
SO YOU'RE STALKING ME NOW?
I DON'T WANNA DO THIS.
NO, I SWEAR. IT'S JUST A COINCIDENCE. GUESS I NEVER REALIZED YOUR HOUSE IS ON OUR WAY HOME.
I'M SORRY. I'M VERY SORRY. I LIKE YOU. BUT I CAN ALSO BE STUBBORN.
YOU DEFINITELY CAN BE, BUT I KINDA LIKE YOU TOO. WHEN YOU'RE NOT BEING ALL PUSHY AND PRYING.
YEAH, I NEED TO WORK ON THAT. MARY IS CONSTANTLY ON ME ABOUT THAT.
WELL, SHE'S NOT WRONG, BUT I GOTTA GO. WE'RE COOL, THOUGH.
I'LL SEE YOU AT RECESS TOMORROW.
COOL. I'LL BRING THE COOKIES.
HEY, IF YOU KNOW ANYONE WHOSE GOT MONSTER PROBLEMS, TELL THEM TO CONTACT US. WE KNOW A THING OR TWO ABOUT MONSTERS.
DON'T LOOK AT ME LIKE THAT. WHAT'S THE POINT OF ALL THIS IF NO ONE KNOWS WE EXIST?
UH, YEAH, I GOTTA GO.

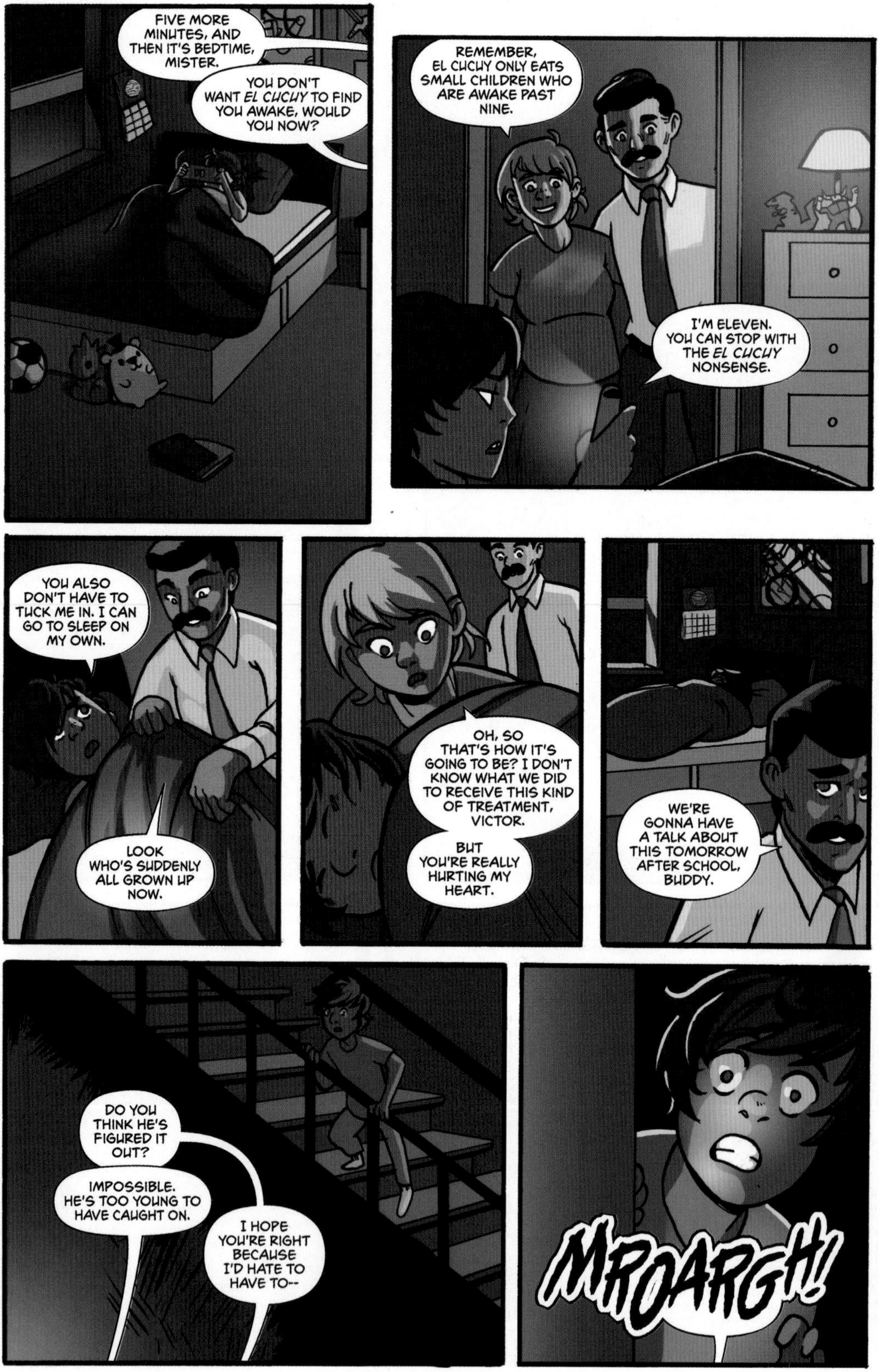
FIVE MORE MINUTES, AND THEN IT'S BEDTIME, MISTER.
YOU DON'T WANT EL CUCUY TO FIND YOU AWAKE, WOULD YOU NOW?
REMEMBER, EL CUCUY ONLY EATS SMALL CHILDREN WHO ARE AWAKE PAST NINE.
I'M ELEVEN. YOU CAN STOP WITH THE EL CUCUY NONSENSE.
YOU ALSO DON'T HAVE TO TUCK ME IN. I CAN GO TO SLEEP ON MY OWN.
LOOK WHO'S SUDDENLY ALL GROWN UP NOW.
OH, SO THAT'S HOW IT'S GOING TO BE? I DON'T KNOW WHAT WE DID TO RECEIVE THIS KIND OF TREATMENT, VICTOR.
BUT YOU'RE REALLY HURTING MY HEART.
WE'RE GONNA HAVE A TALK ABOUT THIS TOMORROW AFTER SCHOOL, BUDDY.
DO YOU THINK HE'S FIGURED IT OUT?
IMPOSSIBLE. HE'S TOO YOUNG TO HAVE CAUGHT ON.
I HOPE YOU'RE RIGHT BECAUSE I'D HATE TO HAVE TO--
MROARGH!

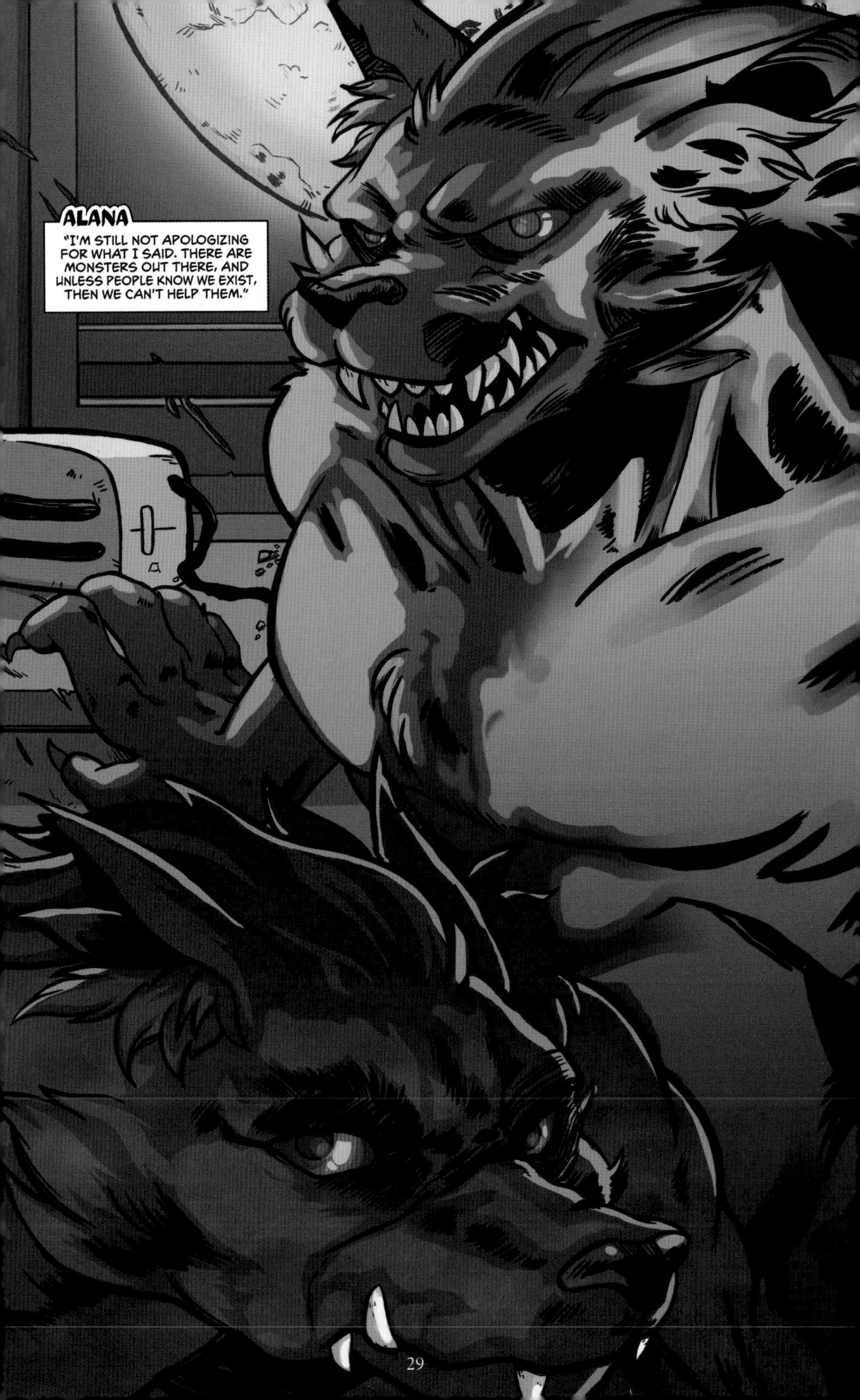
ALANA
"I'M STILL NOT APOLOGIZING FOR WHAT I SAID. THERE ARE MONSTERS OUT THERE, AND UNLESS PEOPLE KNOW WE EXIST, THEN WE CAN'T HELP THEM."

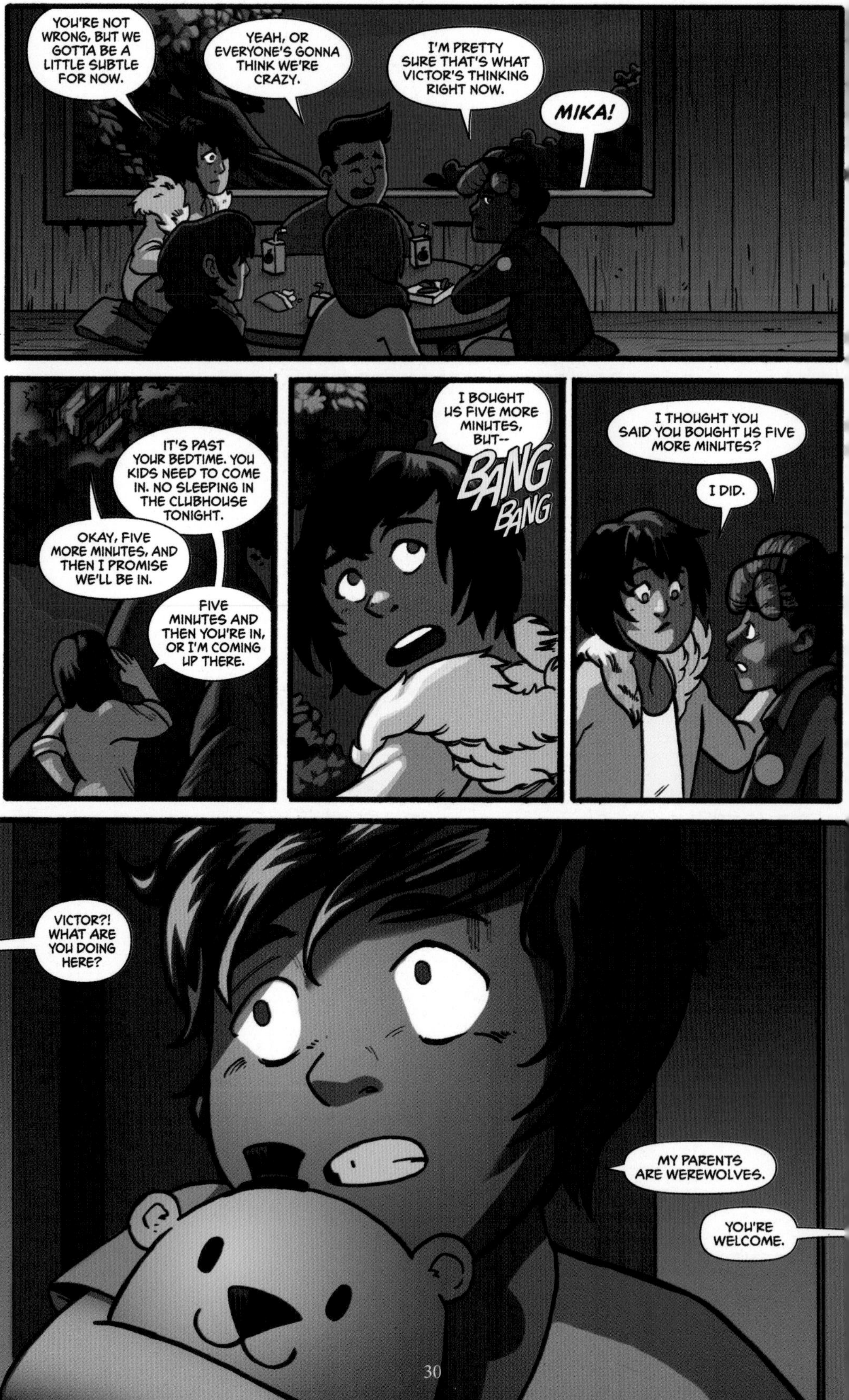
YOU'RE NOT WRONG, BUT WE GOTTA BE A LITTLE SUBTLE FOR NOW.
YEAH, OR EVERYONE'S GONNA THINK WE'RE CRAZY.
I'M PRETTY SURE THAT'S WHAT VICTOR'S THINKING RIGHT NOW.
MIKA!
IT'S PAST YOUR BEDTIME. YOU KIDS NEED TO COME IN. NO SLEEPING IN THE CLUBHOUSE TONIGHT.
OKAY, FIVE MORE MINUTES, AND THEN I PROMISE WE'LL BE IN.
FIVE MINUTES AND THEN YOU'RE IN, OR I'M COMING UP THERE.
I BOUGHT US FIVE MORE MINUTES, BUT--
BANG
BANG
I THOUGHT YOU SAID YOU BOUGHT US FIVE MORE MINUTES?
I DID.
VICTOR?! WHAT ARE YOU DOING HERE?
MY PARENTS ARE WEREWOLVES.
YOU'RE WELCOME.

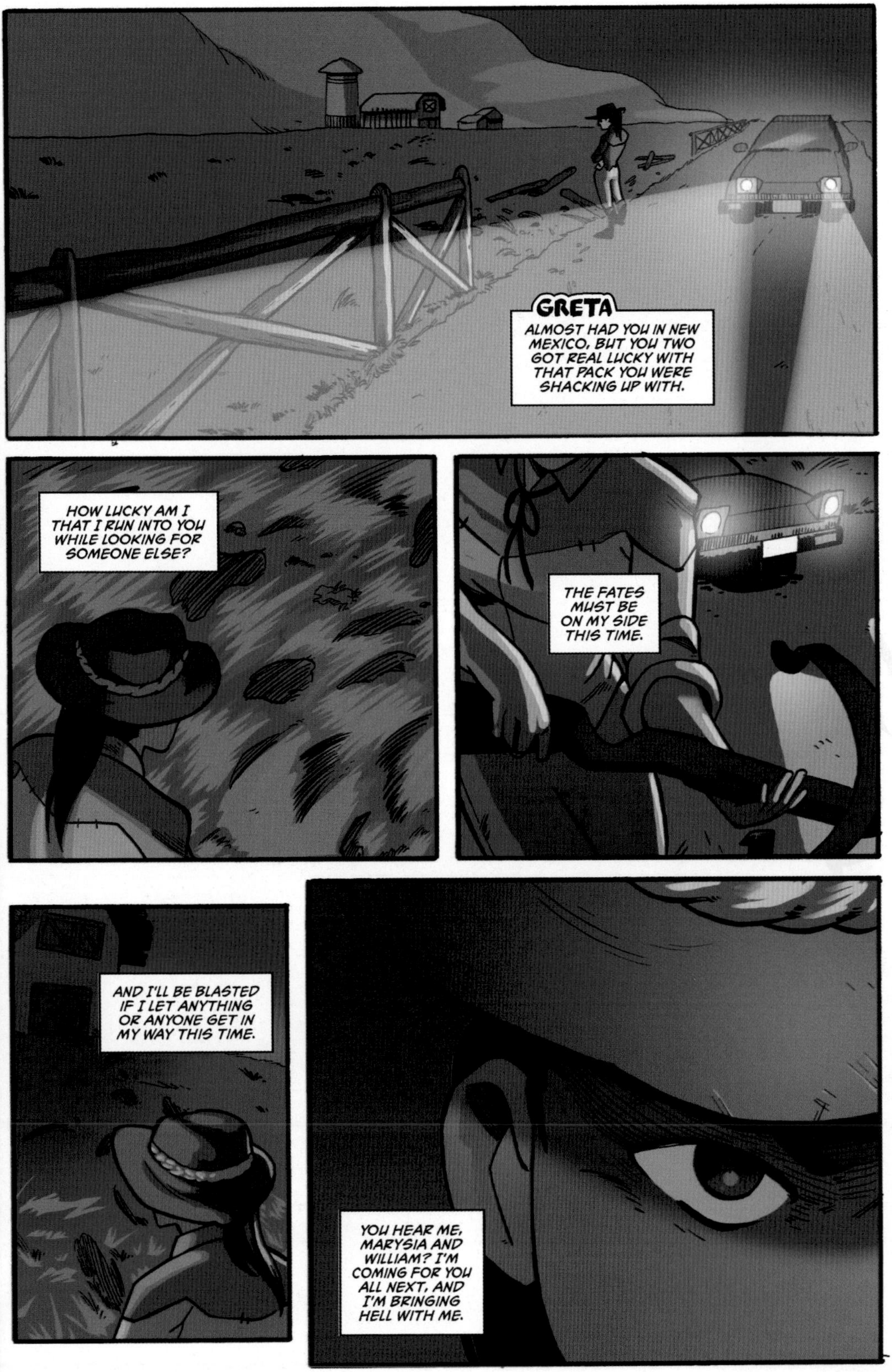
GRETA
ALMOST HAD YOU IN NEW MEXICO, BUT YOU TWO GOT REAL LUCKY WITH THAT PACK YOU WERE SHACKING UP WITH.
HOW LUCKY AM I THAT I RUN INTO YOU WHILE LOOKING FOR SOMEONE ELSE?
THE FATES MUST BE ON MY SIDE THIS TIME.
AND I'LL BE BLASTED IF I LET ANYTHING OR ANYONE GET IN MY WAY THIS TIME.
YOU HEAR ME, MARYSIA AND WILLIAM? I'M COMING FOR YOU ALL NEXT, AND I'M BRINGING HELL WITH ME.

Chapter Two
The Past Will Come Back to Haunt You

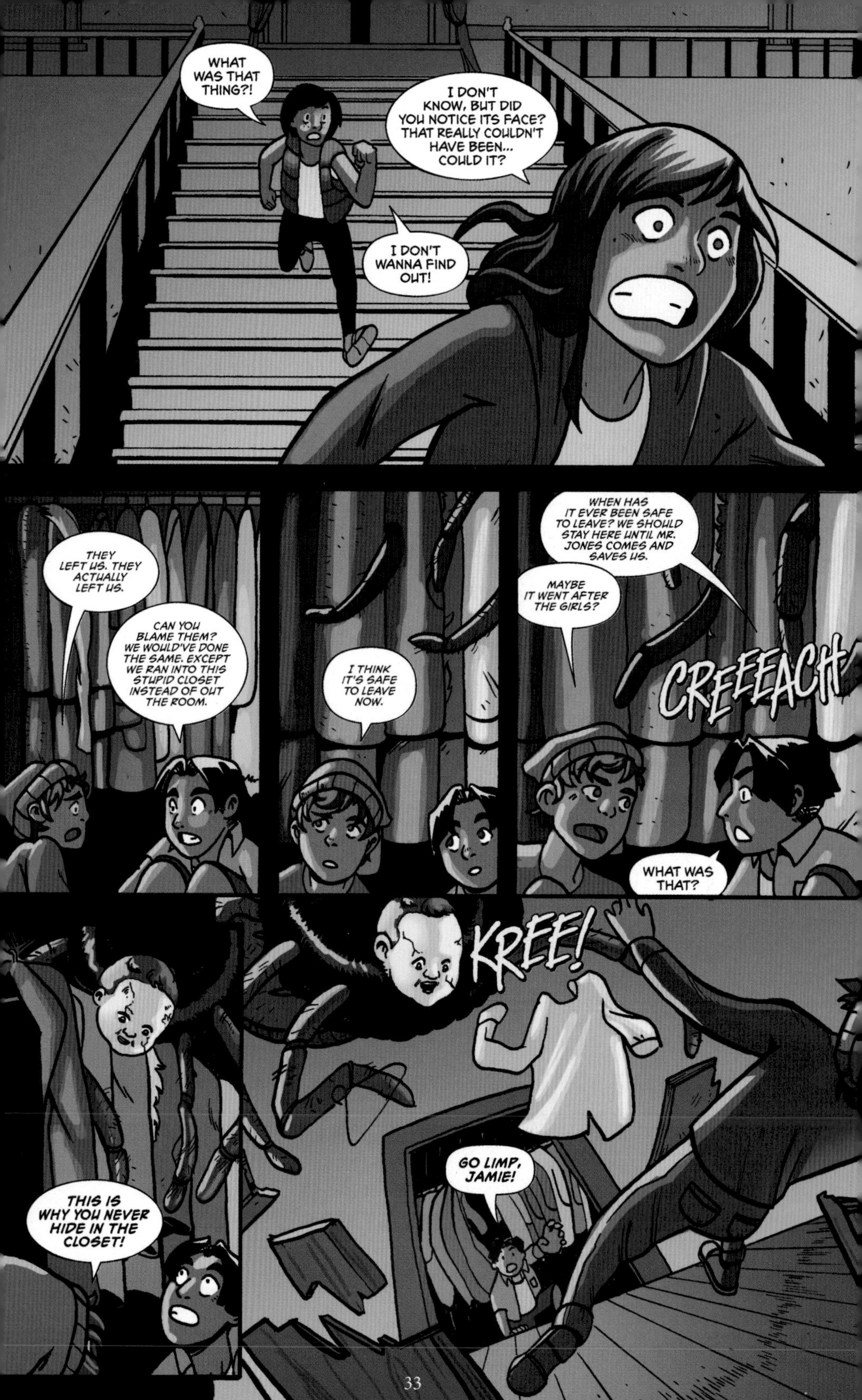
WHAT WAS THAT THING?!
I DON'T KNOW, BUT DID YOU NOTICE ITS FACE? THAT REALLY COULDN'T HAVE BEEN... COULD IT?
I DON'T WANNA FIND OUT!
THEY LEFT US. THEY ACTUALLY LEFT US.
CAN YOU BLAME THEM? WE WOULD'VE DONE THE SAME. EXCEPT WE RAN INTO THIS STUPID CLOSET INSTEAD OF OUT THE ROOM.
I THINK IT'S SAFE TO LEAVE NOW.
WHEN HAS IT EVER BEEN SAFE TO LEAVE? WE SHOULD STAY HERE UNTIL MR. JONES COMES AND SAVES US.
MAYBE IT WENT AFTER THE GIRLS?
CREEEACH
WHAT WAS THAT?
KREE!
THIS IS WHY YOU NEVER HIDE IN THE CLOSET!
GO LIMP, JAMIE!

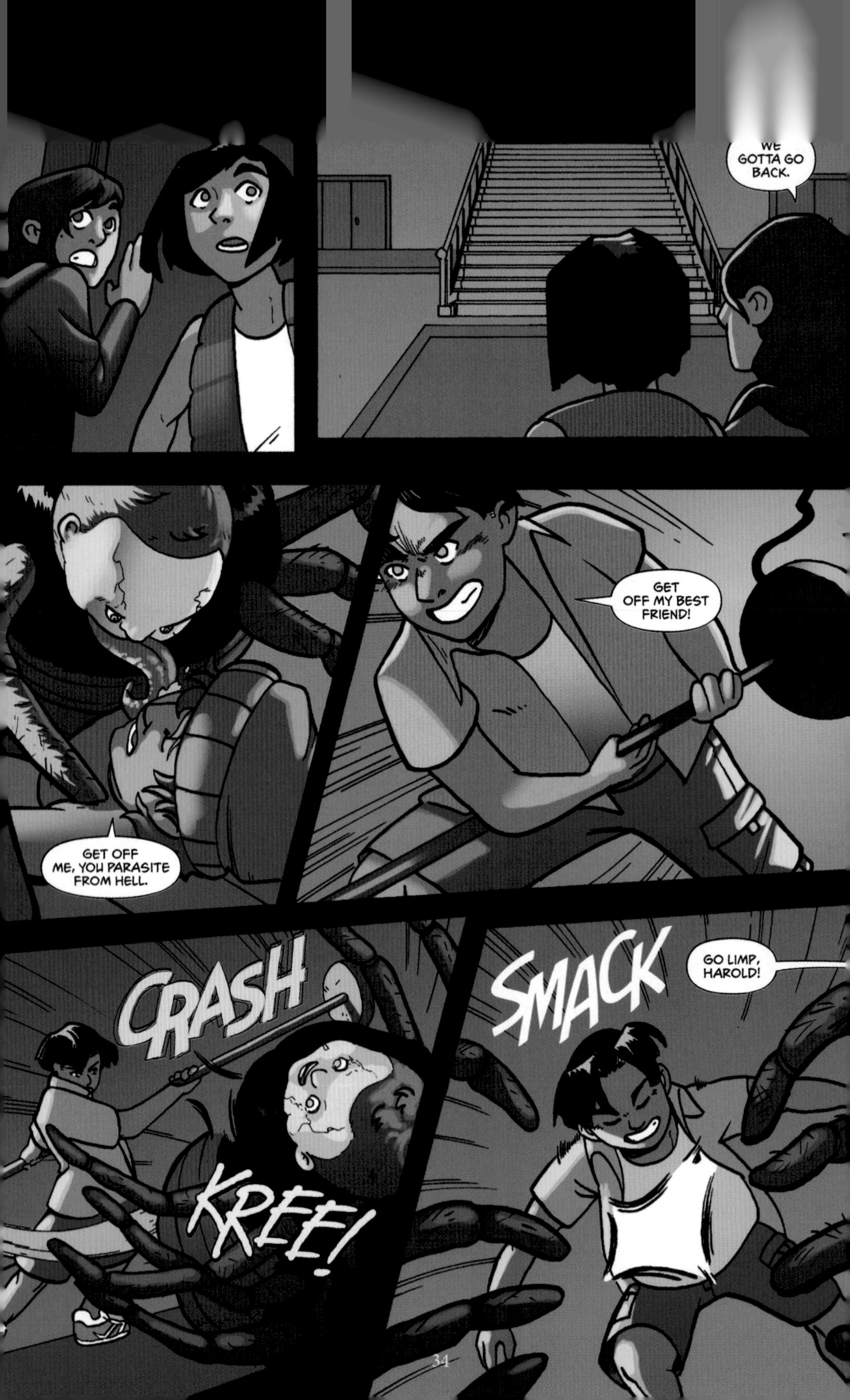
WE GOTTA GO BACK.
GET OFF ME, YOU PARASITE FROM HELL.
GET OFF MY BEST FRIEND!
CRASH
KREE!
SMACK
GO LIMP, HAROLD!

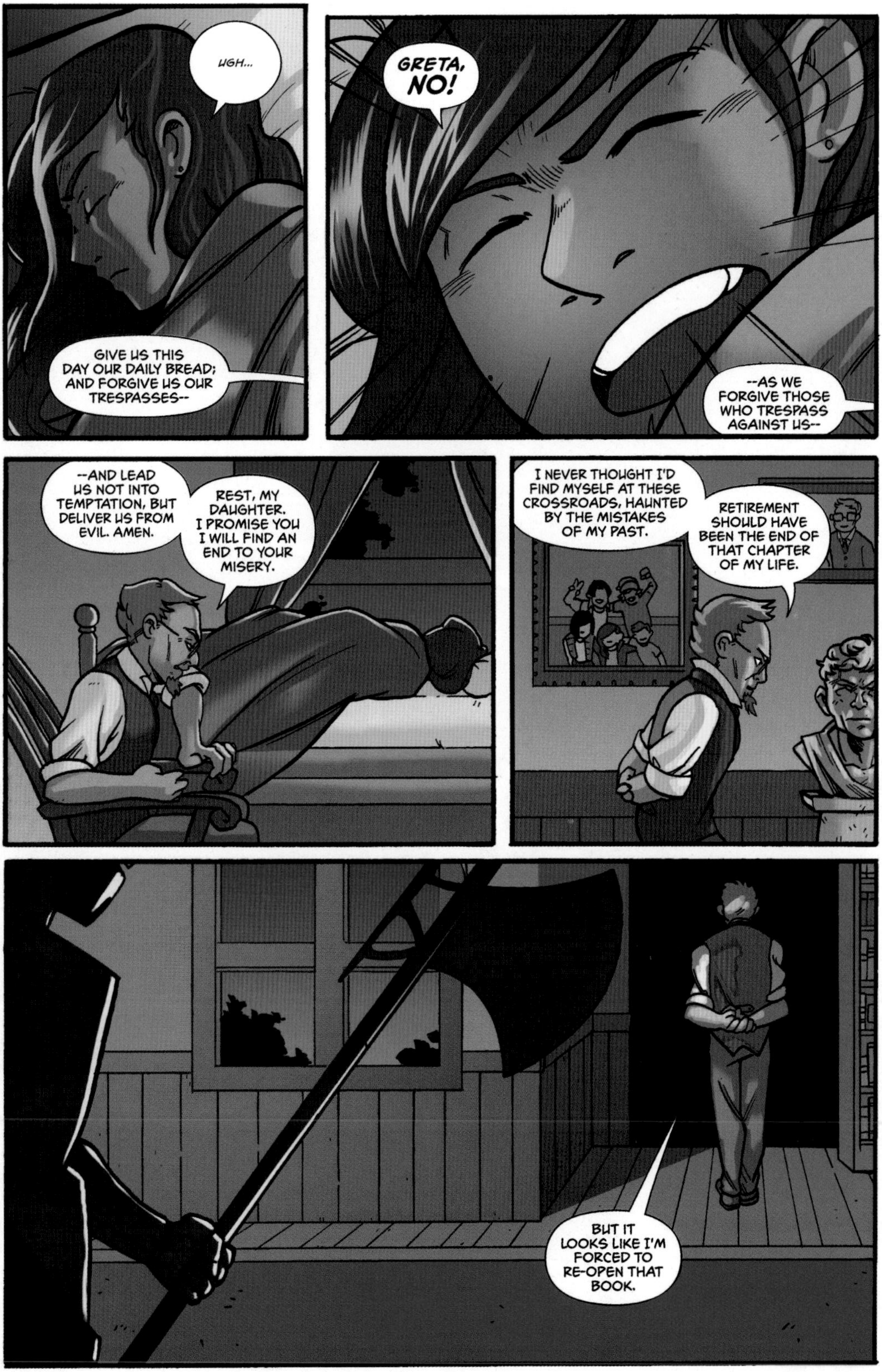
UGH...
GIVE US THIS DAY OUR DAILY BREAD; AND FORGIVE US OUR TRESPASSES--
GRETA, NO!
--AS WE FORGIVE THOSE WHO TRESPASS AGAINST US--
--AND LEAD US NOT INTO TEMPTATION, BUT DELIVER US FROM EVIL. AMEN.
REST, MY DAUGHTER. I PROMISE YOU I WILL FIND AN END TO YOUR MISERY.
I NEVER THOUGHT I'D FIND MYSELF AT THESE CROSSROADS, HAUNTED BY THE MISTAKES OF MY PAST.
RETIREMENT SHOULD HAVE BEEN THE END OF THAT CHAPTER OF MY LIFE.
BUT IT LOOKS LIKE I'M FORCED TO RE-OPEN THAT BOOK.

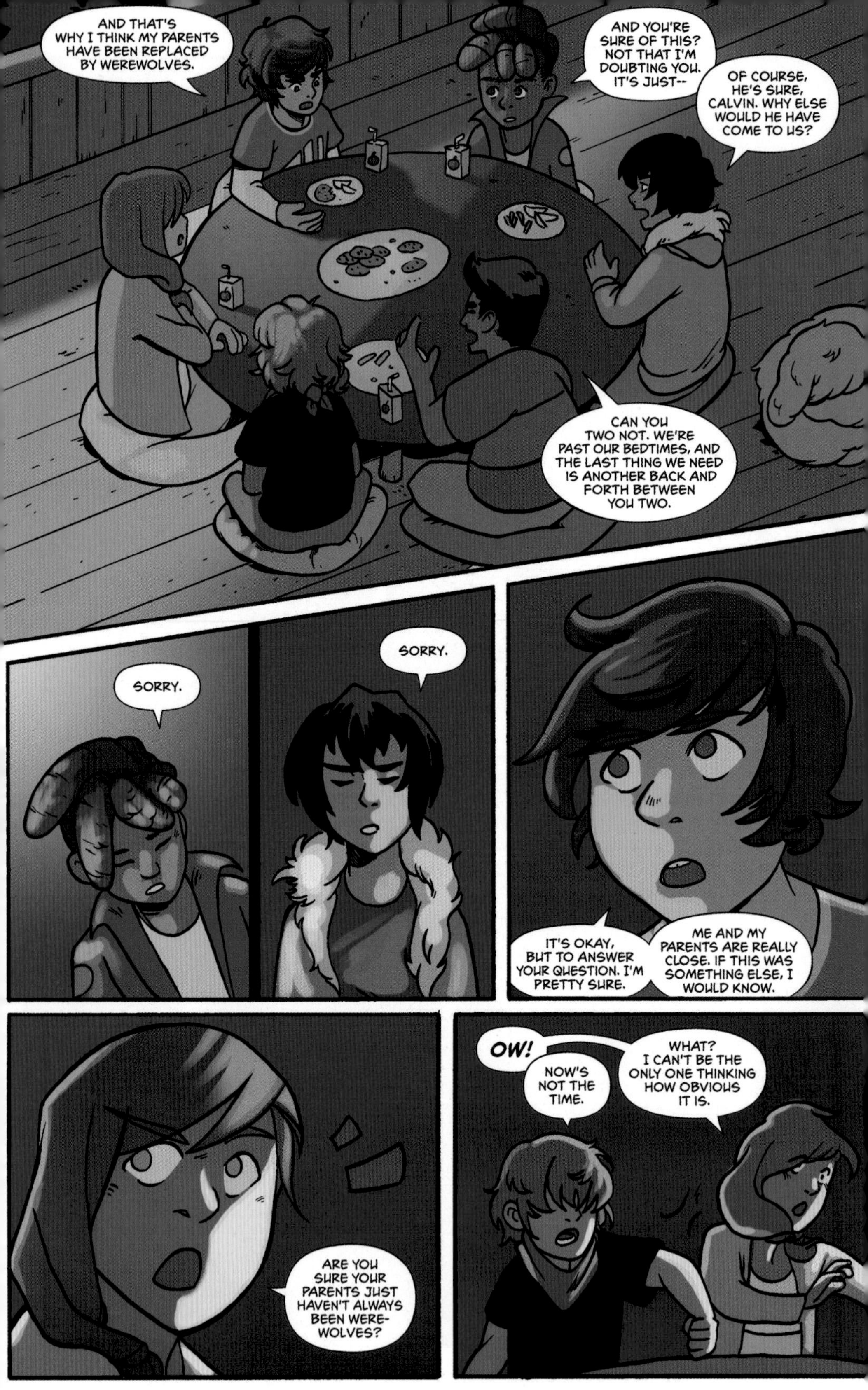
AND THAT'S WHY I THINK MY PARENTS HAVE BEEN REPLACED BY WEREWOLVES.
AND YOU'RE SURE OF THIS? NOT THAT I'M DOUBTING YOU. IT'S JUST--
OF COURSE, HE'S SURE, CALVIN. WHY ELSE WOULD HE HAVE COME TO US?
CAN YOU TWO NOT. WE'RE PAST OUR BEDTIMES, AND THE LAST THING WE NEED IS ANOTHER BACK AND FORTH BETWEEN YOU TWO.
SORRY.
SORRY.
IT'S OKAY, BUT TO ANSWER YOUR QUESTION. I'M PRETTY SURE.
ME AND MY PARENTS ARE REALLY CLOSE. IF THIS WAS SOMETHING ELSE, I WOULD KNOW.
ARE YOU SURE YOUR PARENTS JUST HAVEN'T ALWAYS BEEN WERE-WOLVES?
OW!
NOW'S NOT THE TIME.
WHAT? I CAN'T BE THE ONLY ONE THINKING HOW OBVIOUS IT IS.

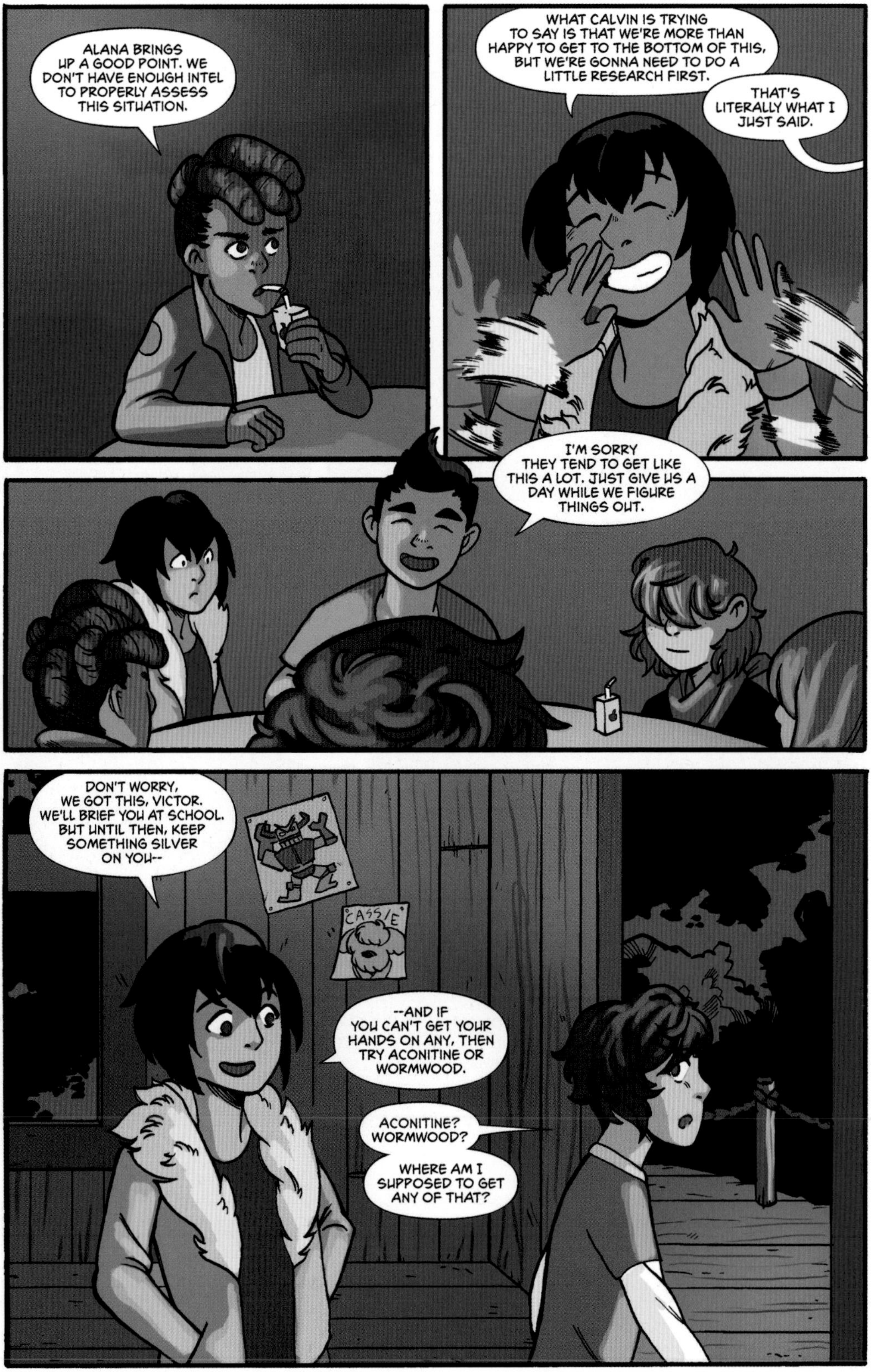
ALANA BRINGS UP A GOOD POINT. WE DON'T HAVE ENOUGH INTEL TO PROPERLY ASSESS THIS SITUATION.
WHAT CALVIN IS TRYING TO SAY IS THAT WE'RE MORE THAN HAPPY TO GET TO THE BOTTOM OF THIS, BUT WE'RE GONNA NEED TO DO A LITTLE RESEARCH FIRST.
THAT'S LITERALLY WHAT I JUST SAID.
I'M SORRY THEY TEND TO GET LIKE THIS A LOT. JUST GIVE US A DAY WHILE WE FIGURE THINGS OUT.
DON'T WORRY, WE GOT THIS, VICTOR. WE'LL BRIEF YOU AT SCHOOL. BUT UNTIL THEN, KEEP SOMETHING SILVER ON YOU--
CASSIE
--AND IF YOU CAN'T GET YOUR HANDS ON ANY, THEN TRY ACONITINE OR WORMWOOD.
ACONITINE? WORMWOOD?
WHERE AM I SUPPOSED TO GET ANY OF THAT?

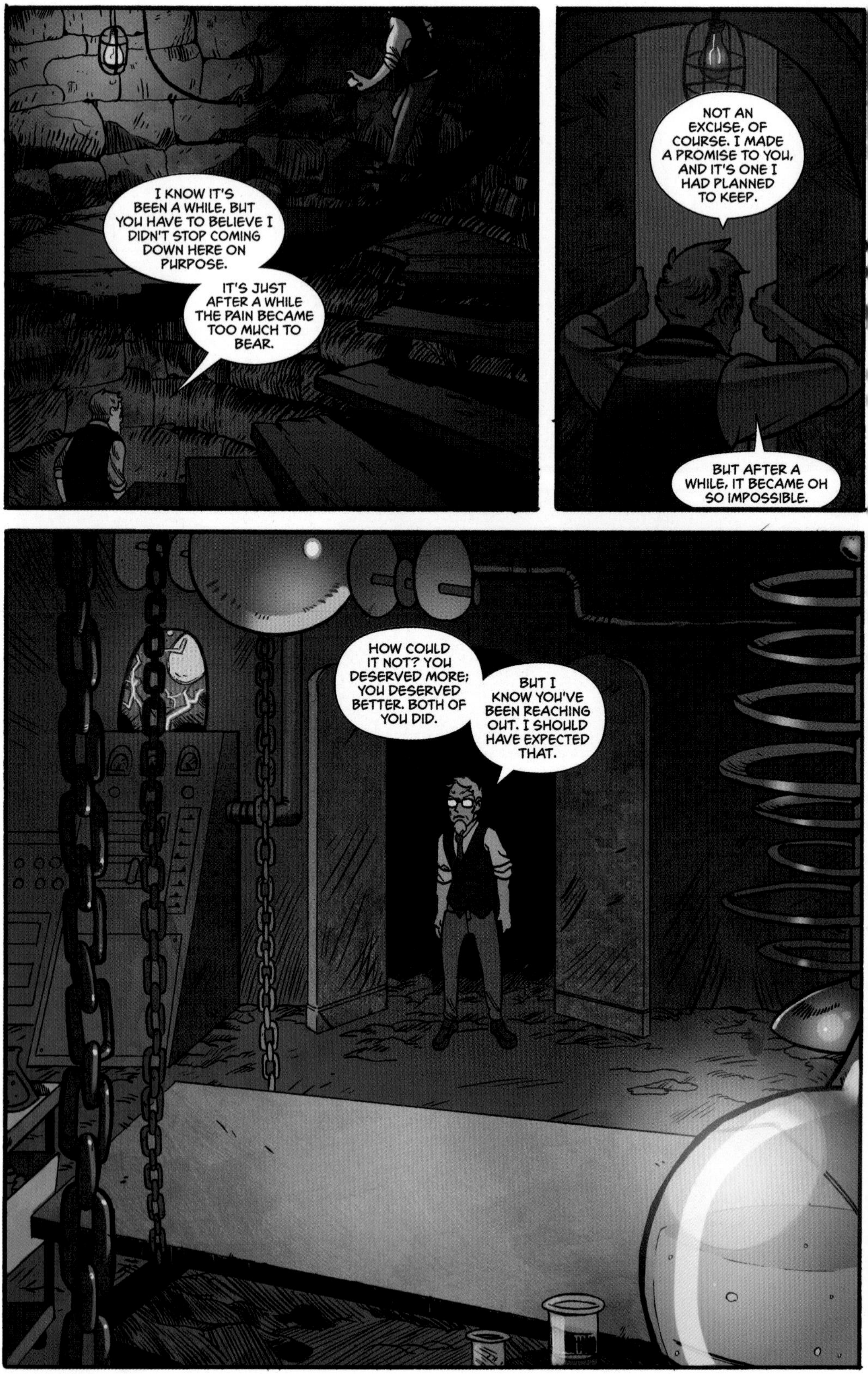
I KNOW IT'S BEEN A WHILE, BUT YOU HAVE TO BELIEVE I DIDN'T STOP COMING DOWN HERE ON PURPOSE.
IT'S JUST AFTER A WHILE THE PAIN BECAME TOO MUCH TO BEAR.
NOT AN EXCUSE, OF COURSE. I MADE A PROMISE TO YOU, AND IT'S ONE I HAD PLANNED TO KEEP.
BUT AFTER A WHILE, IT BECAME OH SO IMPOSSIBLE.
HOW COULD IT NOT? YOU DESERVED MORE; YOU DESERVED BETTER. BOTH OF YOU DID.
BUT I KNOW YOU'VE BEEN REACHING OUT. I SHOULD HAVE EXPECTED THAT.

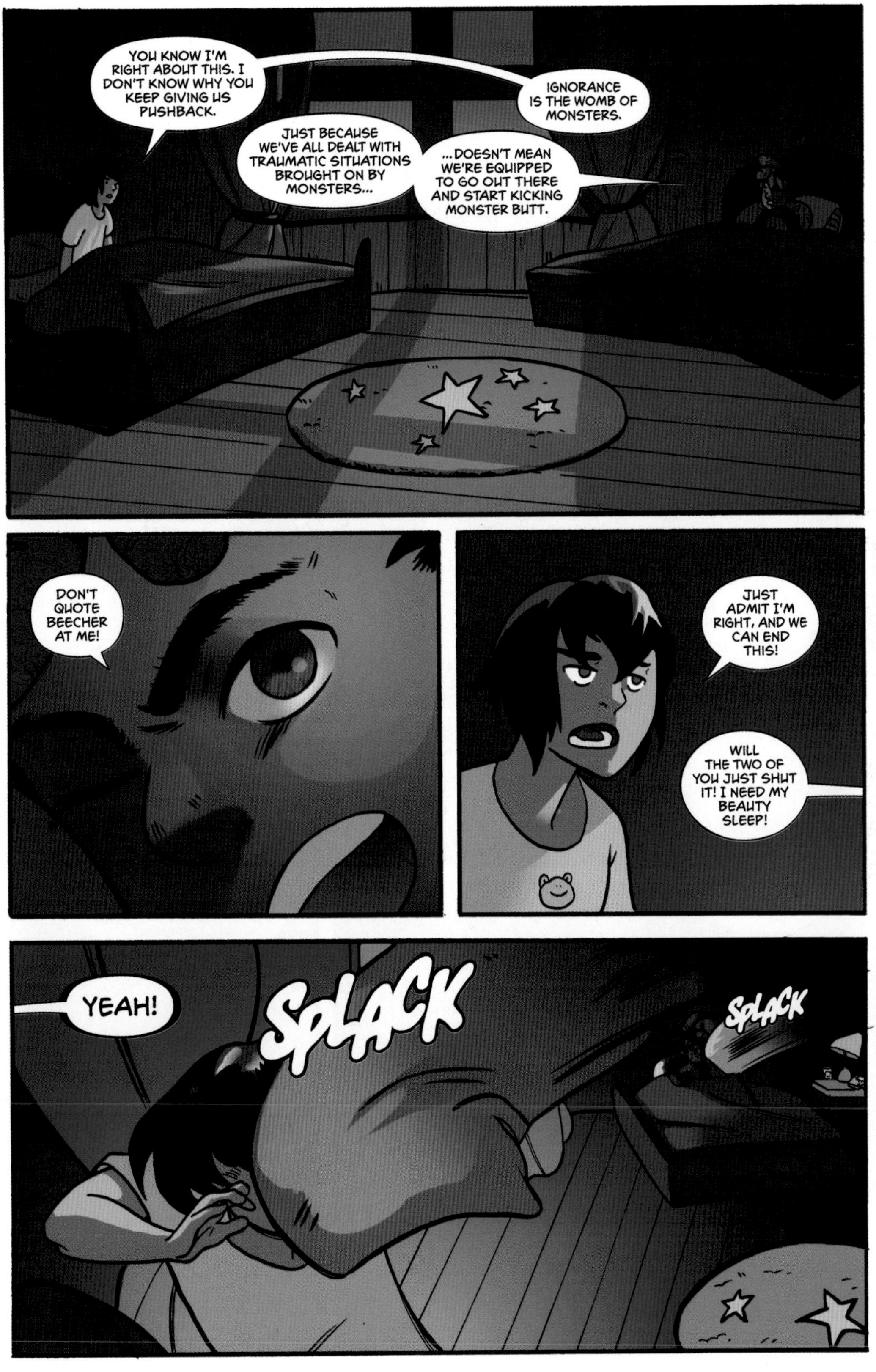
YOU KNOW I'M RIGHT ABOUT THIS. I DON'T KNOW WHY YOU KEEP GIVING US PUSHBACK.
IGNORANCE IS THE WOMB OF MONSTERS.
JUST BECAUSE WE'VE ALL DEALT WITH TRAUMATIC SITUATIONS BROUGHT ON BY MONSTERS...
...DOESN'T MEAN WE'RE EQUIPPED TO GO OUT THERE AND START KICKING MONSTER BUTT.
DON'T QUOTE BEECHER AT ME!
JUST ADMIT I'M RIGHT, AND WE CAN END THIS!
WILL THE TWO OF YOU JUST SHUT IT! I NEED MY BEAUTY SLEEP!
YEAH!
SPLACK
SPLACK

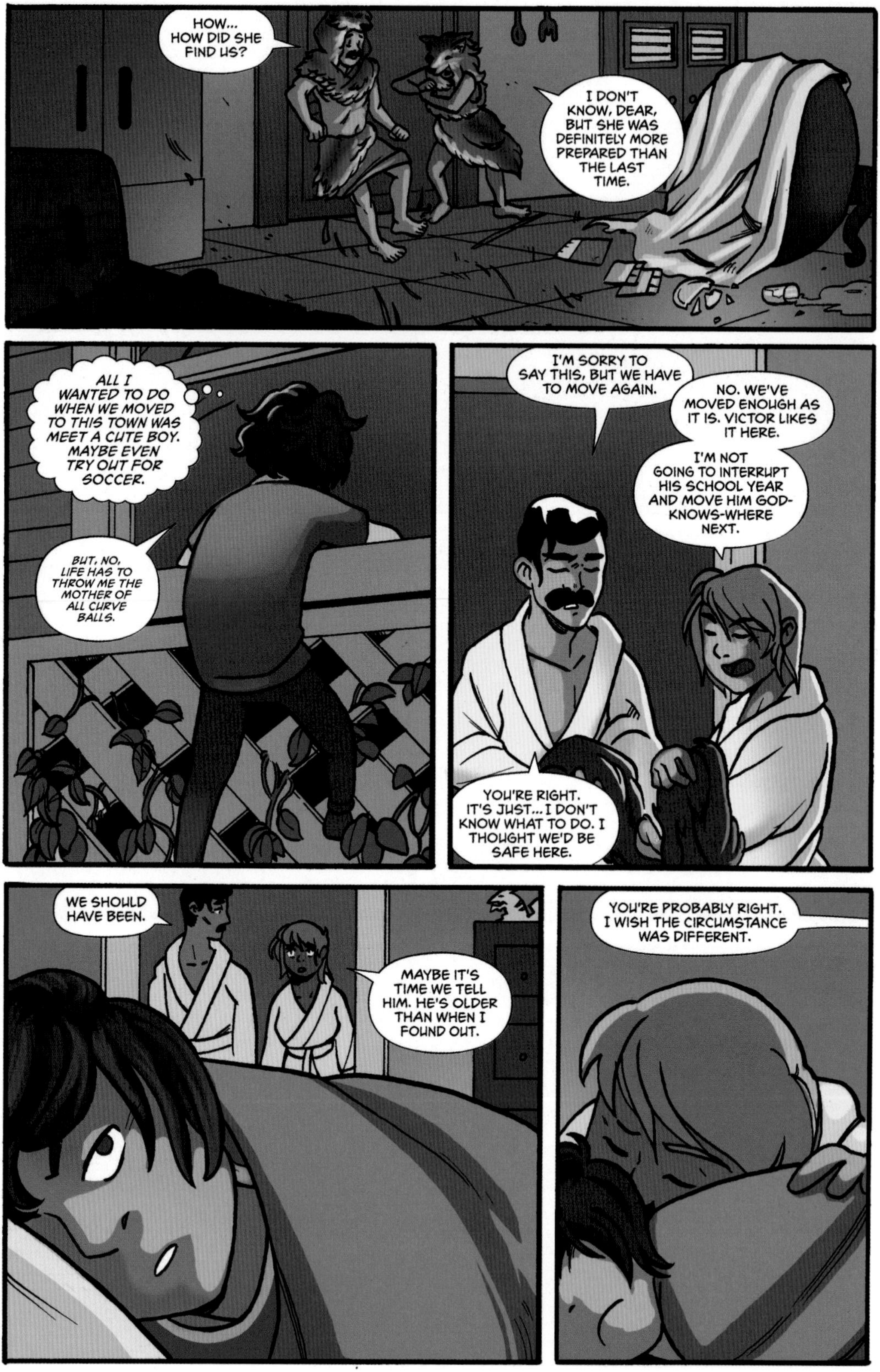
HOW... HOW DID SHE FIND US?
I DON'T KNOW, DEAR, BUT SHE WAS DEFINITELY MORE PREPARED THAN THE LAST TIME.
ALL I WANTED TO DO WHEN WE MOVED TO THIS TOWN WAS MEET A CUTE BOY. MAYBE EVEN TRY OUT FOR SOCCER.
BUT, NO, LIFE HAS TO THROW ME THE MOTHER OF ALL CURVE BALLS.
I'M SORRY TO SAY THIS, BUT WE HAVE TO MOVE AGAIN.
NO. WE'VE MOVED ENOUGH AS IT IS. VICTOR LIKES IT HERE.
I'M NOT GOING TO INTERRUPT HIS SCHOOL YEAR AND MOVE HIM GOD-KNOWS-WHERE NEXT.
YOU'RE RIGHT. IT'S JUST... I DON'T KNOW WHAT TO DO. I THOUGHT WE'D BE SAFE HERE.
WE SHOULD HAVE BEEN.
MAYBE IT'S TIME WE TELL HIM. HE'S OLDER THAN WHEN I FOUND OUT.
YOU'RE PROBABLY RIGHT. I WISH THE CIRCUMSTANCE WAS DIFFERENT.

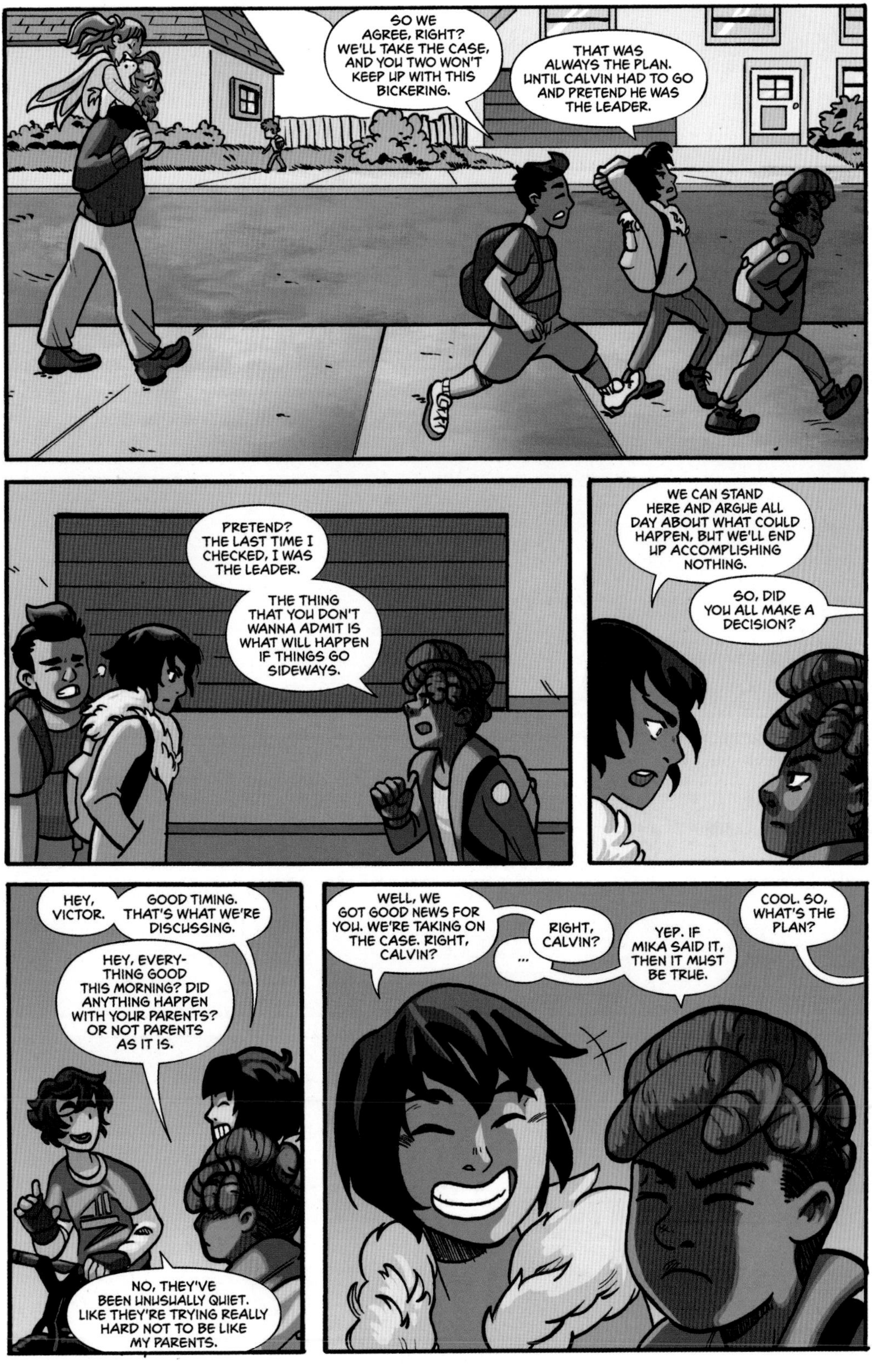

SO WE AGREE, RIGHT? WE'LL TAKE THE CASE, AND YOU TWO WON'T KEEP UP WITH THIS BICKERING.
THAT WAS ALWAYS THE PLAN. UNTIL CALVIN HAD TO GO AND PRETEND HE WAS THE LEADER.
PRETEND? THE LAST TIME I CHECKED, I WAS THE LEADER.
THE THING THAT YOU DON'T WANNA ADMIT IS WHAT WILL HAPPEN IF THINGS GO SIDEWAYS.
WE CAN STAND HERE AND ARGUE ALL DAY ABOUT WHAT COULD HAPPEN, BUT WE'LL END UP ACCOMPLISHING NOTHING.
SO, DID YOU ALL MAKE A DECISION?
HEY, VICTOR.
GOOD TIMING. THAT'S WHAT WE'RE DISCUSSING.
HEY, EVERY-THING GOOD THIS MORNING? DID ANYTHING HAPPEN WITH YOUR PARENTS? OR NOT PARENTS AS IT IS.
NO, THEY'VE BEEN UNUSUALLY QUIET. LIKE THEY'RE TRYING REALLY HARD NOT TO BE LIKE MY PARENTS.
WELL, WE GOT GOOD NEWS FOR YOU. WE'RE TAKING ON THE CASE. RIGHT, CALVIN?
RIGHT, CALVIN?
...
YEP. IF MIKA SAID IT, THEN IT MUST BE TRUE.
COOL. SO, WHAT'S THE PLAN?

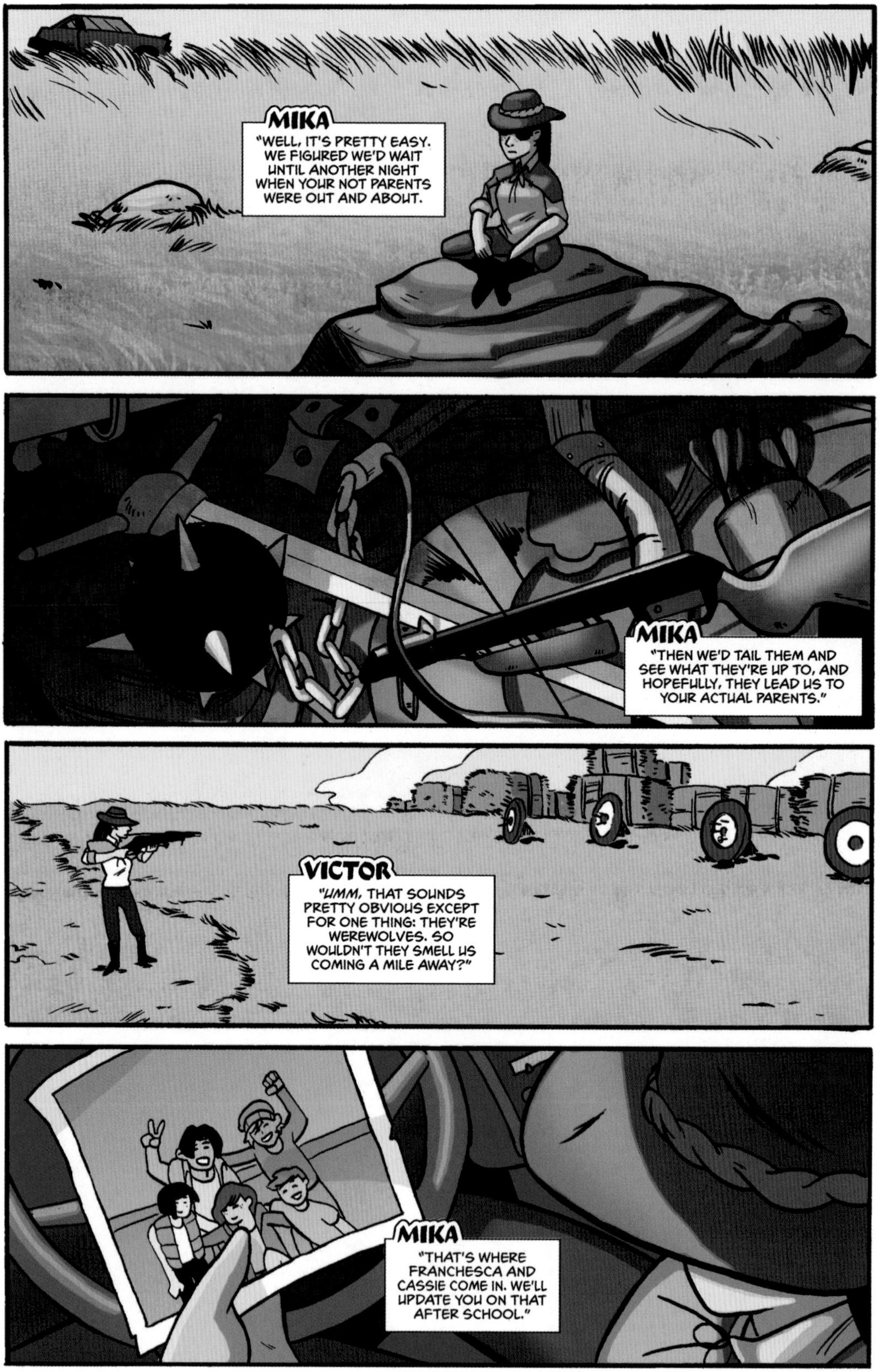
MIKA
"WELL, IT'S PRETTY EASY. WE FIGURED WE'D WAIT UNTIL ANOTHER NIGHT WHEN YOUR NOT PARENTS WERE OUT AND ABOUT.
MIKA
"THEN WE'D TAIL THEM AND SEE WHAT THEY'RE UP TO, AND HOPEFULLY, THEY LEAD US TO YOUR ACTUAL PARENTS."
VICTOR
"UMM, THAT SOUNDS PRETTY OBVIOUS EXCEPT FOR ONE THING: THEY'RE WEREWOLVES. SO WOULDN'T THEY SMELL US COMING A MILE AWAY?"
MIKA
"THAT'S WHERE FRANCHESCA AND CASSIE COME IN. WE'LL UPDATE YOU ON THAT AFTER SCHOOL."

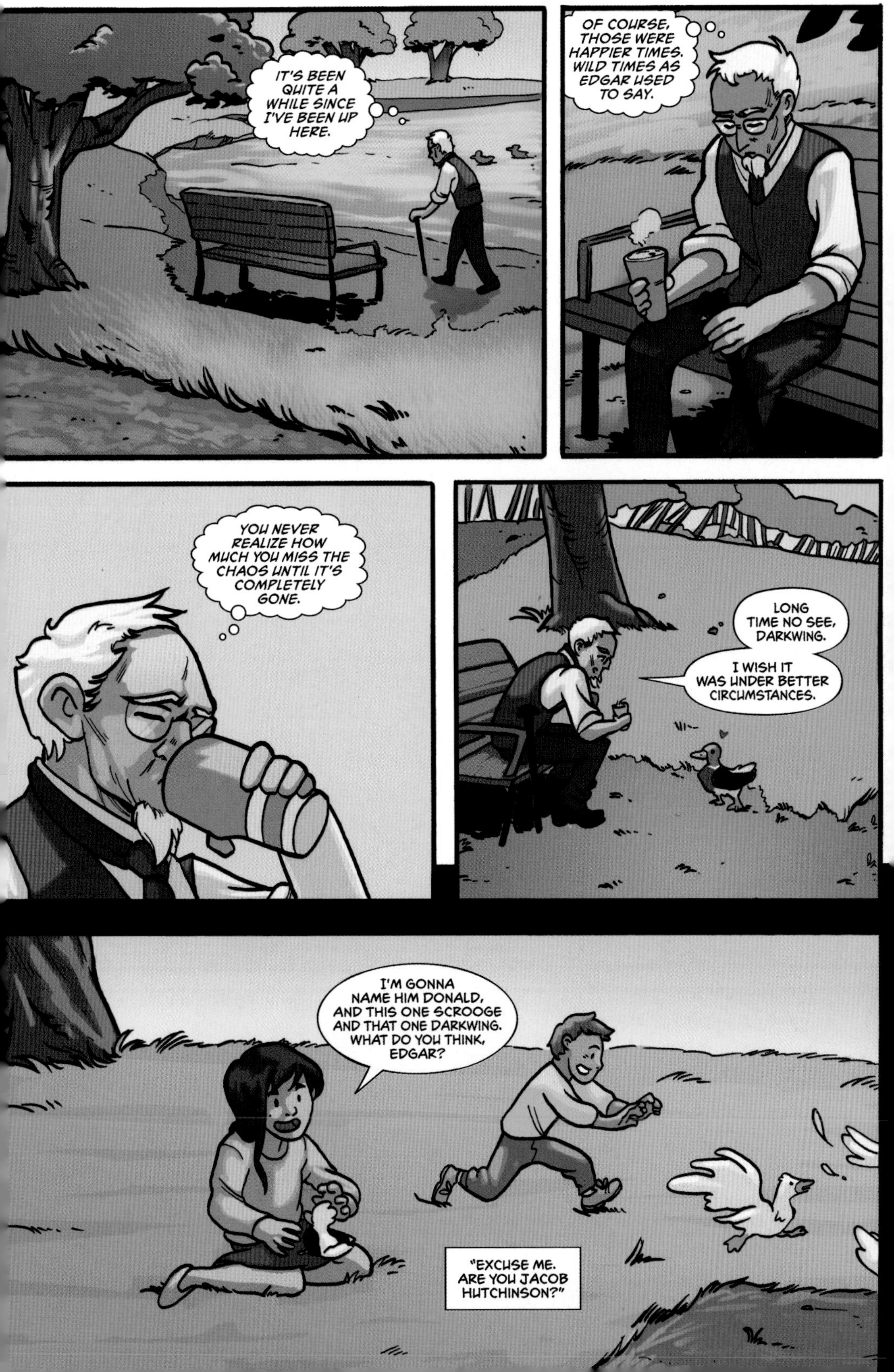
IT'S BEEN QUITE A WHILE SINCE I'VE BEEN UP HERE.
OF COURSE, THOSE WERE HAPPIER TIMES. WILD TIMES AS EDGAR USED TO SAY.
YOU NEVER REALIZE HOW MUCH YOU MISS THE CHAOS UNTIL IT'S COMPLETELY GONE.
LONG TIME NO SEE, DARKWING.
I WISH IT WAS UNDER BETTER CIRCUMSTANCES.
I'M GONNA NAME HIM DONALD, AND THIS ONE SCROOGE AND THAT ONE DARKWING. WHAT DO YOU THINK, EDGAR?
"EXCUSE ME. ARE YOU JACOB HUTCHINSON?"

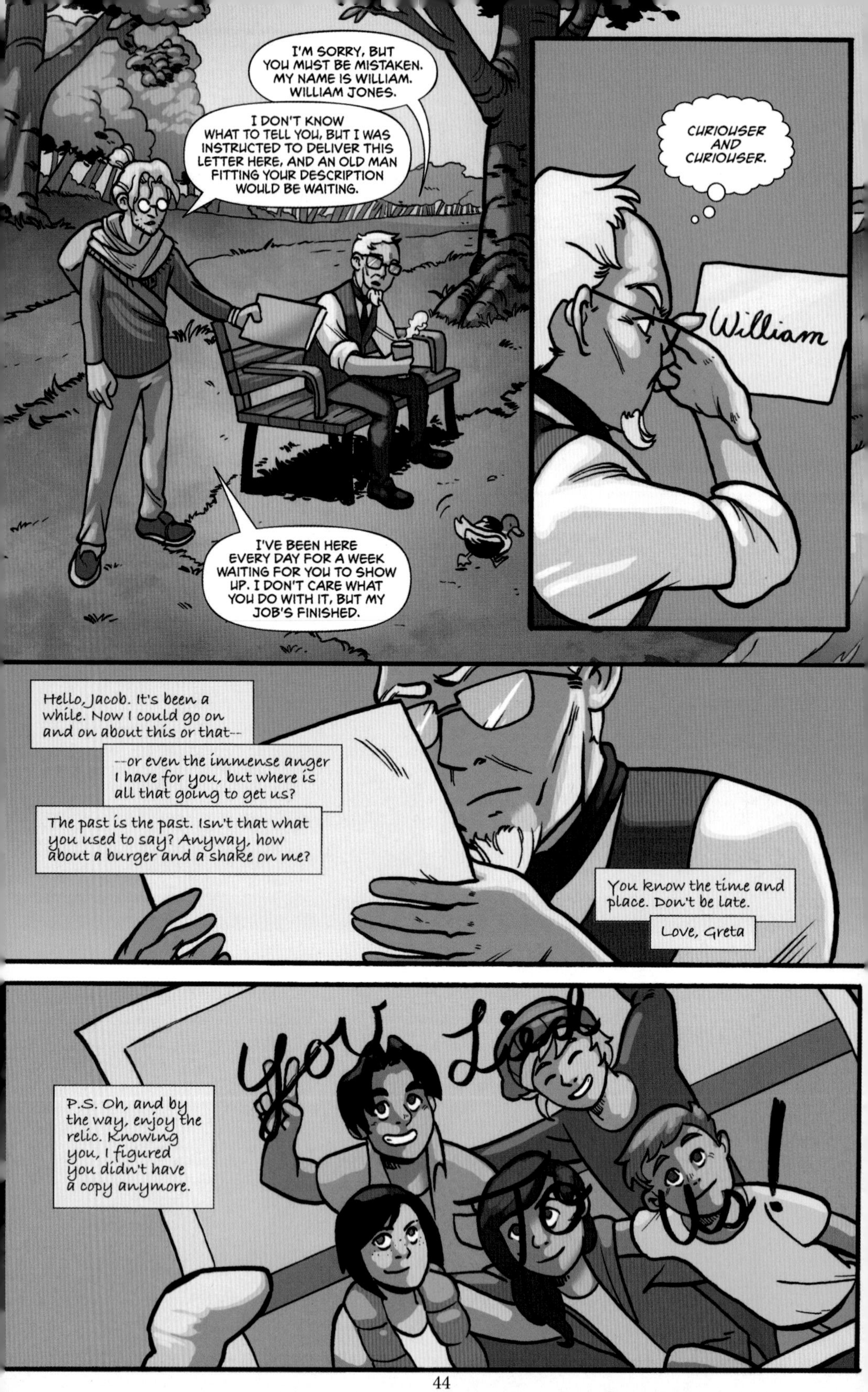
I'M SORRY, BUT YOU MUST BE MISTAKEN. MY NAME IS WILLIAM. WILLIAM JONES.
I DON'T KNOW WHAT TO TELL YOU, BUT I WAS INSTRUCTED TO DELIVER THIS LETTER HERE, AND AN OLD MAN FITTING YOUR DESCRIPTION WOULD BE WAITING.
I'VE BEEN HERE EVERY DAY FOR A WEEK WAITING FOR YOU TO SHOW UP. I DON'T CARE WHAT YOU DO WITH IT, BUT MY JOB'S FINISHED.
CURIOUSER AND CURIOUSER.
William
Hello, Jacob. It's been a while. Now I could go on and on about this or that--
--or even the immense anger I have for you, but where is all that going to get us?
The past is the past. Isn't that what you used to say? Anyway, how about a burger and a shake on me?
You know the time and place. Don't be late.
Love, Greta
You Lied!
P.S. Oh, and by the way, enjoy the relic. Knowing you, I figured you didn't have a copy anymore.

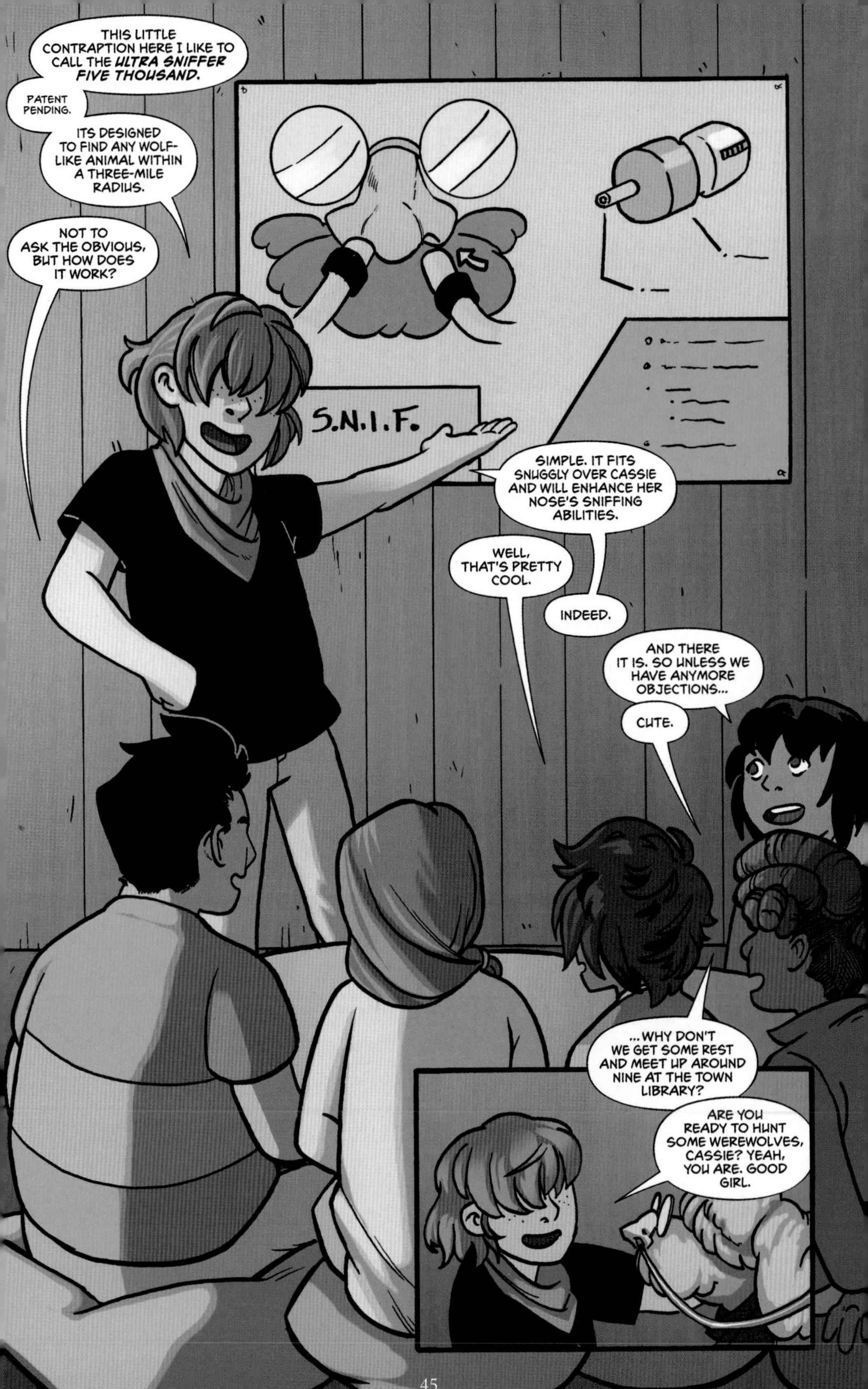
THIS LITTLE CONTRAPTION HERE I LIKE TO CALL THE *ULTRA SNIFFER FIVE THOUSAND.*
PATENT PENDING.
ITS DESIGNED TO FIND ANY WOLF-LIKE ANIMAL WITHIN A THREE-MILE RADIUS.
NOT TO ASK THE OBVIOUS, BUT HOW DOES IT WORK?
S.N.I.F.
SIMPLE. IT FITS SNUGGLY OVER CASSIE AND WILL ENHANCE HER NOSE'S SNIFFING ABILITIES.
WELL, THAT'S PRETTY COOL.
INDEED.
AND THERE IT IS. SO UNLESS WE HAVE ANYMORE OBJECTIONS...
CUTE.
...WHY DON'T WE GET SOME REST AND MEET UP AROUND NINE AT THE TOWN LIBRARY?
ARE YOU READY TO HUNT SOME WEREWOLVES, CASSIE? YEAH, YOU ARE. GOOD GIRL.

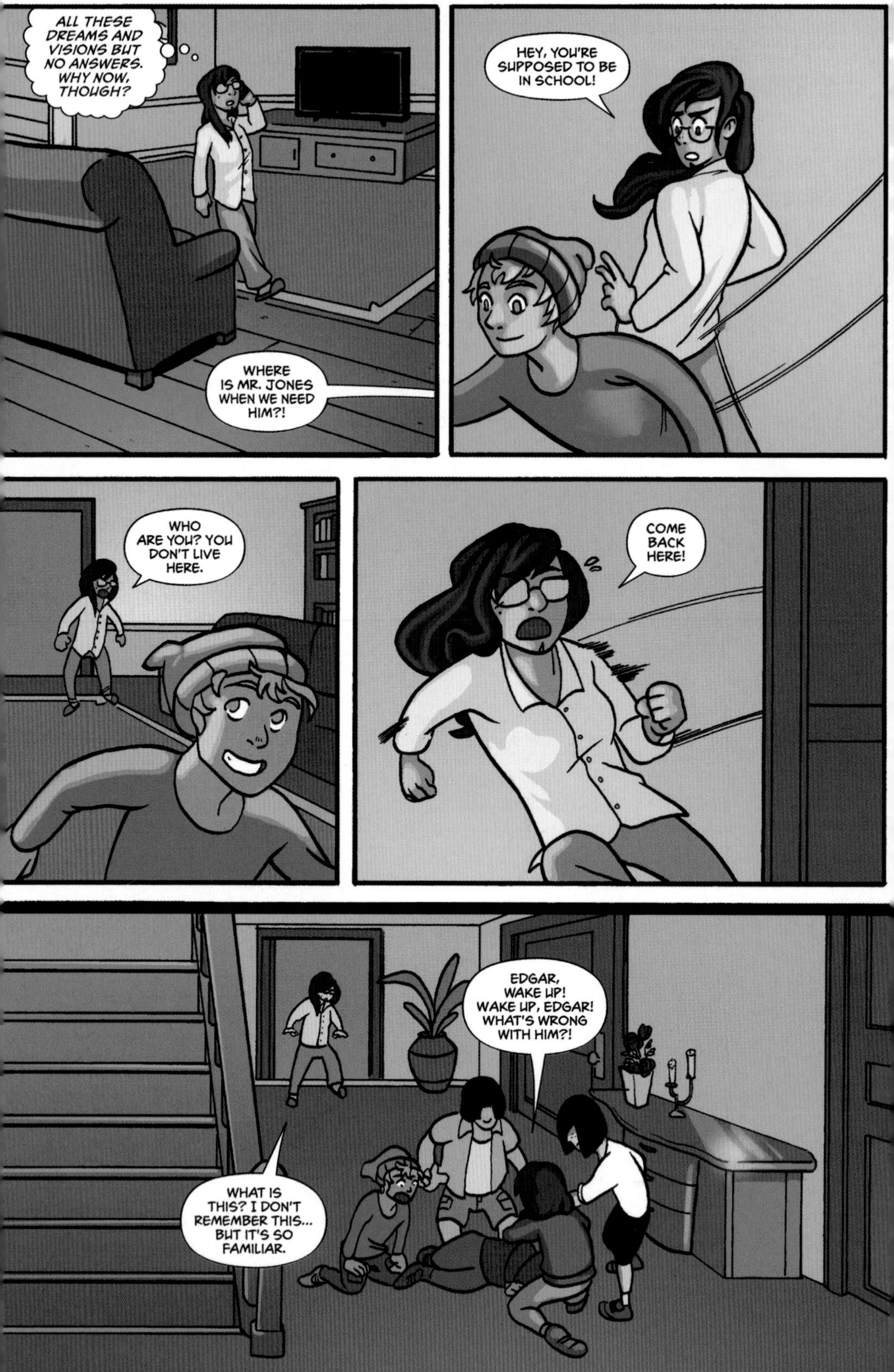
ALL THESE DREAMS AND VISIONS BUT NO ANSWERS. WHY NOW, THOUGH?
WHERE IS MR. JONES WHEN WE NEED HIM?!
HEY, YOU'RE SUPPOSED TO BE IN SCHOOL!
WHO ARE YOU? YOU DON'T LIVE HERE.
COME BACK HERE!
EDGAR, WAKE UP! WAKE UP, EDGAR! WHAT'S WRONG WITH HIM?!
WHAT IS THIS? I DON'T REMEMBER THIS... BUT IT'S SO FAMILIAR.

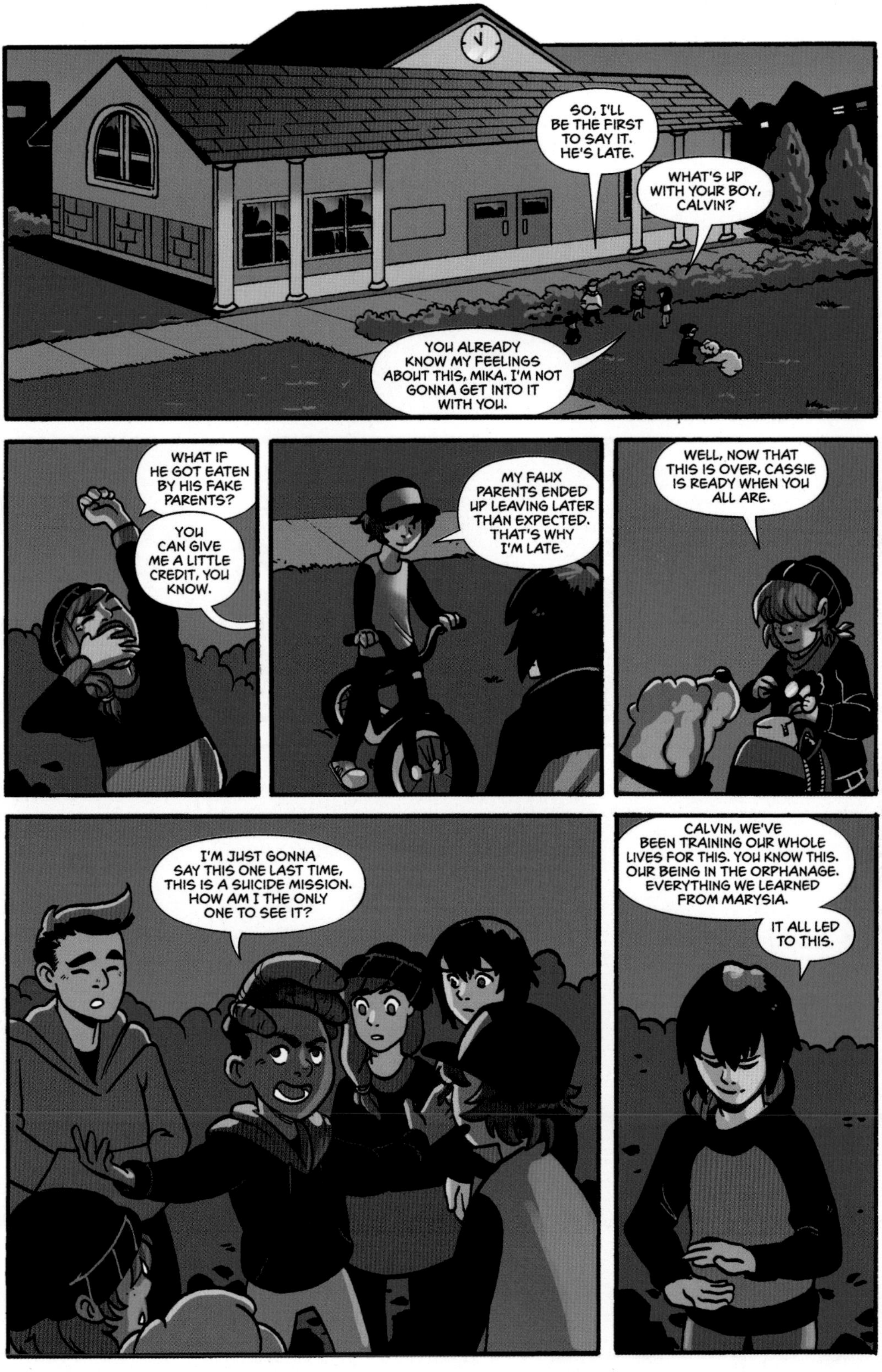
SO, I'LL BE THE FIRST TO SAY IT. HE'S LATE.
WHAT'S UP WITH YOUR BOY, CALVIN?
YOU ALREADY KNOW MY FEELINGS ABOUT THIS, MIKA. I'M NOT GONNA GET INTO IT WITH YOU.
WHAT IF HE GOT EATEN BY HIS FAKE PARENTS?
YOU CAN GIVE ME A LITTLE CREDIT, YOU KNOW.
MY FAUX PARENTS ENDED UP LEAVING LATER THAN EXPECTED. THAT'S WHY I'M LATE.
WELL, NOW THAT THIS IS OVER, CASSIE IS READY WHEN YOU ALL ARE.
I'M JUST GONNA SAY THIS ONE LAST TIME, THIS IS A SUICIDE MISSION. HOW AM I THE ONLY ONE TO SEE IT?
CALVIN, WE'VE BEEN TRAINING OUR WHOLE LIVES FOR THIS. YOU KNOW THIS. OUR BEING IN THE ORPHANAGE. EVERYTHING WE LEARNED FROM MARYSIA.
IT ALL LED TO THIS.

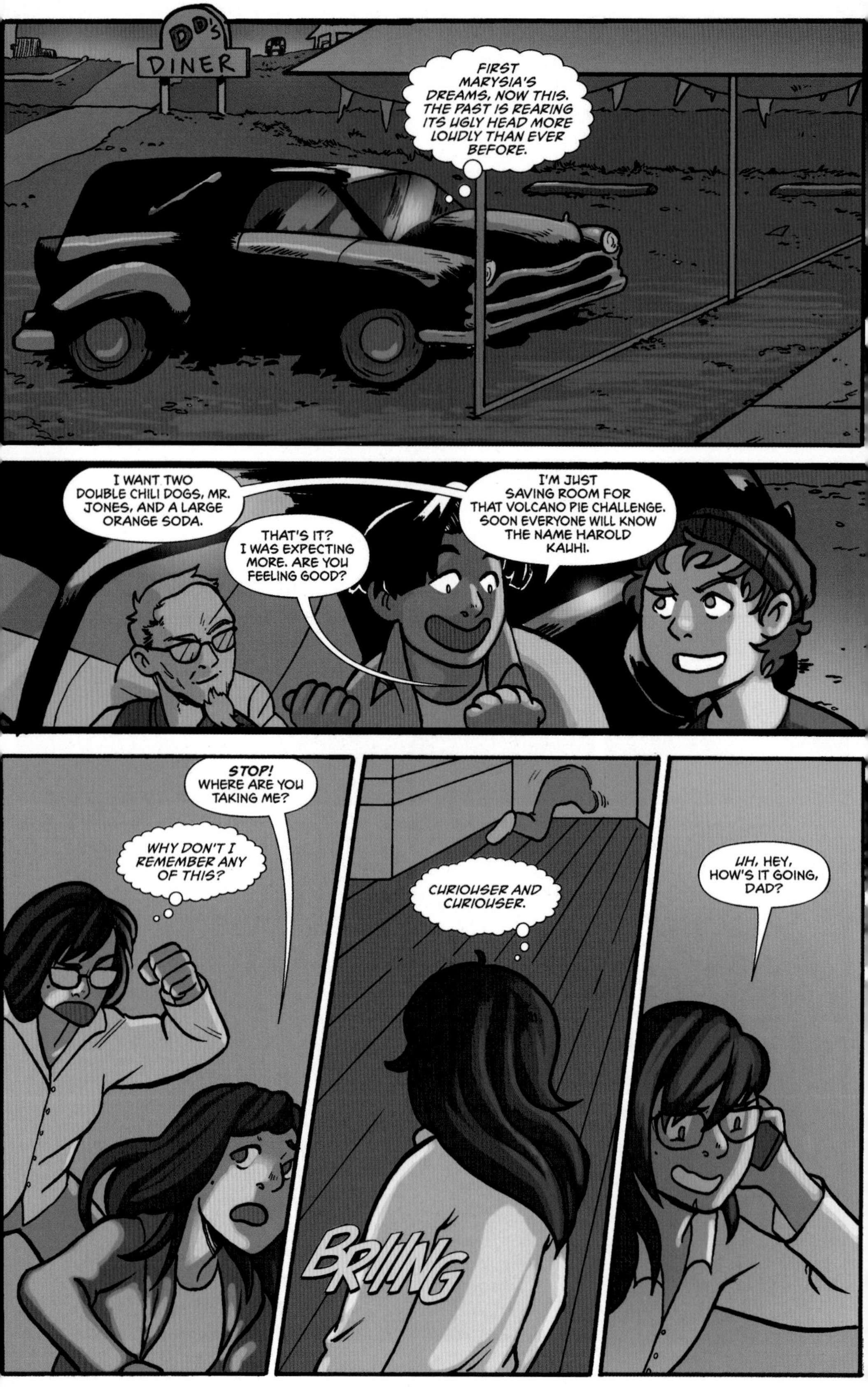
DD's
DINER
FIRST MARYSIA'S DREAMS, NOW THIS. THE PAST IS REARING ITS UGLY HEAD MORE LOUDLY THAN EVER BEFORE.
I WANT TWO DOUBLE CHILI DOGS, MR. JONES, AND A LARGE ORANGE SODA.
THAT'S IT? I WAS EXPECTING MORE. ARE YOU FEELING GOOD?
I'M JUST SAVING ROOM FOR THAT VOLCANO PIE CHALLENGE. SOON EVERYONE WILL KNOW THE NAME HAROLD KAUHI.
STOP! WHERE ARE YOU TAKING ME?
WHY DON'T I REMEMBER ANY OF THIS?
CURIOUSER AND CURIOUSER.
BRIIING
UH, HEY, HOW'S IT GOING, DAD?

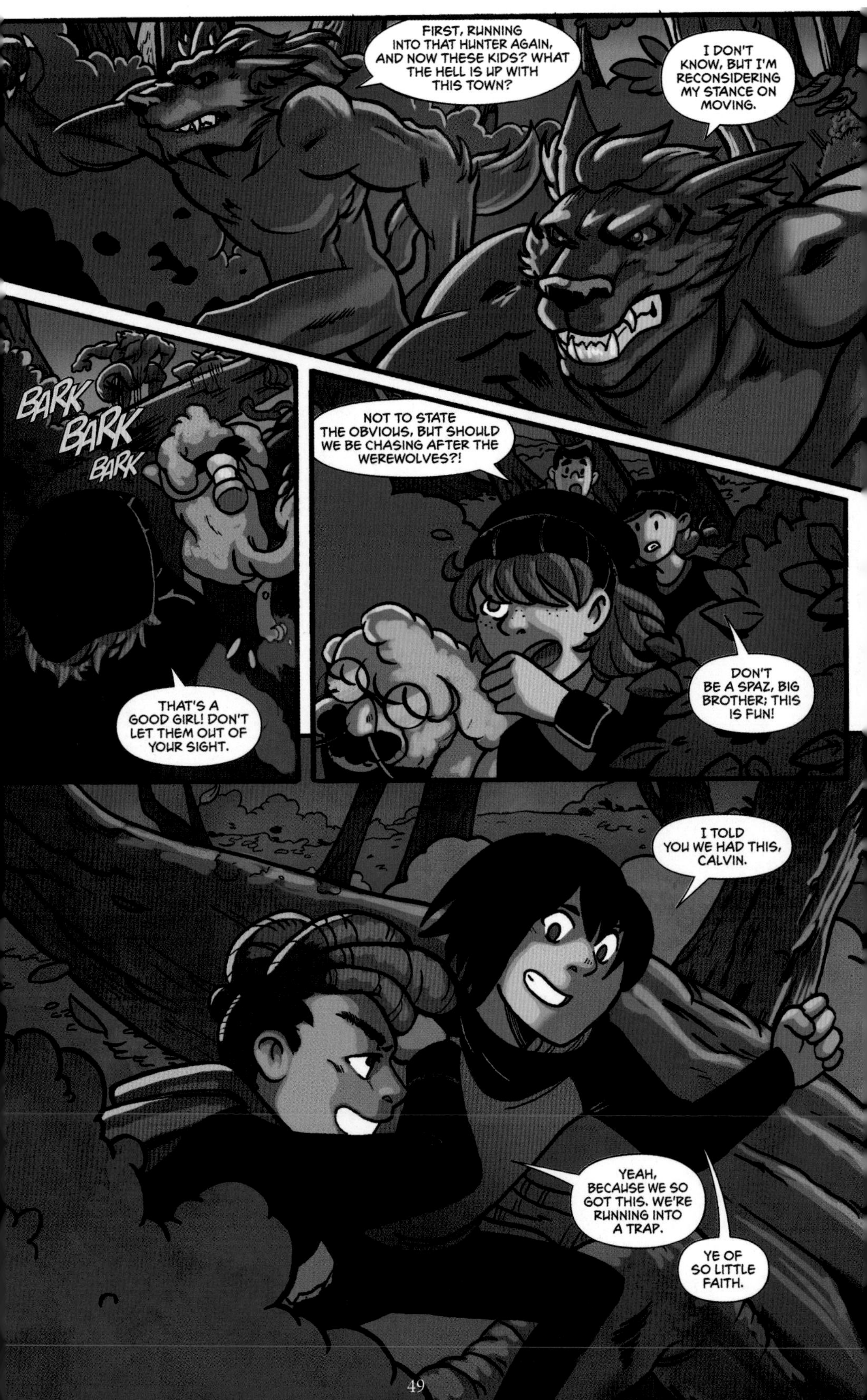
FIRST, RUNNING INTO THAT HUNTER AGAIN, AND NOW THESE KIDS? WHAT THE HELL IS UP WITH THIS TOWN?
I DON'T KNOW, BUT I'M RECONSIDERING MY STANCE ON MOVING.
BARK
BARK
BARK
THAT'S A GOOD GIRL! DON'T LET THEM OUT OF YOUR SIGHT.
NOT TO STATE THE OBVIOUS, BUT SHOULD WE BE CHASING AFTER THE WEREWOLVES?!
DON'T BE A SPAZ, BIG BROTHER; THIS IS FUN!
I TOLD YOU WE HAD THIS, CALVIN.
YEAH, BECAUSE WE SO GOT THIS. WE'RE RUNNING INTO A TRAP.
YE OF SO LITTLE FAITH.

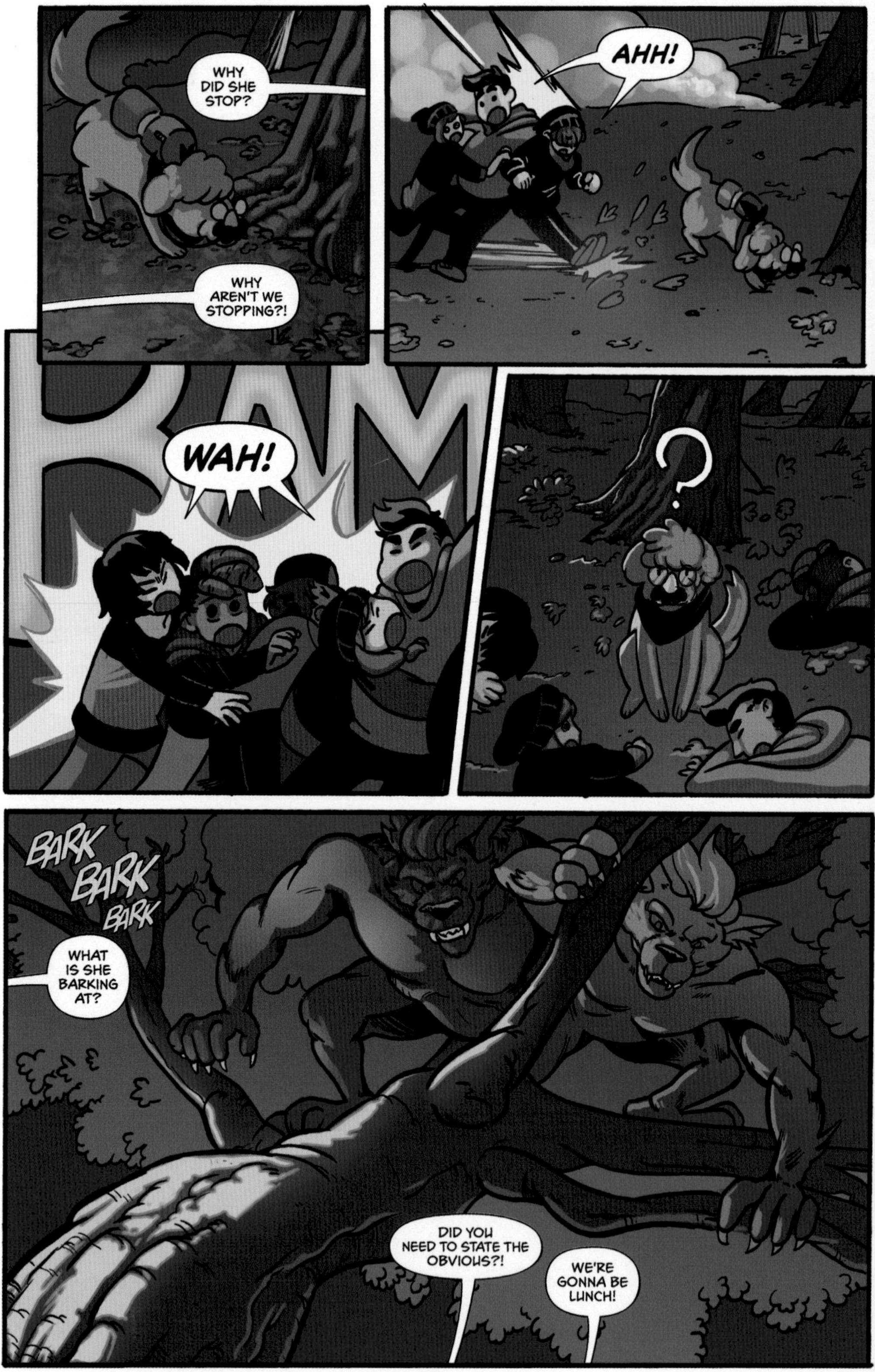
WHY DID SHE STOP?
WHY AREN'T WE STOPPING?!
AHH!
WAH!
?
BARK
BARK
BARK
WHAT IS SHE BARKING AT?
DID YOU NEED TO STATE THE OBVIOUS?!
WE'RE GONNA BE LUNCH!

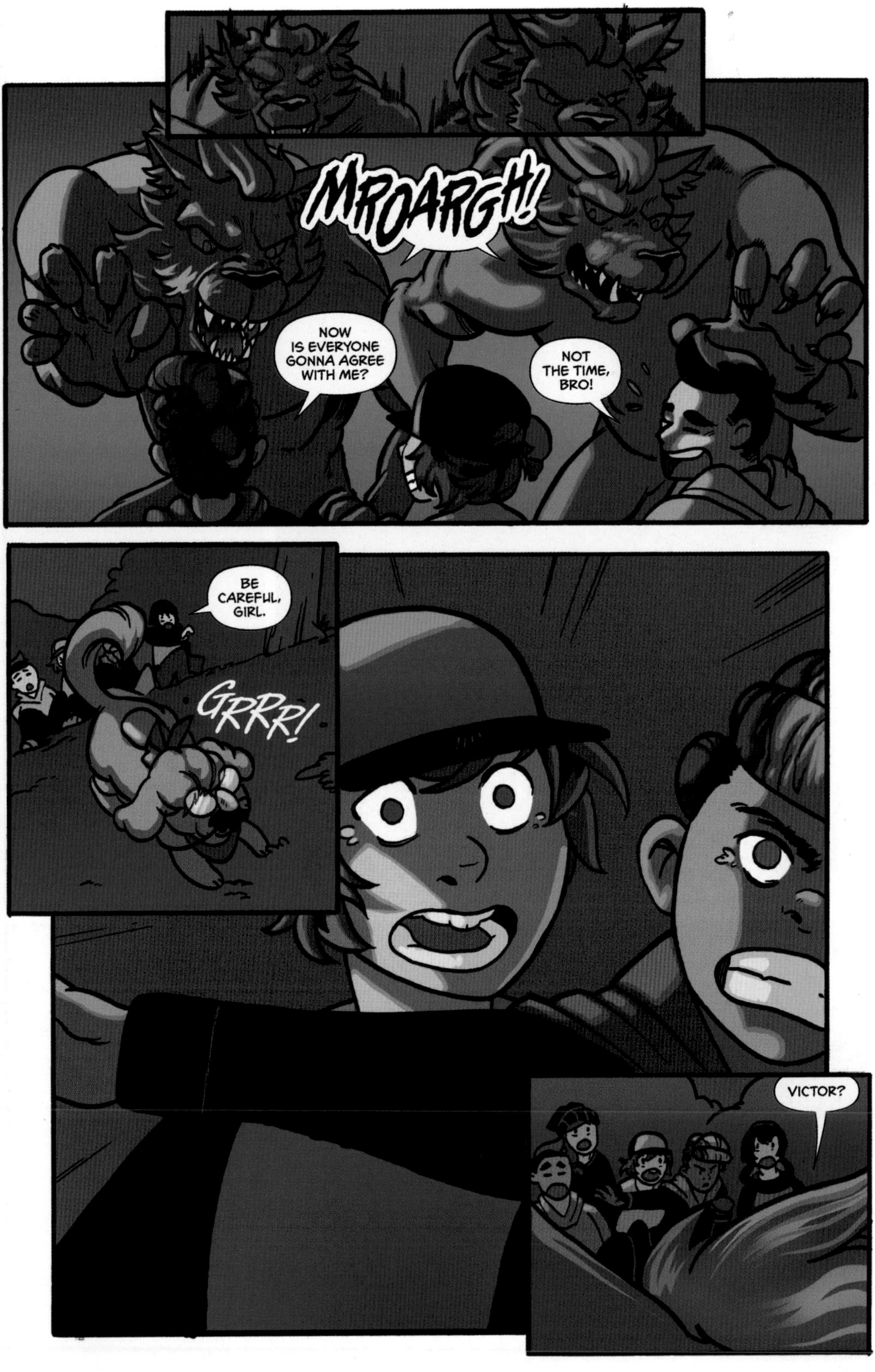
MROARGH!
NOW IS EVERYONE GONNA AGREE WITH ME?
NOT THE TIME, BRO!
BE CAREFUL, GIRL.
GRRR!
VICTOR?

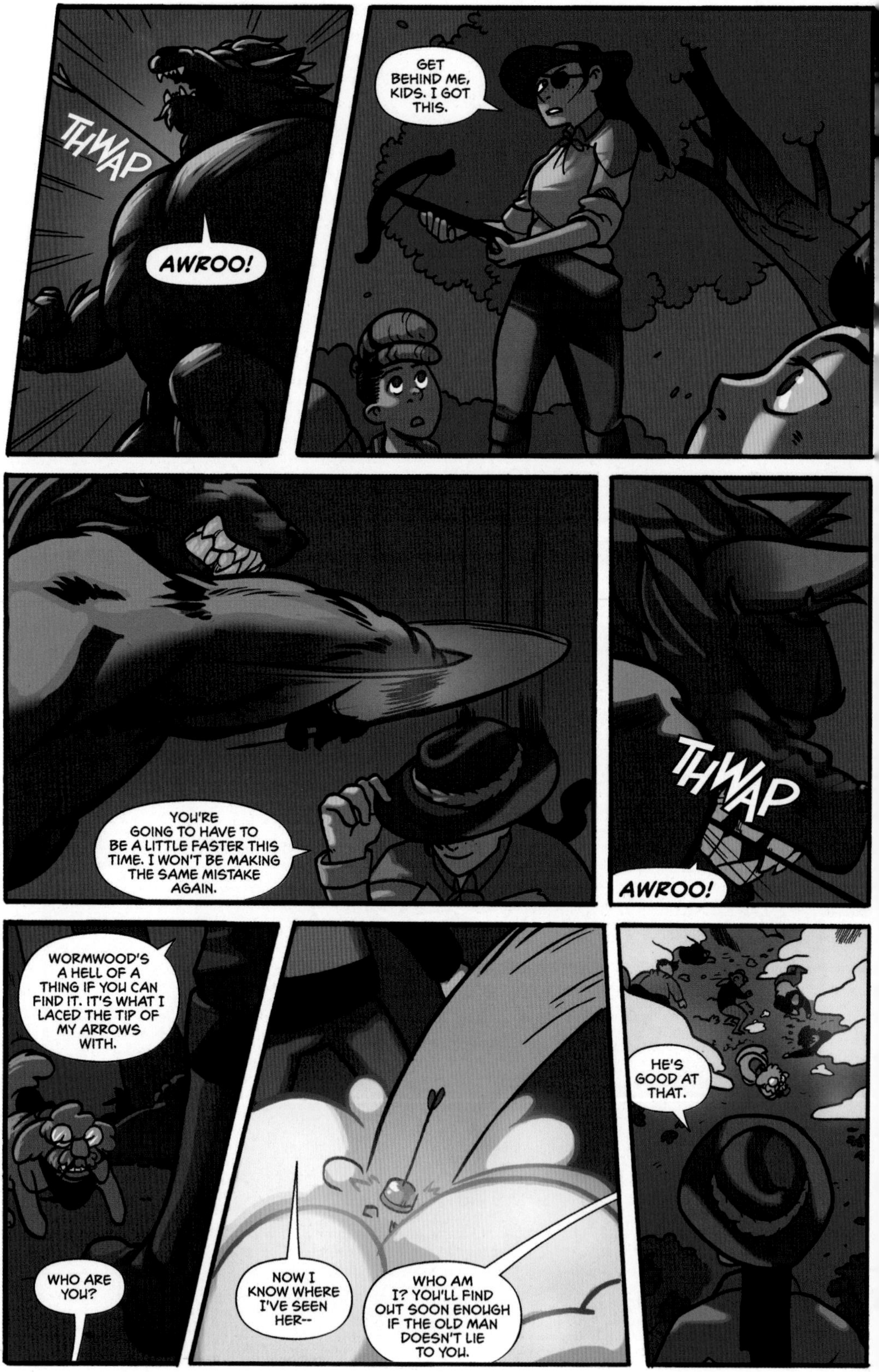
THWAP
AWROO!
GET BEHIND ME, KIDS. I GOT THIS.
YOU'RE GOING TO HAVE TO BE A LITTLE FASTER THIS TIME. I WON'T BE MAKING THE SAME MISTAKE AGAIN.
THWAP
AWROO!
WORMWOOD'S A HELL OF A THING IF YOU CAN FIND IT. IT'S WHAT I LACED THE TIP OF MY ARROWS WITH.
WHO ARE YOU?
NOW I KNOW WHERE I'VE SEEN HER--
WHO AM I? YOU'LL FIND OUT SOON ENOUGH IF THE OLD MAN DOESN'T LIE TO YOU.
HE'S GOOD AT THAT.

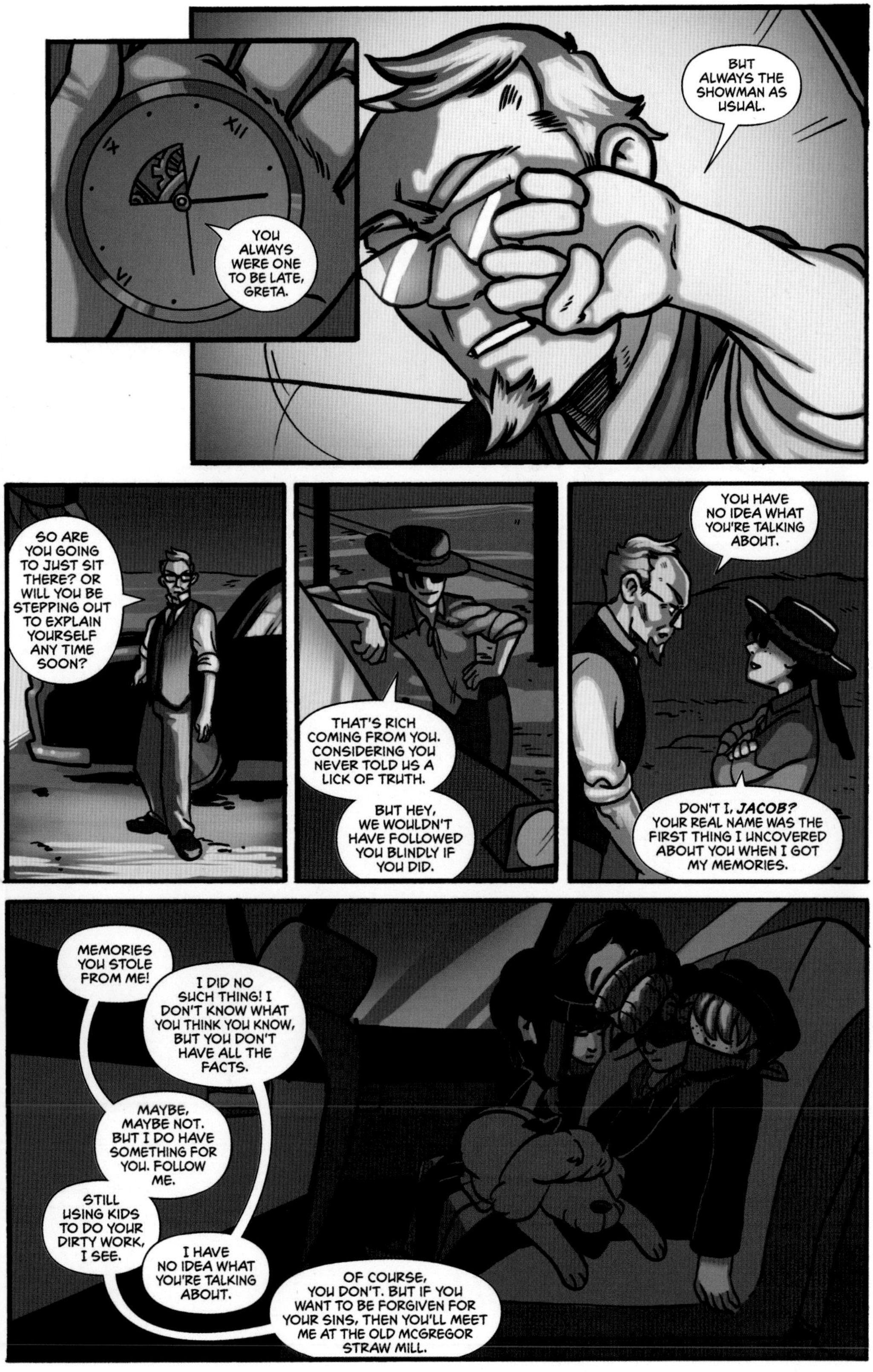
YOU ALWAYS WERE ONE TO BE LATE, GRETA.
BUT ALWAYS THE SHOWMAN AS USUAL.
SO ARE YOU GOING TO JUST SIT THERE? OR WILL YOU BE STEPPING OUT TO EXPLAIN YOURSELF ANY TIME SOON?
THAT'S RICH COMING FROM YOU. CONSIDERING YOU NEVER TOLD US A LICK OF TRUTH.
BUT HEY, WE WOULDN'T HAVE FOLLOWED YOU BLINDLY IF YOU DID.
YOU HAVE NO IDEA WHAT YOU'RE TALKING ABOUT.
DON'T I, JACOB? YOUR REAL NAME WAS THE FIRST THING I UNCOVERED ABOUT YOU WHEN I GOT MY MEMORIES.
MEMORIES YOU STOLE FROM ME!
I DID NO SUCH THING! I DON'T KNOW WHAT YOU THINK YOU KNOW, BUT YOU DON'T HAVE ALL THE FACTS.
MAYBE, MAYBE NOT. BUT I DO HAVE SOMETHING FOR YOU. FOLLOW ME.
STILL USING KIDS TO DO YOUR DIRTY WORK, I SEE.
I HAVE NO IDEA WHAT YOU'RE TALKING ABOUT.
OF COURSE, YOU DON'T. BUT IF YOU WANT TO BE FORGIVEN FOR YOUR SINS, THEN YOU'LL MEET ME AT THE OLD MCGREGOR STRAW MILL.

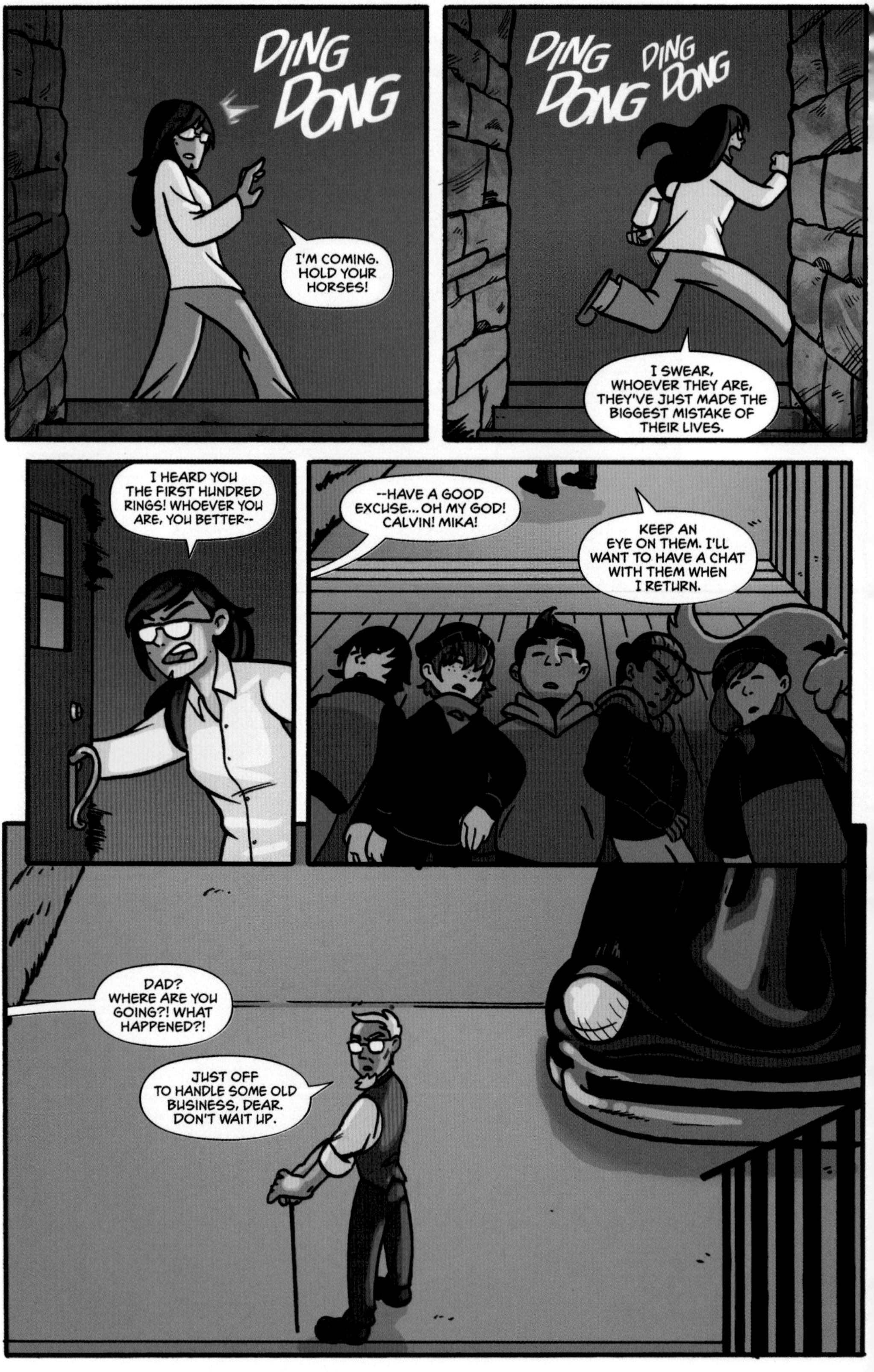
DING DONG
I'M COMING. HOLD YOUR HORSES!
DING DONG DING DONG
I SWEAR, WHOEVER THEY ARE, THEY'VE JUST MADE THE BIGGEST MISTAKE OF THEIR LIVES.
I HEARD YOU THE FIRST HUNDRED RINGS! WHOEVER YOU ARE, YOU BETTER--
--HAVE A GOOD EXCUSE... OH MY GOD! CALVIN! MIKA!
KEEP AN EYE ON THEM. I'LL WANT TO HAVE A CHAT WITH THEM WHEN I RETURN.
DAD? WHERE ARE YOU GOING?! WHAT HAPPENED?!
JUST OFF TO HANDLE SOME OLD BUSINESS, DEAR. DON'T WAIT UP.

Chapter Three
Truth Can Be a
Painful Reminder

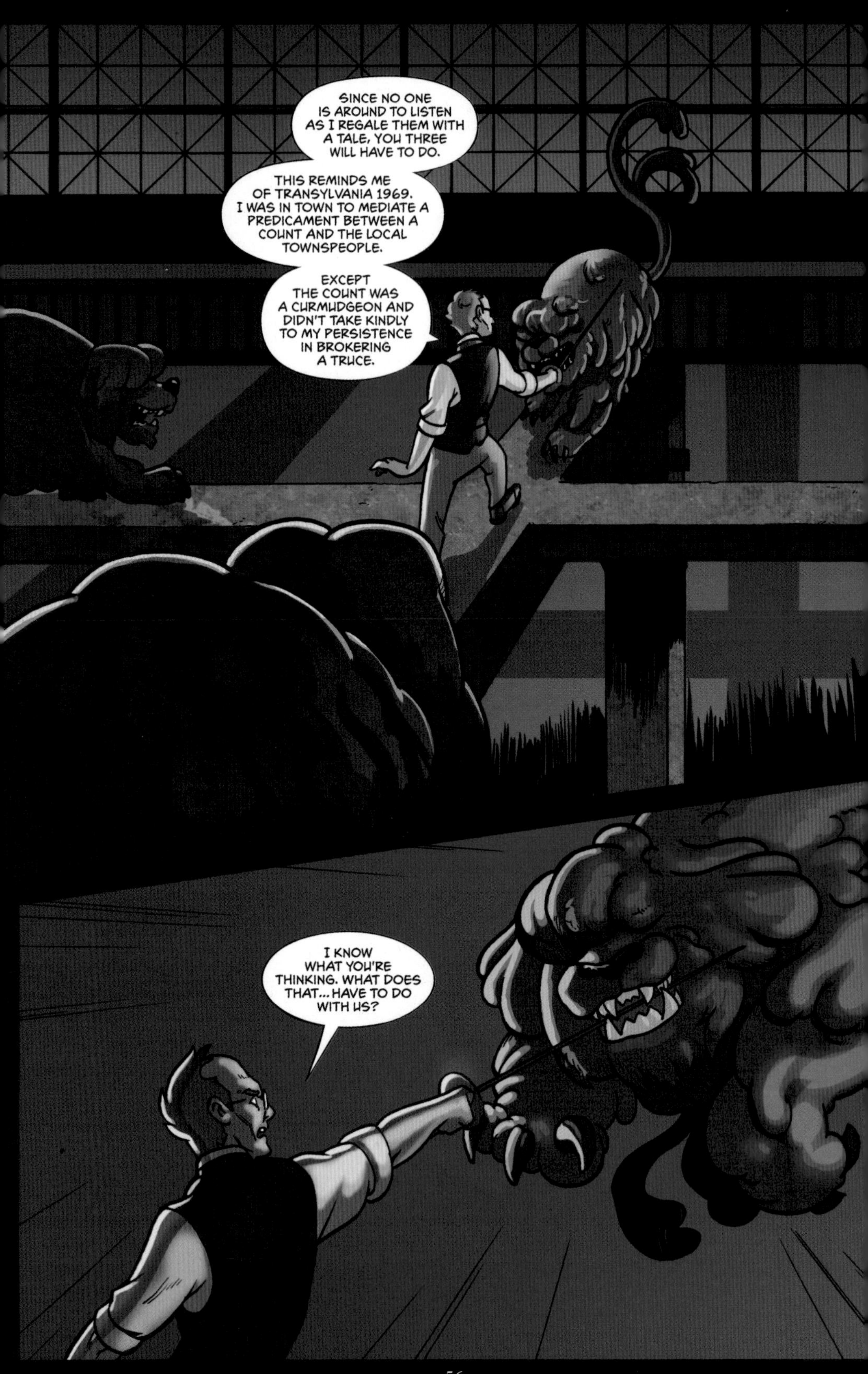
SINCE NO ONE IS AROUND TO LISTEN AS I REGALE THEM WITH A TALE, YOU THREE WILL HAVE TO DO.
THIS REMINDS ME OF TRANSYLVANIA 1969. I WAS IN TOWN TO MEDIATE A PREDICAMENT BETWEEN A COUNT AND THE LOCAL TOWNSPEOPLE.
EXCEPT THE COUNT WAS A CURMUDGEON AND DIDN'T TAKE KINDLY TO MY PERSISTENCE IN BROKERING A TRUCE.
I KNOW WHAT YOU'RE THINKING. WHAT DOES THAT... HAVE TO DO WITH US?

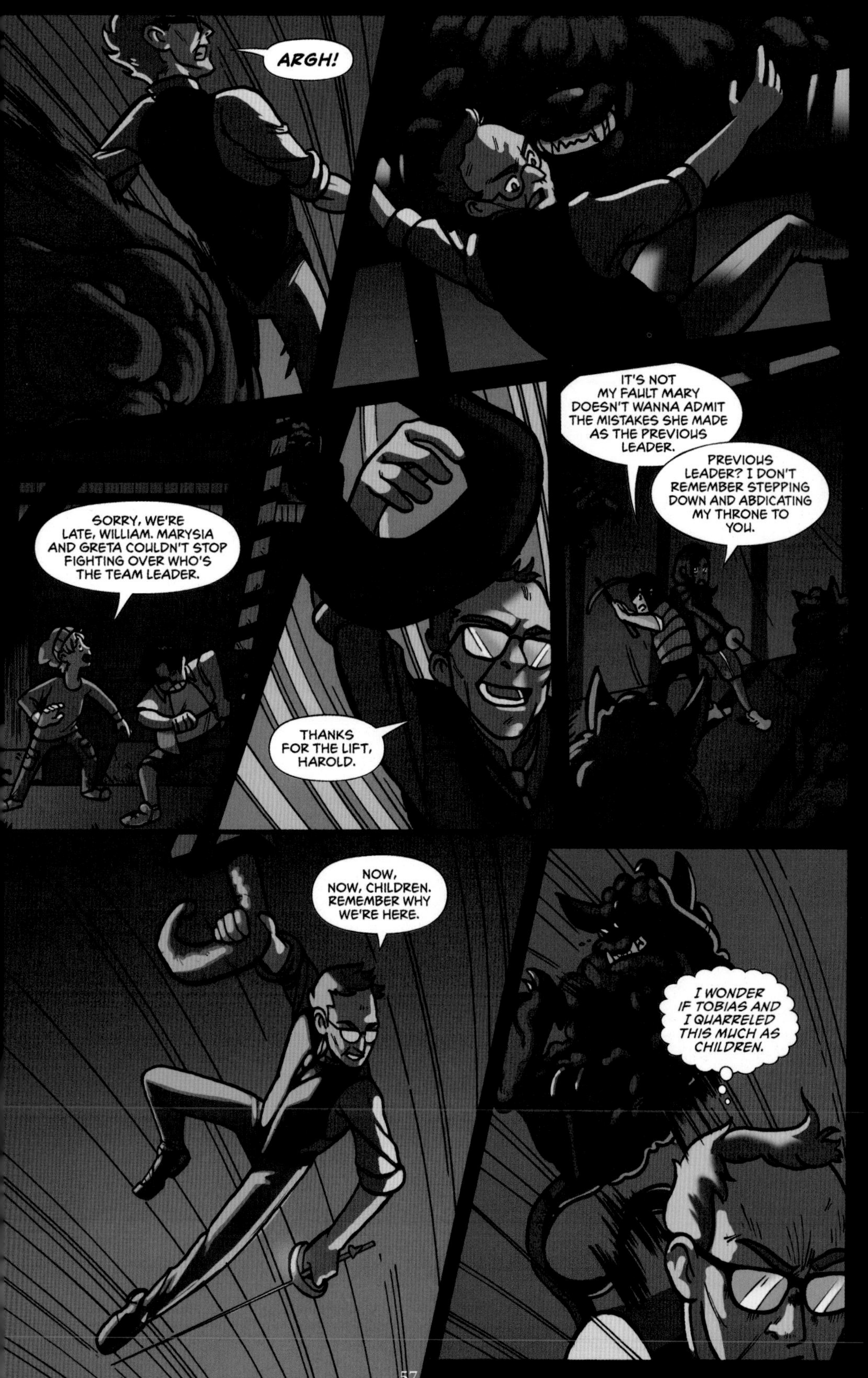
ARGH!
IT'S NOT MY FAULT MARY DOESN'T WANNA ADMIT THE MISTAKES SHE MADE AS THE PREVIOUS LEADER.
PREVIOUS LEADER? I DON'T REMEMBER STEPPING DOWN AND ABDICATING MY THRONE TO YOU.
SORRY, WE'RE LATE, WILLIAM. MARYSIA AND GRETA COULDN'T STOP FIGHTING OVER WHO'S THE TEAM LEADER.
THANKS FOR THE LIFT, HAROLD.
NOW, NOW, CHILDREN. REMEMBER WHY WE'RE HERE.
I WONDER IF TOBIAS AND I QUARRELED THIS MUCH AS CHILDREN.

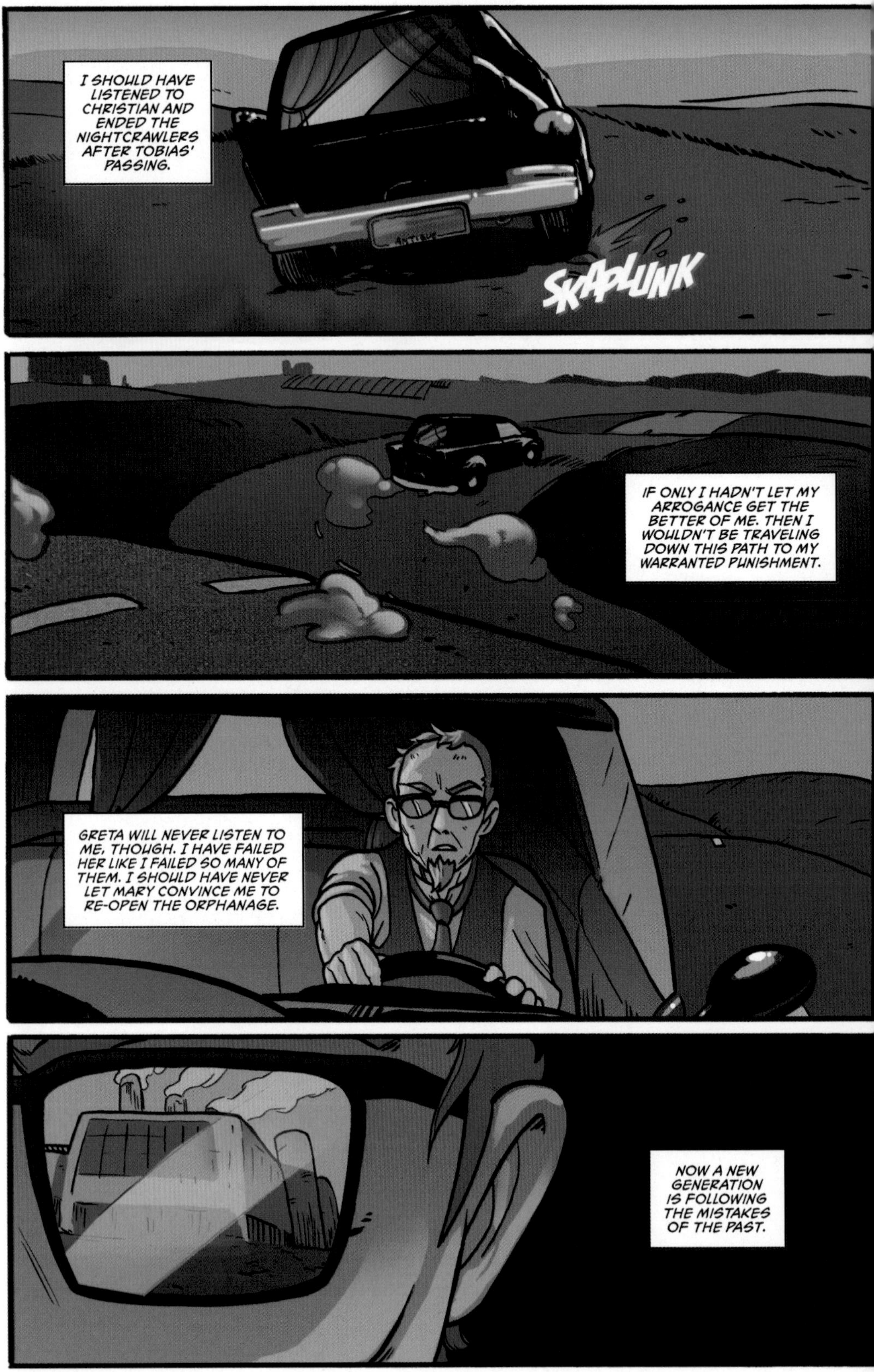
I SHOULD HAVE LISTENED TO CHRISTIAN AND ENDED THE NIGHTCRAWLERS AFTER TOBIAS' PASSING.
SKAPLUNK
IF ONLY I HADN'T LET MY ARROGANCE GET THE BETTER OF ME. THEN I WOULDN'T BE TRAVELING DOWN THIS PATH TO MY WARRANTED PUNISHMENT.
GRETA WILL NEVER LISTEN TO ME, THOUGH. I HAVE FAILED HER LIKE I FAILED SO MANY OF THEM. I SHOULD HAVE NEVER LET MARY CONVINCE ME TO RE-OPEN THE ORPHANAGE.
NOW A NEW GENERATION IS FOLLOWING THE MISTAKES OF THE PAST.

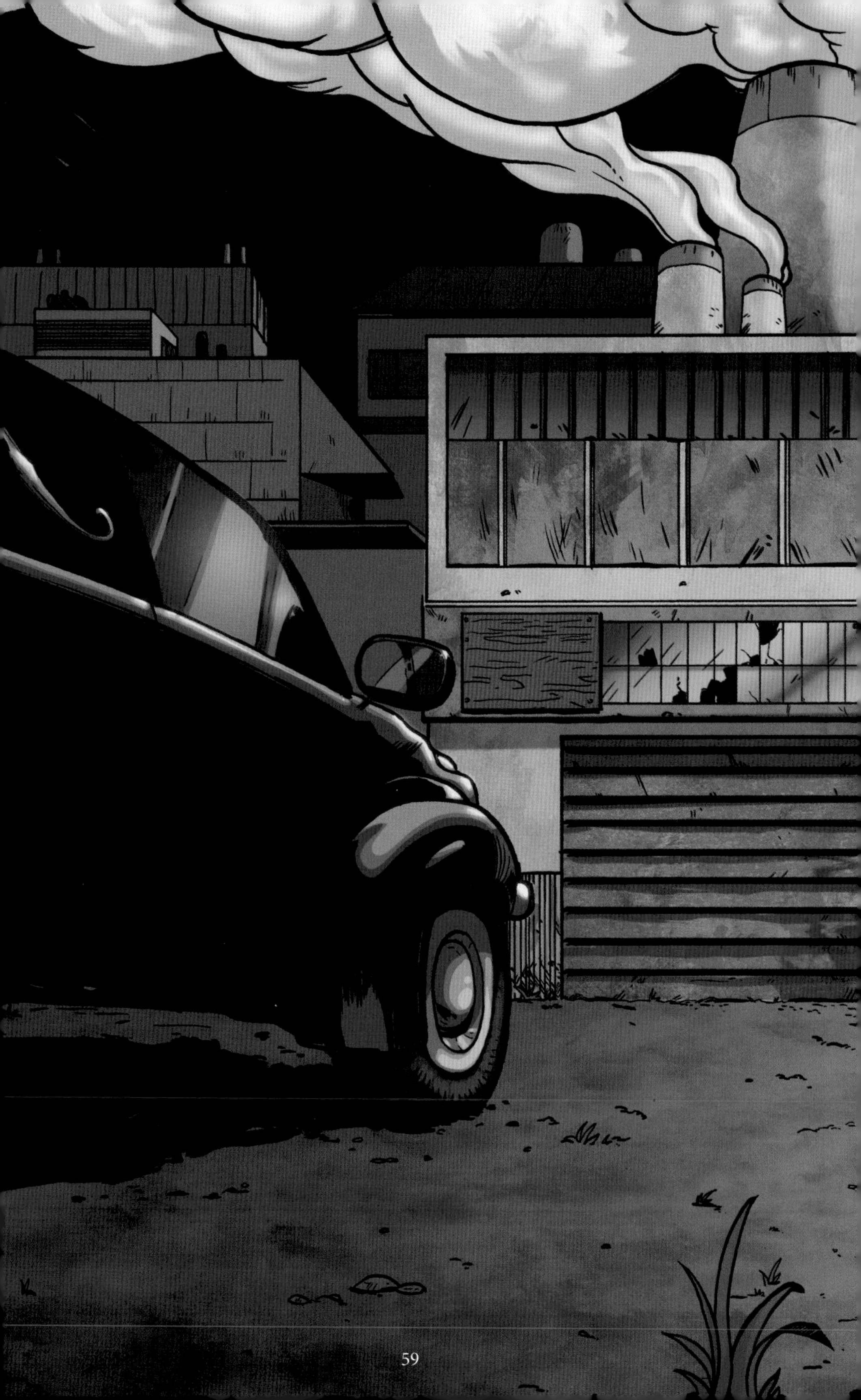

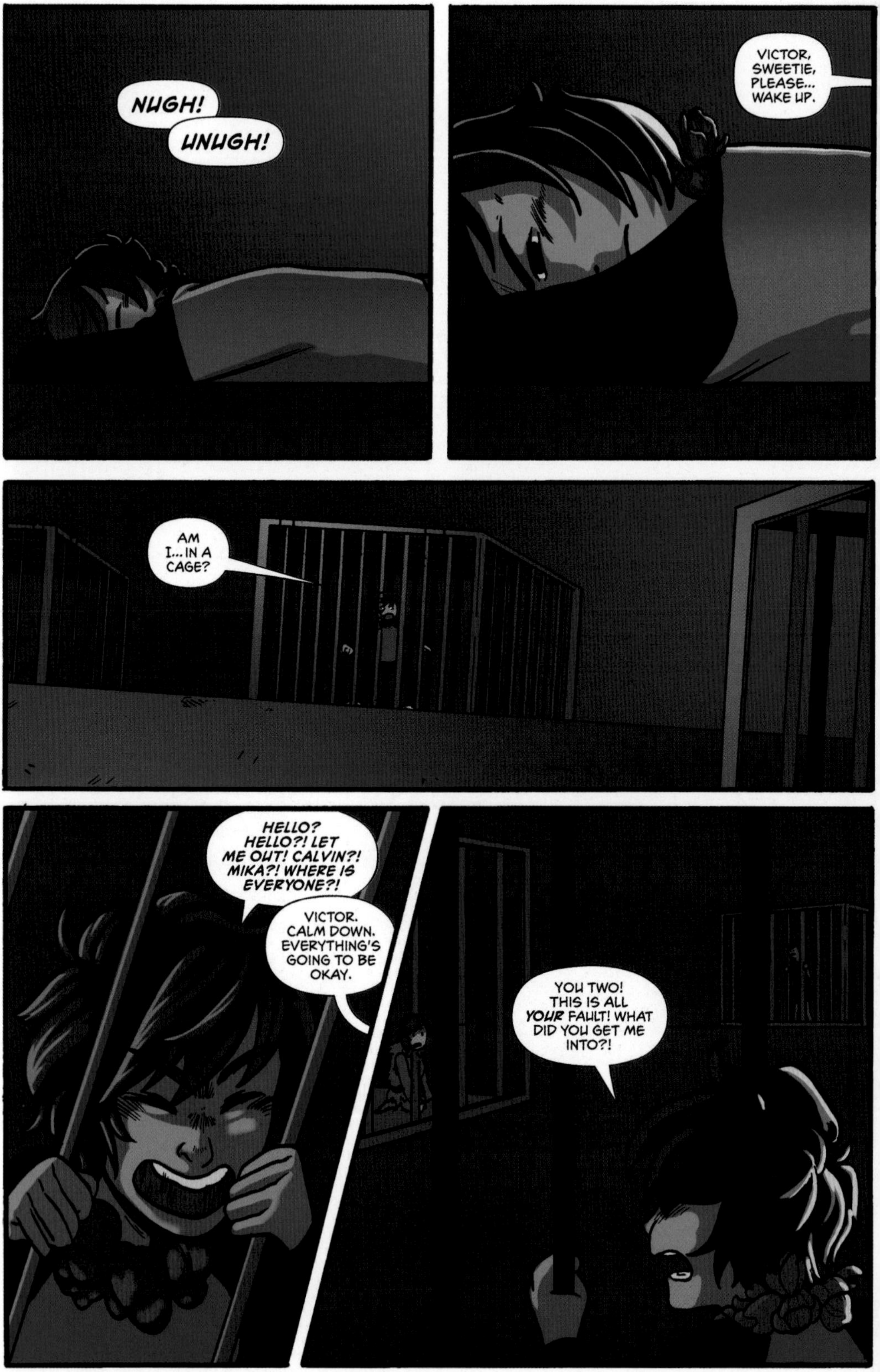
NUGH!
UNUGH!
VICTOR, SWEETIE, PLEASE... WAKE UP.
AM I...IN A CAGE?
HELLO? HELLO?! LET ME OUT! CALVIN?! MIKA?! WHERE IS EVERYONE?!
VICTOR. CALM DOWN. EVERYTHING'S GOING TO BE OKAY.
YOU TWO! THIS IS ALL YOUR FAULT! WHAT DID YOU GET ME INTO?!

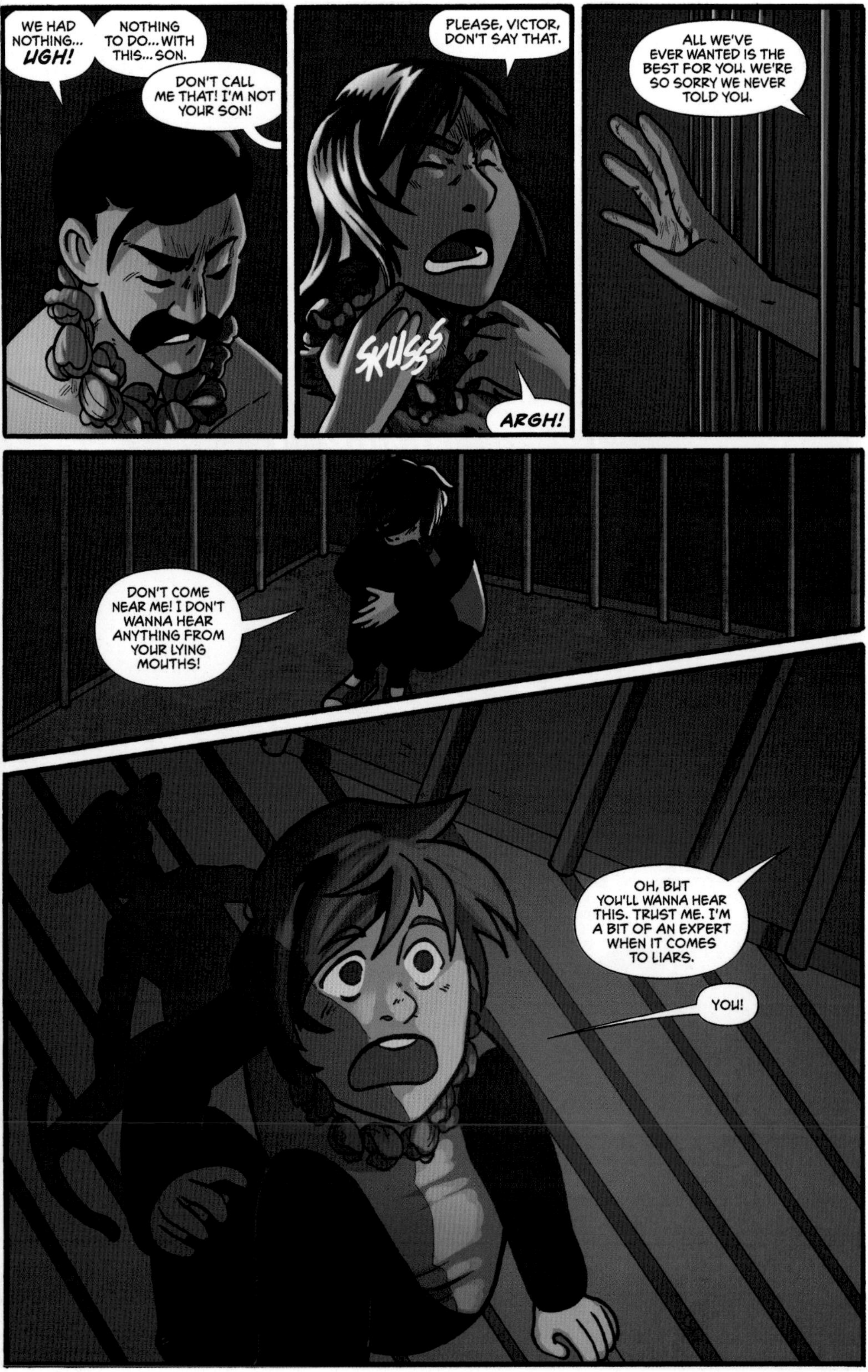
WE HAD NOTHING... UGH!
NOTHING TO DO... WITH THIS... SON.
DON'T CALL ME THAT! I'M NOT YOUR SON!
PLEASE, VICTOR, DON'T SAY THAT.
SKUSSS
ARGH!
ALL WE'VE EVER WANTED IS THE BEST FOR YOU. WE'RE SO SORRY WE NEVER TOLD YOU.
DON'T COME NEAR ME! I DON'T WANNA HEAR ANYTHING FROM YOUR LYING MOUTHS!
OH, BUT YOU'LL WANNA HEAR THIS. TRUST ME. I'M A BIT OF AN EXPERT WHEN IT COMES TO LIARS.
YOU!

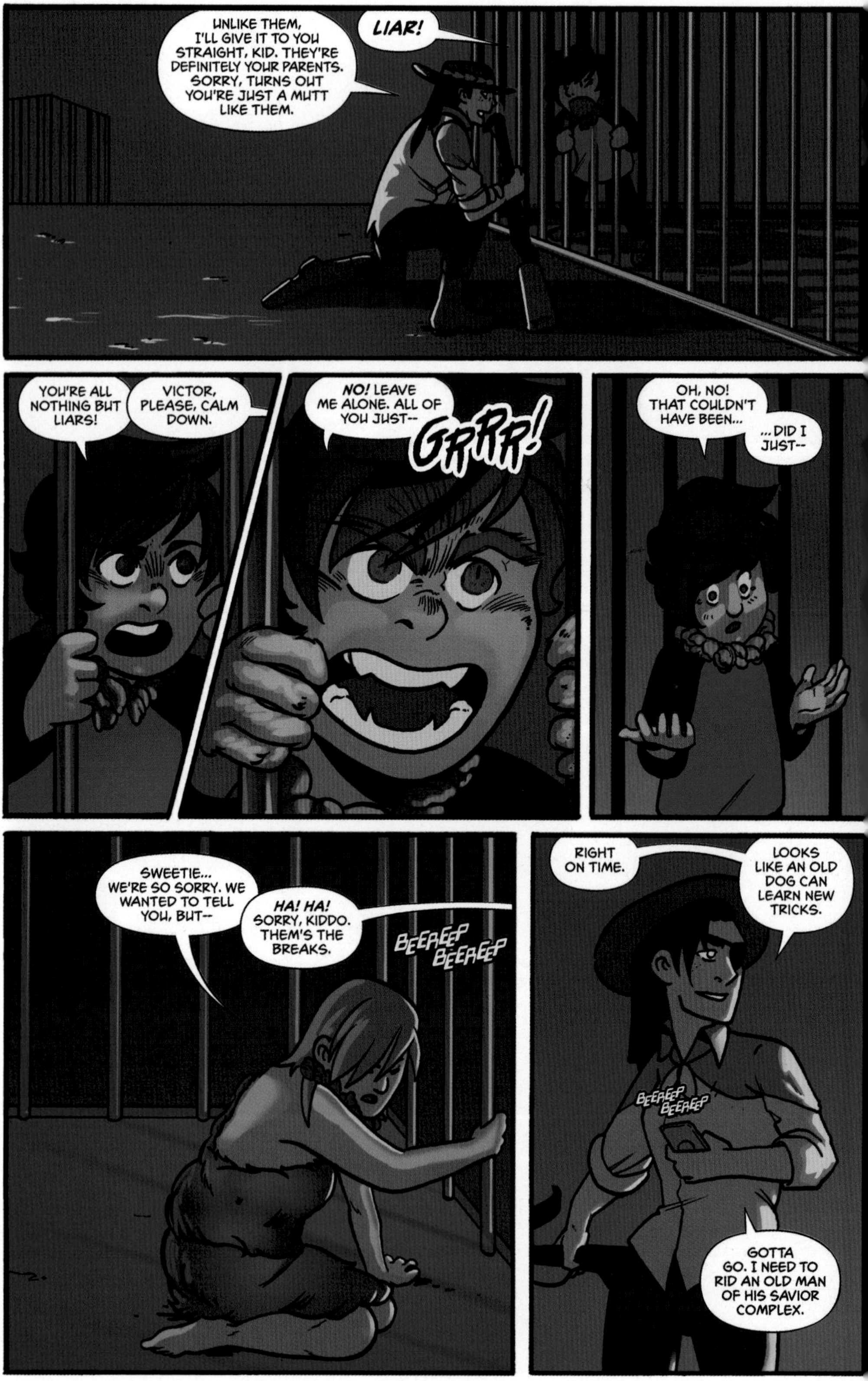
UNLIKE THEM, I'LL GIVE IT TO YOU STRAIGHT, KID. THEY'RE DEFINITELY YOUR PARENTS. SORRY, TURNS OUT YOU'RE JUST A MUTT LIKE THEM.
LIAR!
YOU'RE ALL NOTHING BUT LIARS!
VICTOR, PLEASE, CALM DOWN.
NO! LEAVE ME ALONE. ALL OF YOU JUST--
GRRR!
OH, NO! THAT COULDN'T HAVE BEEN...
...DID I JUST--
SWEETIE... WE'RE SO SORRY. WE WANTED TO TELL YOU, BUT--
HA! HA! SORRY, KIDDO. THEM'S THE BREAKS.
BEEREEP BEEREEP
RIGHT ON TIME.
LOOKS LIKE AN OLD DOG CAN LEARN NEW TRICKS.
BEEREEP BEEREEP
GOTTA GO. I NEED TO RID AN OLD MAN OF HIS SAVIOR COMPLEX.

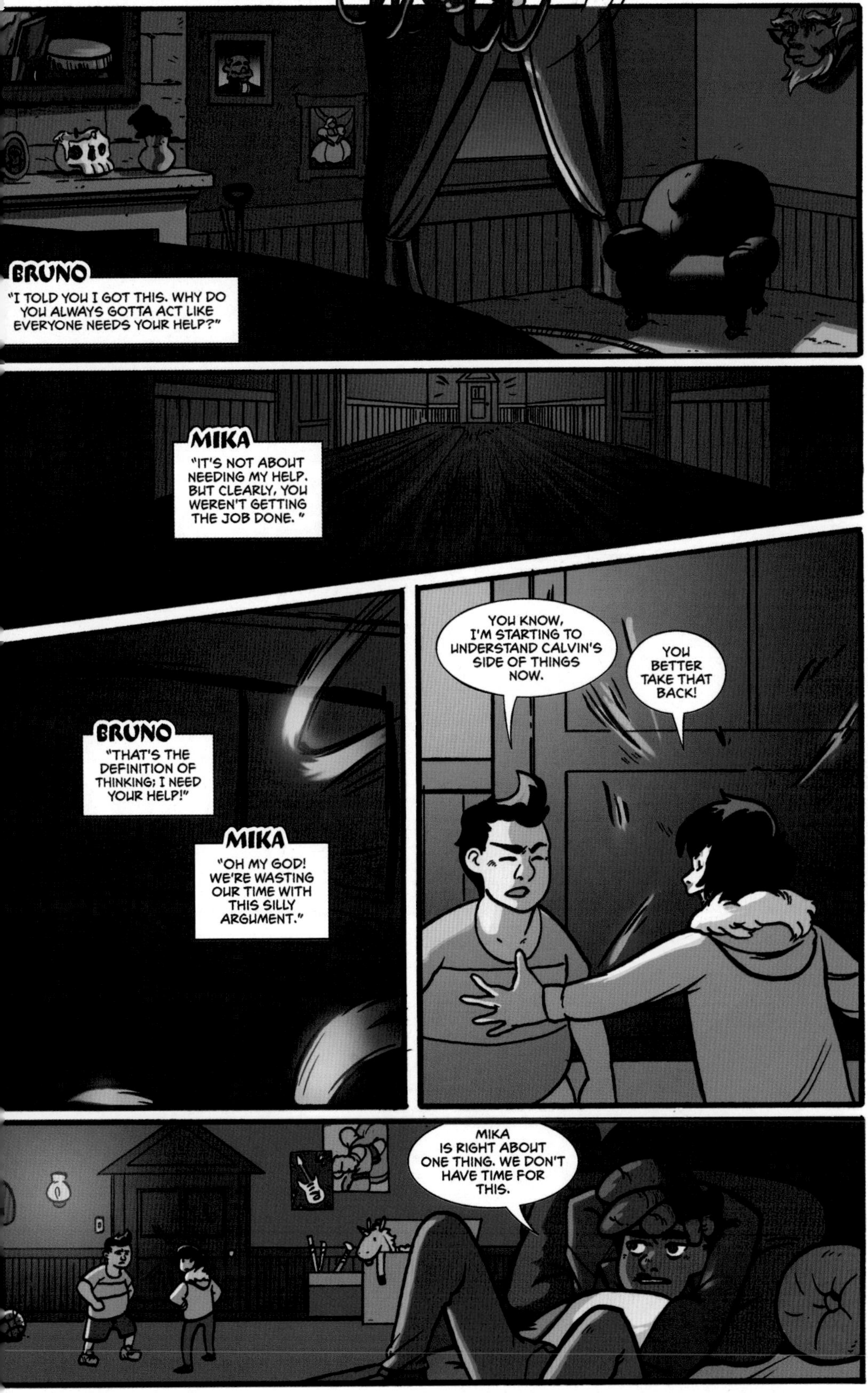
BRUNO
"I TOLD YOU I GOT THIS. WHY DO YOU ALWAYS GOTTA ACT LIKE EVERYONE NEEDS YOUR HELP?"
MIKA
"IT'S NOT ABOUT NEEDING MY HELP. BUT CLEARLY, YOU WEREN'T GETTING THE JOB DONE."
BRUNO
"THAT'S THE DEFINITION OF THINKING; I NEED YOUR HELP!"
MIKA
"OH MY GOD! WE'RE WASTING OUR TIME WITH THIS SILLY ARGUMENT."
YOU KNOW, I'M STARTING TO UNDERSTAND CALVIN'S SIDE OF THINGS NOW.
YOU BETTER TAKE THAT BACK!
MIKA IS RIGHT ABOUT ONE THING. WE DON'T HAVE TIME FOR THIS.

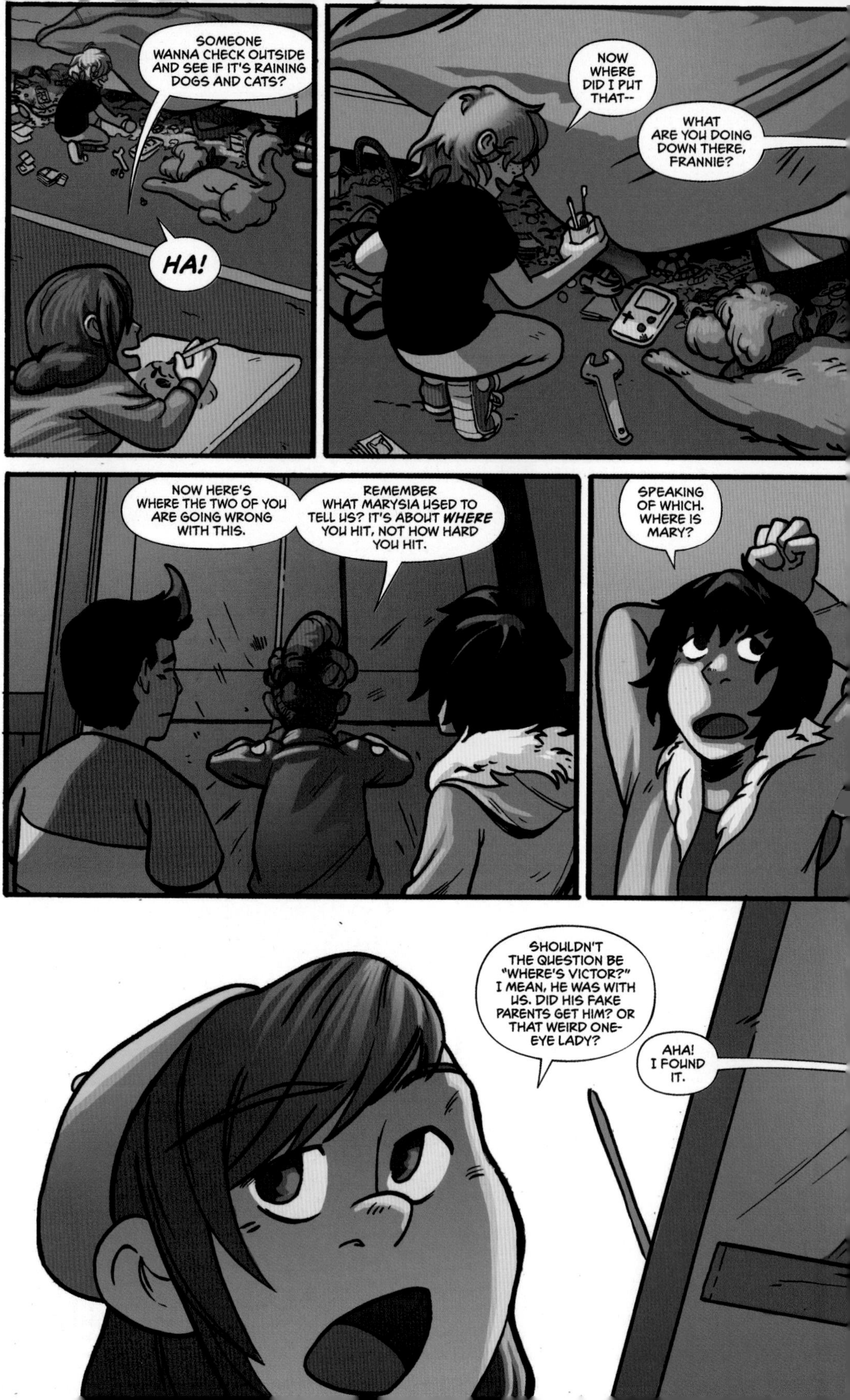
SOMEONE WANNA CHECK OUTSIDE AND SEE IF IT'S RAINING DOGS AND CATS?
HA!
NOW WHERE DID I PUT THAT--
WHAT ARE YOU DOING DOWN THERE, FRANNIE?
NOW HERE'S WHERE THE TWO OF YOU ARE GOING WRONG WITH THIS.
REMEMBER WHAT MARYSIA USED TO TELL US? IT'S ABOUT *WHERE* YOU HIT, NOT HOW HARD YOU HIT.
SPEAKING OF WHICH. WHERE IS MARY?
SHOULDN'T THE QUESTION BE "WHERE'S VICTOR?" I MEAN, HE WAS WITH US. DID HIS FAKE PARENTS GET HIM? OR THAT WEIRD ONE-EYE LADY?
AHA! I FOUND IT.

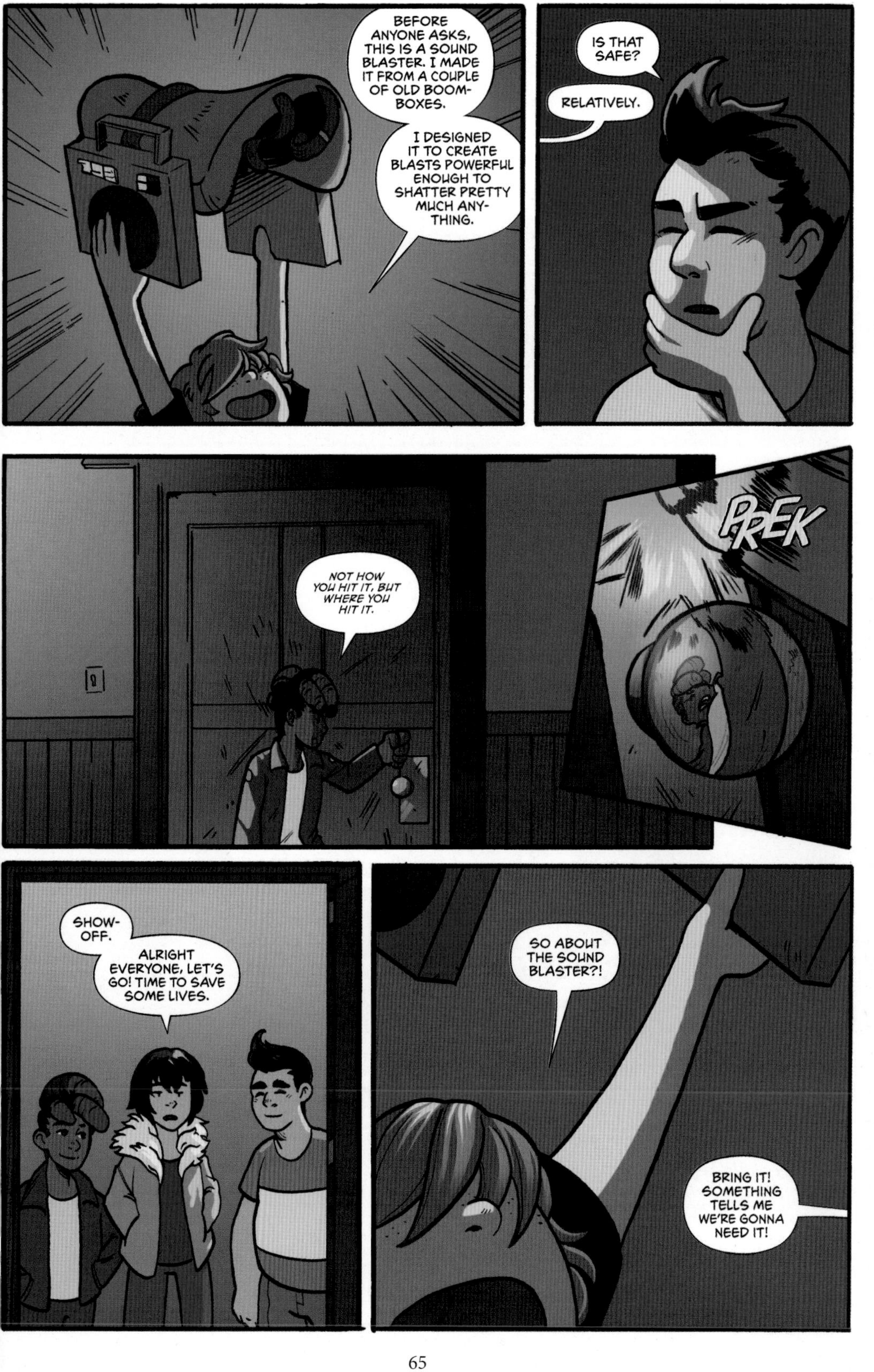
BEFORE ANYONE ASKS, THIS IS A SOUND BLASTER. I MADE IT FROM A COUPLE OF OLD BOOM-BOXES.
I DESIGNED IT TO CREATE BLASTS POWERFUL ENOUGH TO SHATTER PRETTY MUCH ANY-THING.
IS THAT SAFE?
RELATIVELY.
NOT HOW YOU HIT IT, BUT WHERE YOU HIT IT.
PREK
SHOW-OFF.
ALRIGHT EVERYONE, LET'S GO! TIME TO SAVE SOME LIVES.
SO ABOUT THE SOUND BLASTER?!
BRING IT! SOMETHING TELLS ME WE'RE GONNA NEED IT!

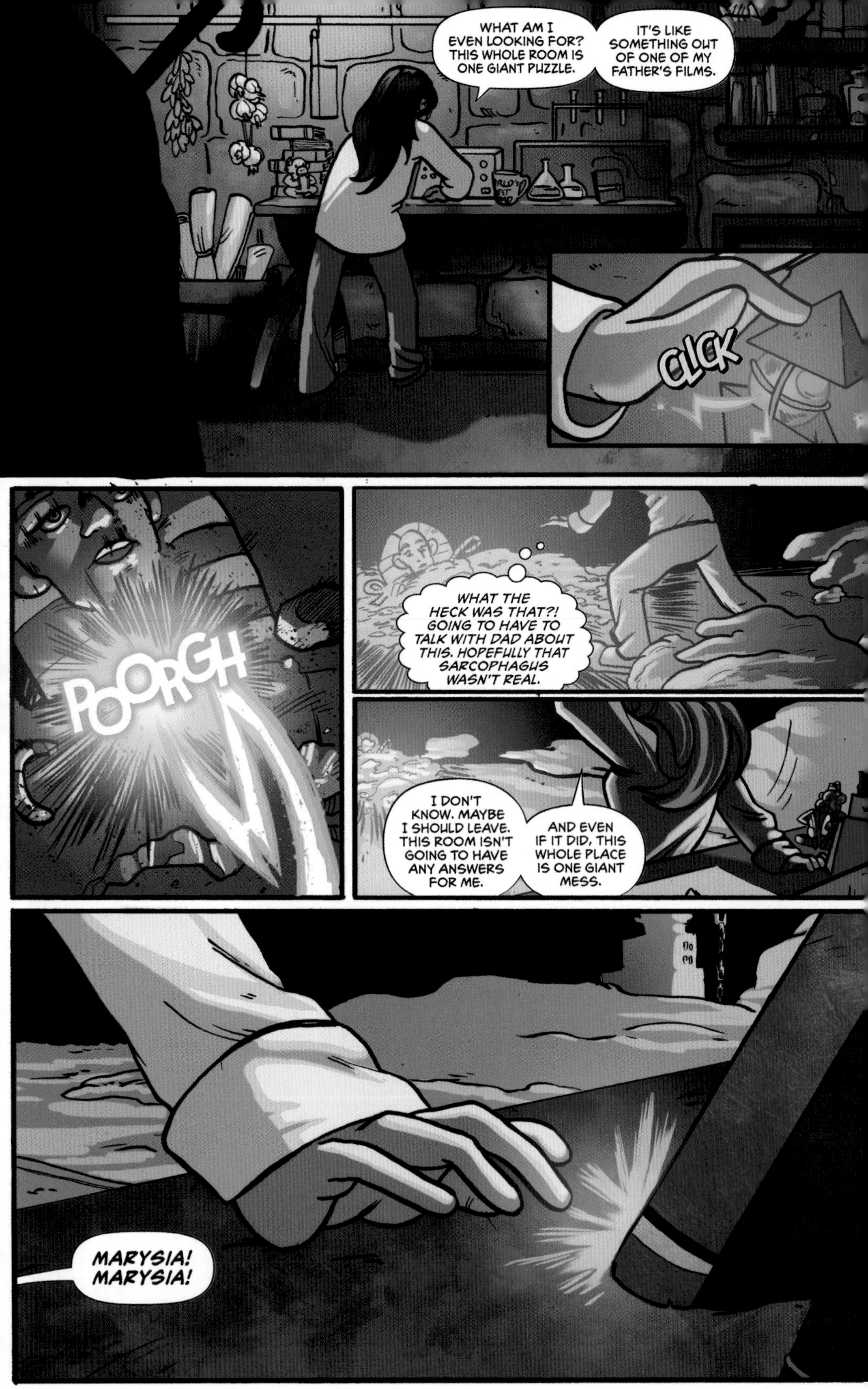
WHAT AM I EVEN LOOKING FOR? THIS WHOLE ROOM IS ONE GIANT PUZZLE.
IT'S LIKE SOMETHING OUT OF ONE OF MY FATHER'S FILMS.
CLICK
POORGH
WHAT THE HECK WAS THAT?! GOING TO HAVE TO TALK WITH DAD ABOUT THIS. HOPEFULLY THAT SARCOPHAGUS WASN'T REAL.
I DON'T KNOW. MAYBE I SHOULD LEAVE. THIS ROOM ISN'T GOING TO HAVE ANY ANSWERS FOR ME.
AND EVEN IF IT DID, THIS WHOLE PLACE IS ONE GIANT MESS.
MARYSIA! MARYSIA!

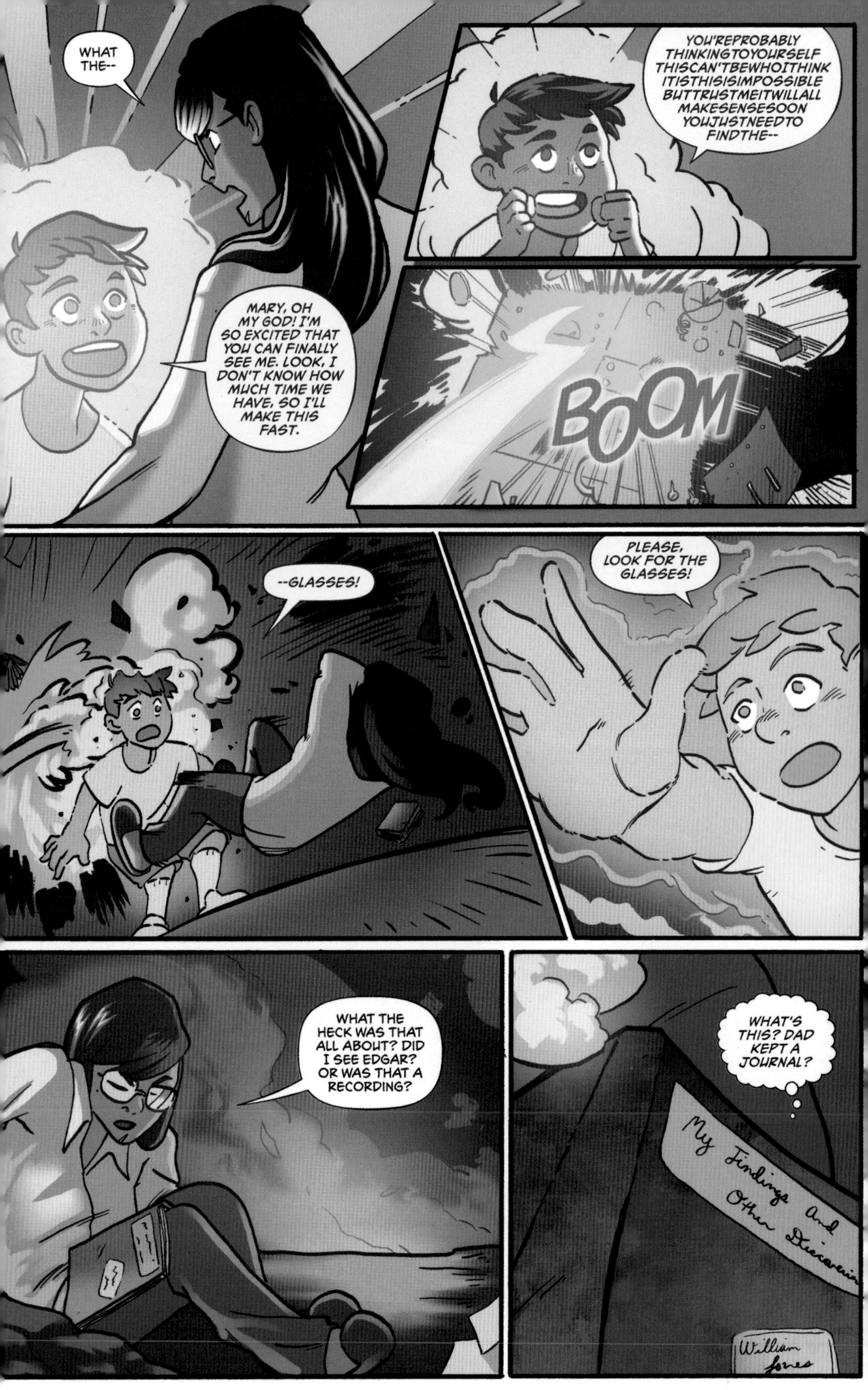
WHAT THE--
YOU'REPROBABLY THINKINGTOYOURSELF THISCAN'TBEWHOITHINK ITISTHISISIMPOSSIBLE BUTTRUSTMEITWILLALL MAKESENSESOON YOUJUSTNEEDTO FINDTHE--
MARY, OH MY GOD! I'M SO EXCITED THAT YOU CAN FINALLY SEE ME. LOOK, I DON'T KNOW HOW MUCH TIME WE HAVE, SO I'LL MAKE THIS FAST.
BOOM
--GLASSES!
PLEASE, LOOK FOR THE GLASSES!
WHAT THE HECK WAS THAT ALL ABOUT? DID I SEE EDGAR? OR WAS THAT A RECORDING?
WHAT'S THIS? DAD KEPT A JOURNAL?
My Findings and Other Discoveries
William Jones

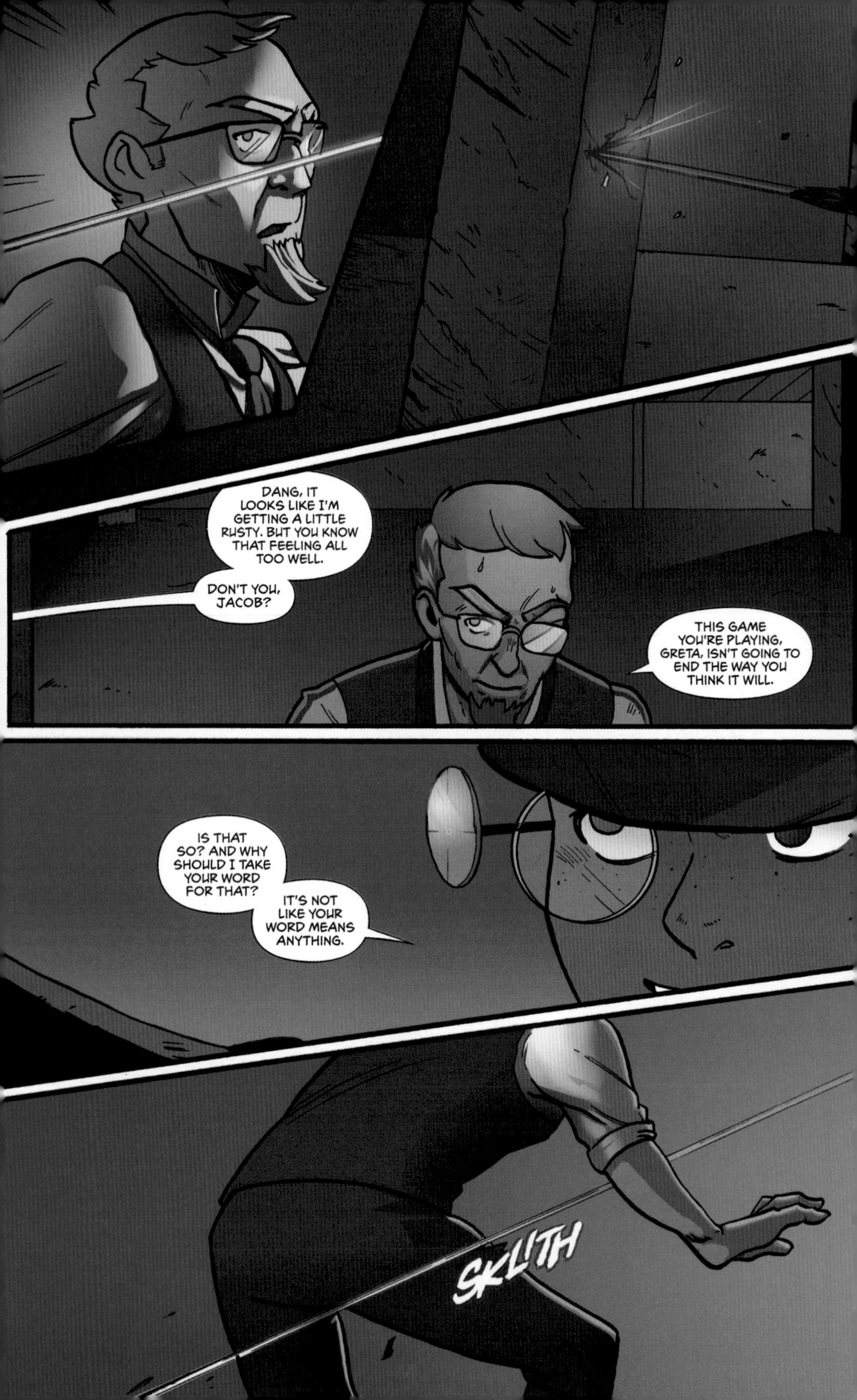
DANG, IT LOOKS LIKE I'M GETTING A LITTLE RUSTY. BUT YOU KNOW THAT FEELING ALL TOO WELL.
DON'T YOU, JACOB?
THIS GAME YOU'RE PLAYING, GRETA, ISN'T GOING TO END THE WAY YOU THINK IT WILL.
IS THAT SO? AND WHY SHOULD I TAKE YOUR WORD FOR THAT?
IT'S NOT LIKE YOUR WORD MEANS ANYTHING.
SKLITH

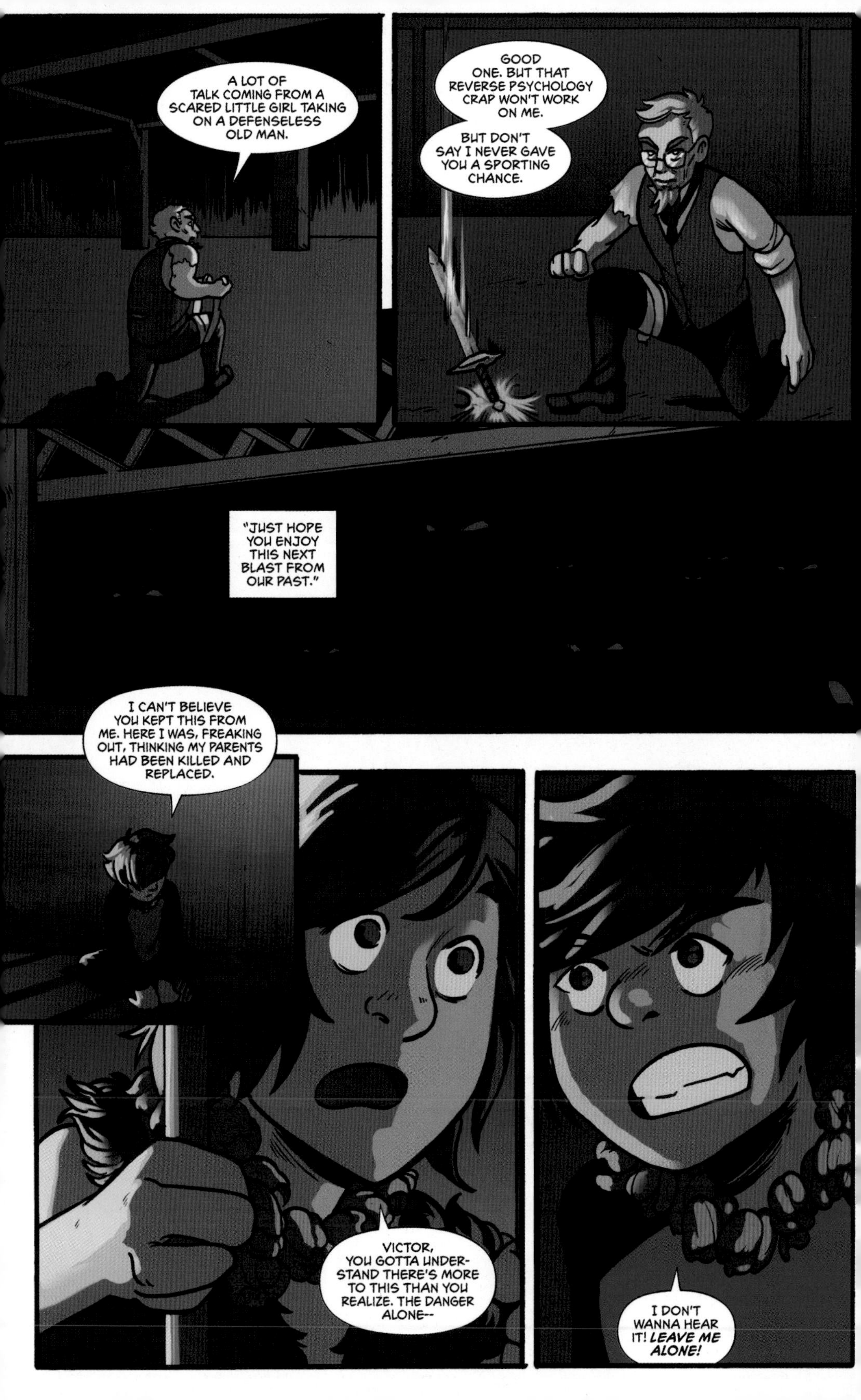
A LOT OF TALK COMING FROM A SCARED LITTLE GIRL TAKING ON A DEFENSELESS OLD MAN.
GOOD ONE. BUT THAT REVERSE PSYCHOLOGY CRAP WON'T WORK ON ME.
BUT DON'T SAY I NEVER GAVE YOU A SPORTING CHANCE.
"JUST HOPE YOU ENJOY THIS NEXT BLAST FROM OUR PAST."
I CAN'T BELIEVE YOU KEPT THIS FROM ME. HERE I WAS, FREAKING OUT, THINKING MY PARENTS HAD BEEN KILLED AND REPLACED.
VICTOR, YOU GOTTA UNDER-STAND THERE'S MORE TO THIS THAN YOU REALIZE. THE DANGER ALONE--
I DON'T WANNA HEAR IT! *LEAVE ME ALONE!*

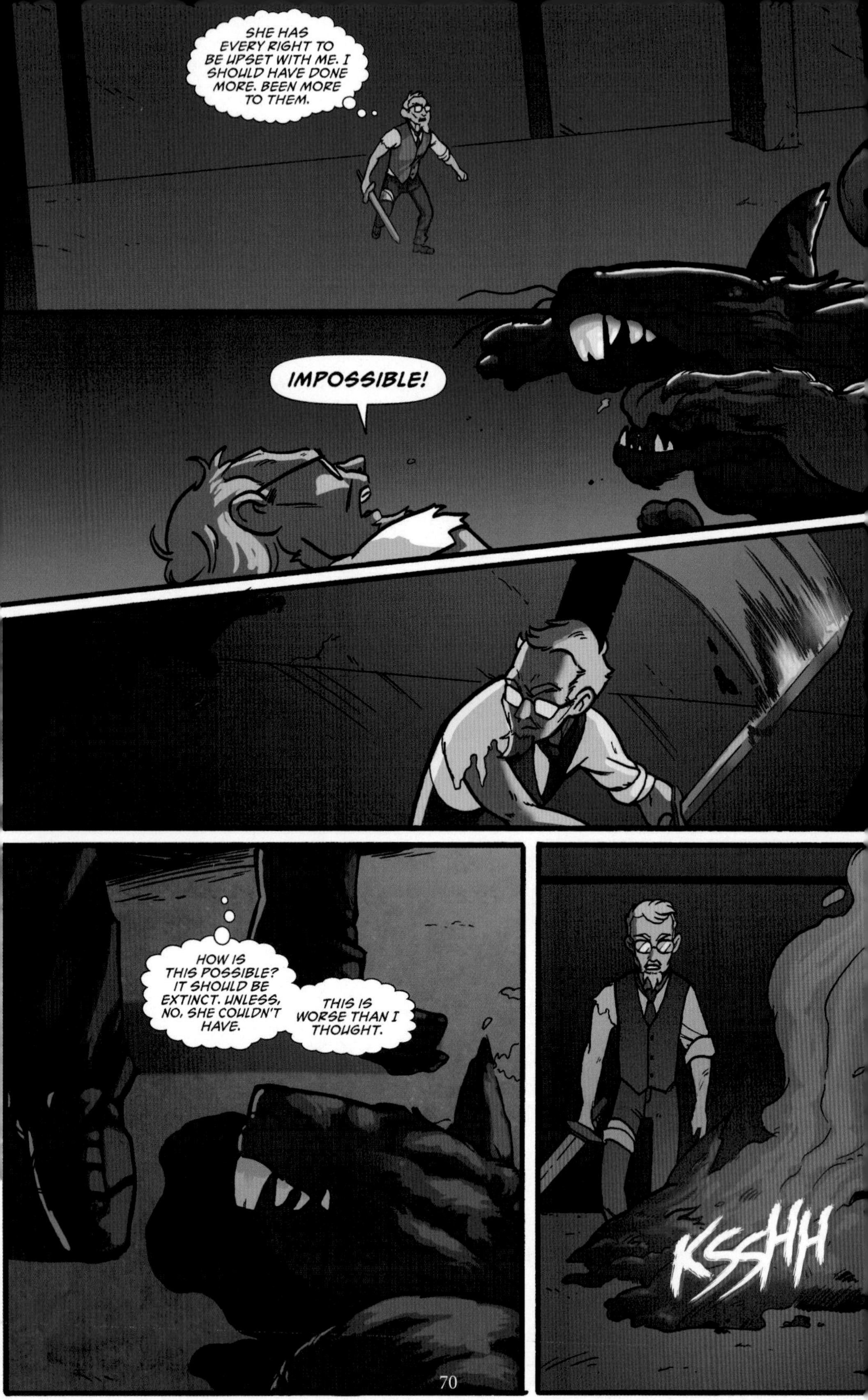
SHE HAS EVERY RIGHT TO BE UPSET WITH ME. I SHOULD HAVE DONE MORE. BEEN MORE TO THEM.
IMPOSSIBLE!
HOW IS THIS POSSIBLE? IT SHOULD BE EXTINCT. UNLESS, NO, SHE COULDN'T HAVE.
THIS IS WORSE THAN I THOUGHT.
KSSHH

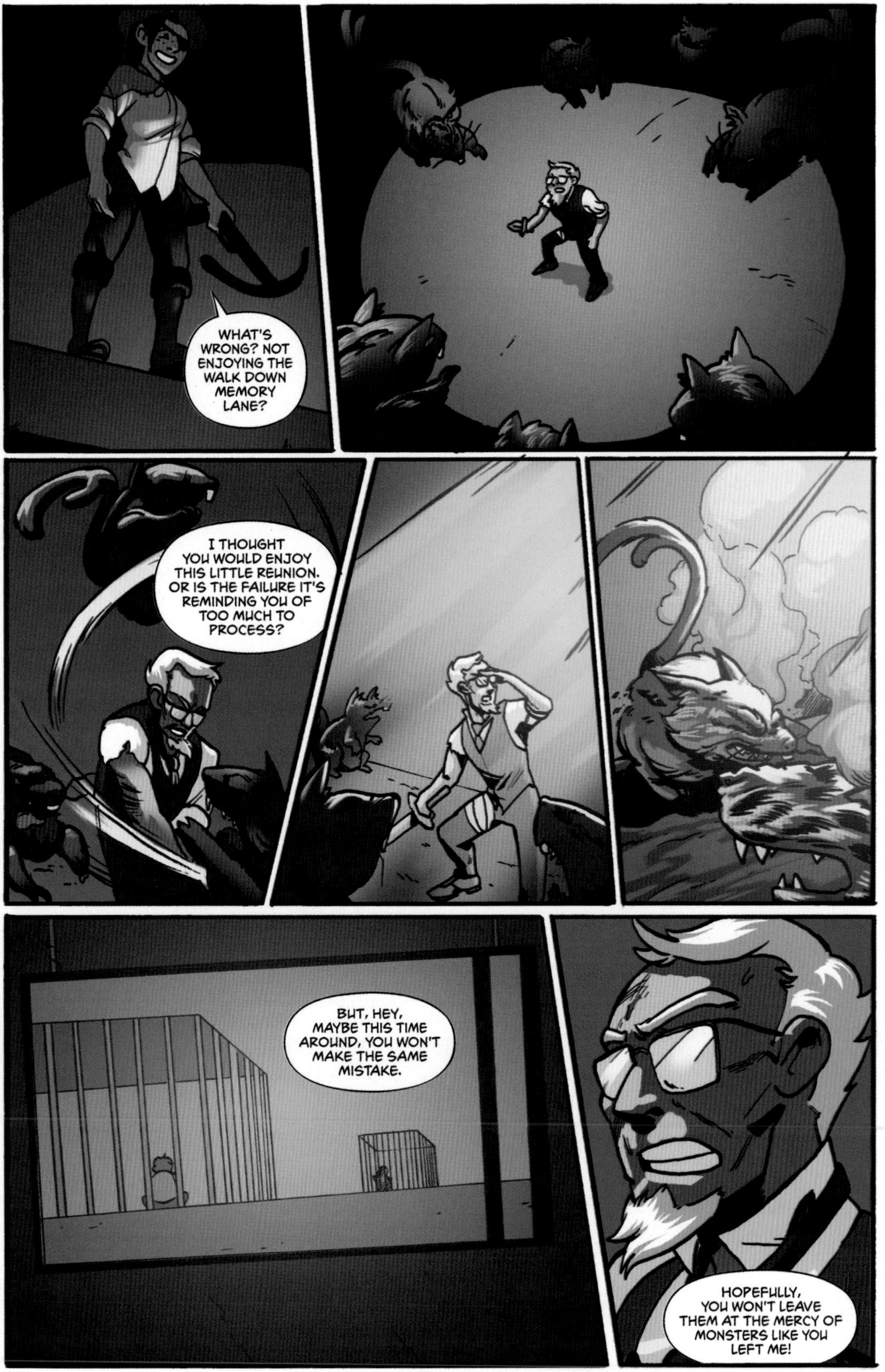
WHAT'S WRONG? NOT ENJOYING THE WALK DOWN MEMORY LANE?
I THOUGHT YOU WOULD ENJOY THIS LITTLE REUNION. OR IS THE FAILURE IT'S REMINDING YOU OF TOO MUCH TO PROCESS?
BUT, HEY, MAYBE THIS TIME AROUND, YOU WON'T MAKE THE SAME MISTAKE.
HOPEFULLY, YOU WON'T LEAVE THEM AT THE MERCY OF MONSTERS LIKE YOU LEFT ME!

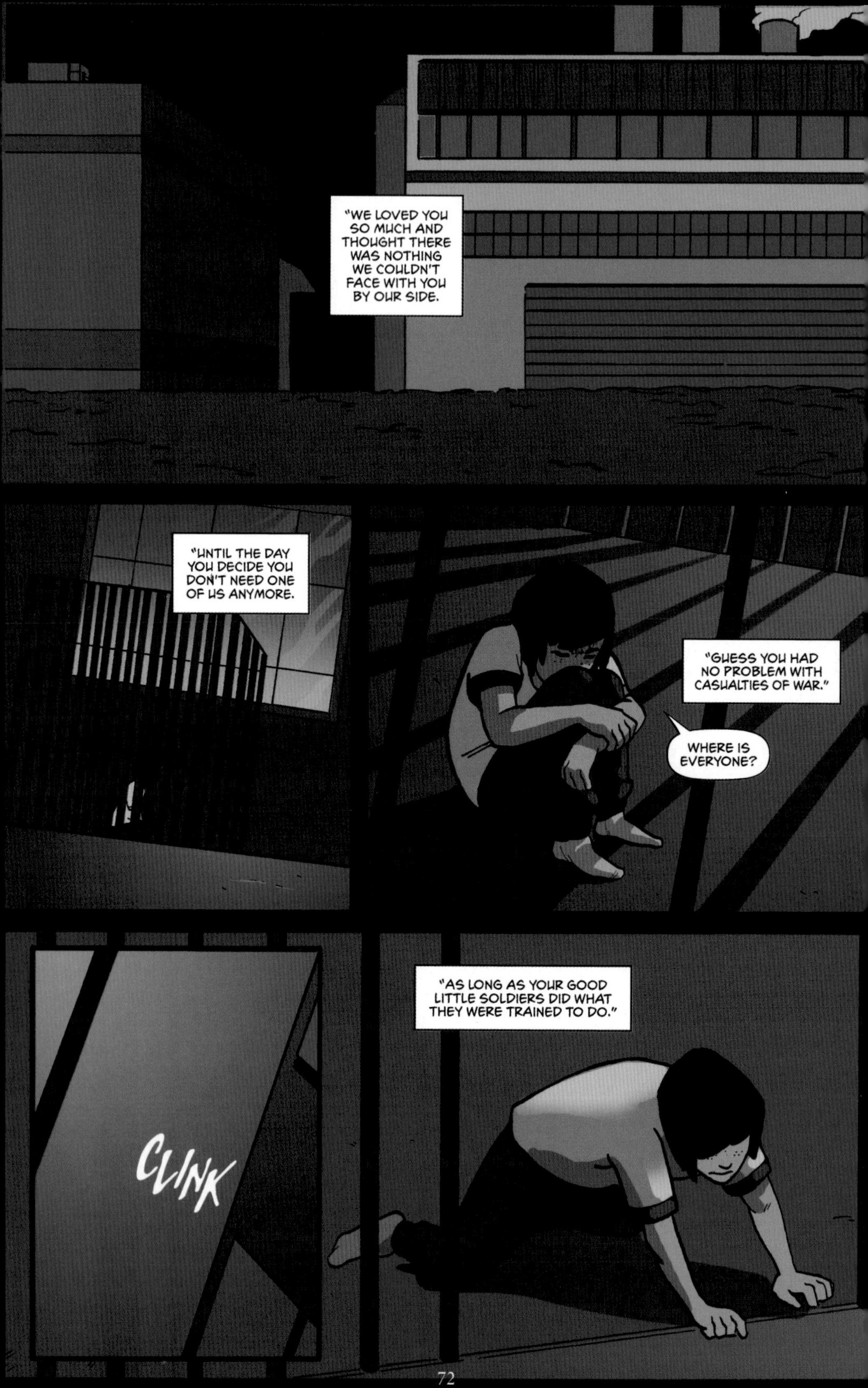
"WE LOVED YOU SO MUCH AND THOUGHT THERE WAS NOTHING WE COULDN'T FACE WITH YOU BY OUR SIDE.
"UNTIL THE DAY YOU DECIDE YOU DON'T NEED ONE OF US ANYMORE.
"GUESS YOU HAD NO PROBLEM WITH CASUALTIES OF WAR."
WHERE IS EVERYONE?
CLINK
"AS LONG AS YOUR GOOD LITTLE SOLDIERS DID WHAT THEY WERE TRAINED TO DO."

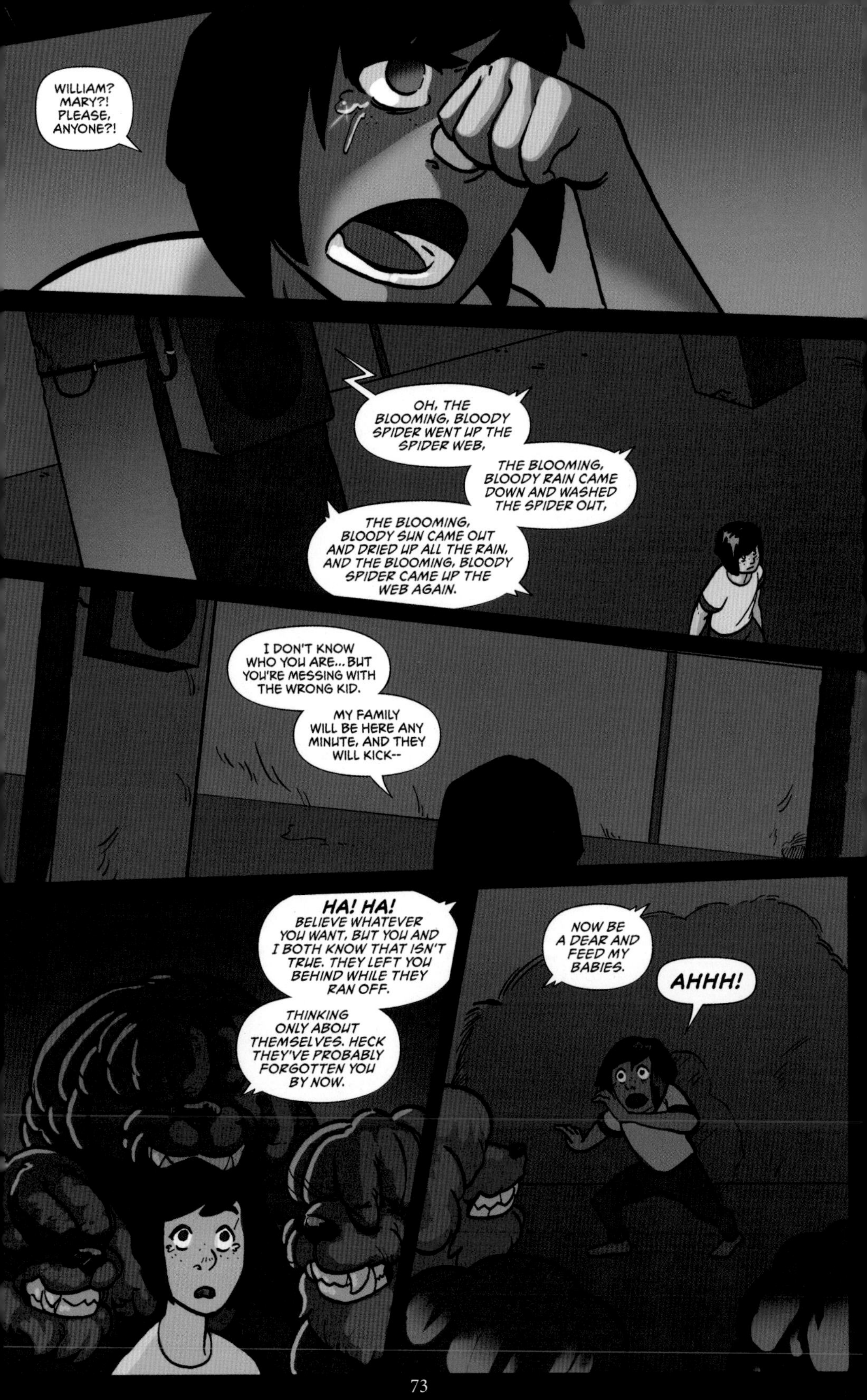
WILLIAM? MARY?! PLEASE, ANYONE?!
OH, THE BLOOMING, BLOODY SPIDER WENT UP THE SPIDER WEB,
THE BLOOMING, BLOODY RAIN CAME DOWN AND WASHED THE SPIDER OUT,
THE BLOOMING, BLOODY SUN CAME OUT AND DRIED UP ALL THE RAIN, AND THE BLOOMING, BLOODY SPIDER CAME UP THE WEB AGAIN.
I DON'T KNOW WHO YOU ARE... BUT YOU'RE MESSING WITH THE WRONG KID.
MY FAMILY WILL BE HERE ANY MINUTE, AND THEY WILL KICK--
HA! HA! BELIEVE WHATEVER YOU WANT, BUT YOU AND I BOTH KNOW THAT ISN'T TRUE. THEY LEFT YOU BEHIND WHILE THEY RAN OFF.
THINKING ONLY ABOUT THEMSELVES. HECK THEY'VE PROBABLY FORGOTTEN YOU BY NOW.
NOW BE A DEAR AND FEED MY BABIES.
AHHH!

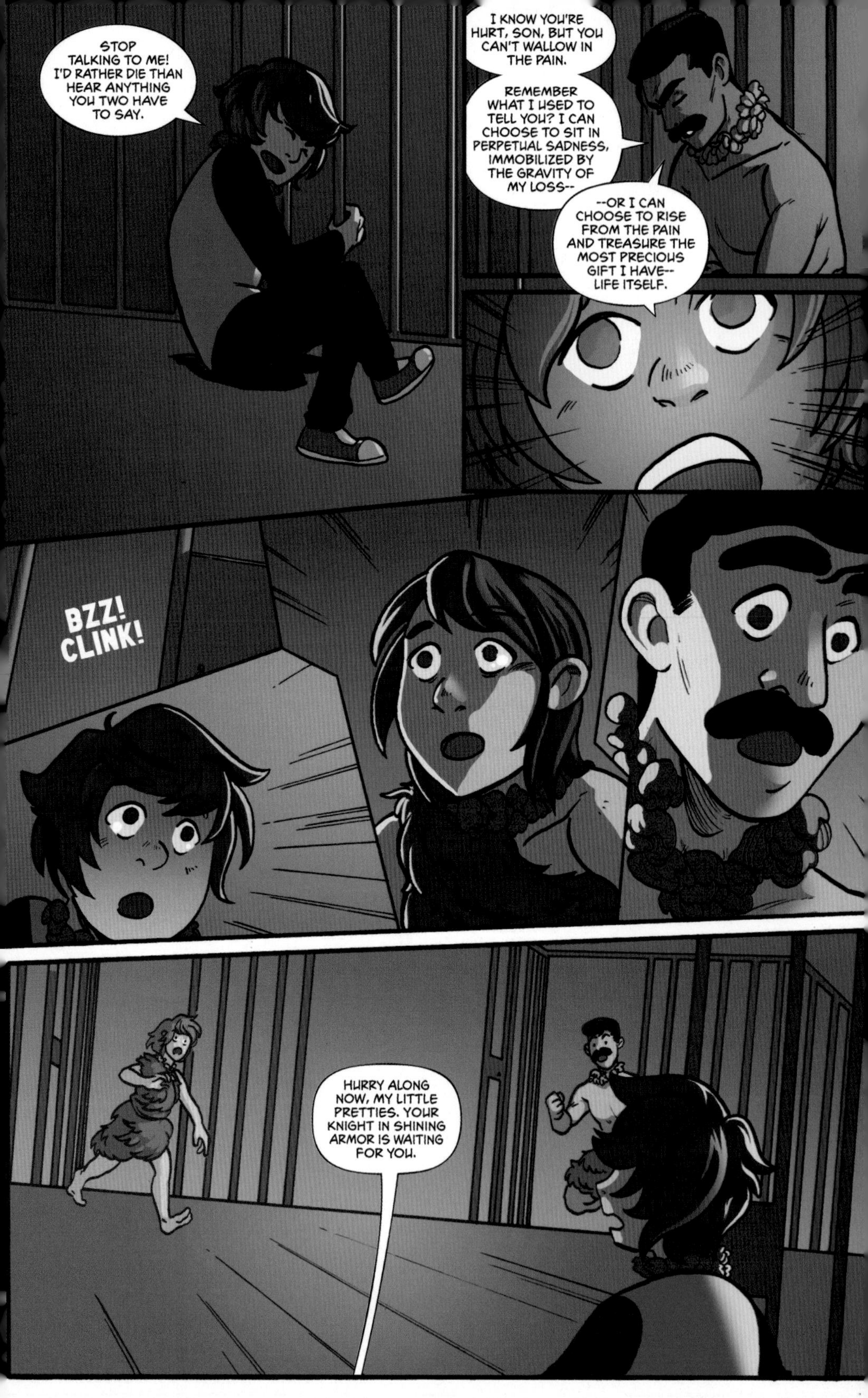
STOP TALKING TO ME! I'D RATHER DIE THAN HEAR ANYTHING YOU TWO HAVE TO SAY.
I KNOW YOU'RE HURT, SON, BUT YOU CAN'T WALLOW IN THE PAIN.
REMEMBER WHAT I USED TO TELL YOU? I CAN CHOOSE TO SIT IN PERPETUAL SADNESS, IMMOBILIZED BY THE GRAVITY OF MY LOSS--
--OR I CAN CHOOSE TO RISE FROM THE PAIN AND TREASURE THE MOST PRECIOUS GIFT I HAVE-- LIFE ITSELF.
BZZ! CLINK!
HURRY ALONG NOW, MY LITTLE PRETTIES. YOUR KNIGHT IN SHINING ARMOR IS WAITING FOR YOU.

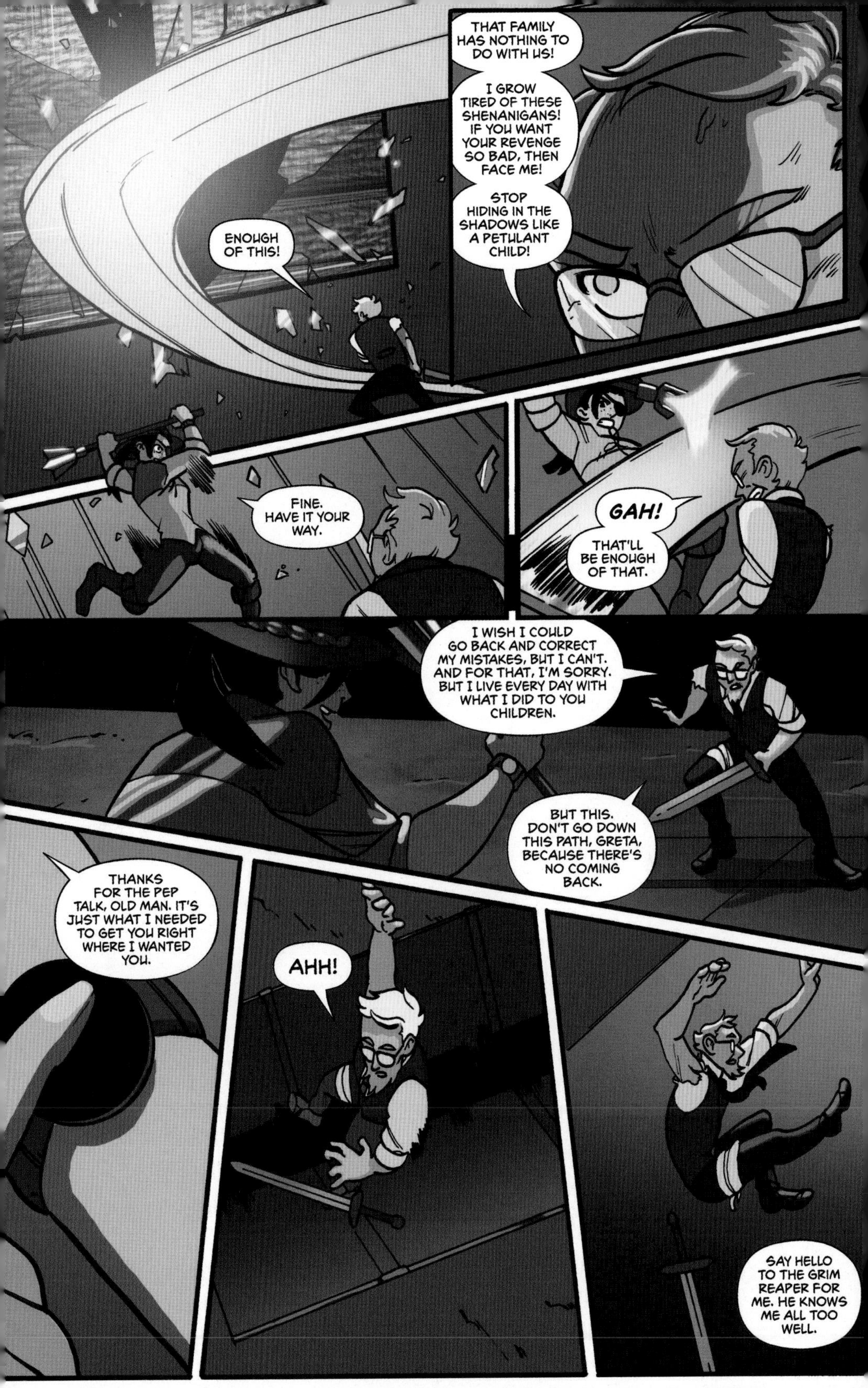
ENOUGH OF THIS!
THAT FAMILY HAS NOTHING TO DO WITH US!
I GROW TIRED OF THESE SHENANIGANS! IF YOU WANT YOUR REVENGE SO BAD, THEN FACE ME!
STOP HIDING IN THE SHADOWS LIKE A PETHLANT CHILD!
FINE. HAVE IT YOUR WAY.
GAH!
THAT'LL BE ENOUGH OF THAT.
I WISH I COULD GO BACK AND CORRECT MY MISTAKES, BUT I CAN'T. AND FOR THAT, I'M SORRY. BUT I LIVE EVERY DAY WITH WHAT I DID TO YOU CHILDREN.
BUT THIS. DON'T GO DOWN THIS PATH, GRETA, BECAUSE THERE'S NO COMING BACK.
THANKS FOR THE PEP TALK, OLD MAN. IT'S JUST WHAT I NEEDED TO GET YOU RIGHT WHERE I WANTED YOU.
AHH!
SAY HELLO TO THE GRIM REAPER FOR ME. HE KNOWS ME ALL TOO WELL.

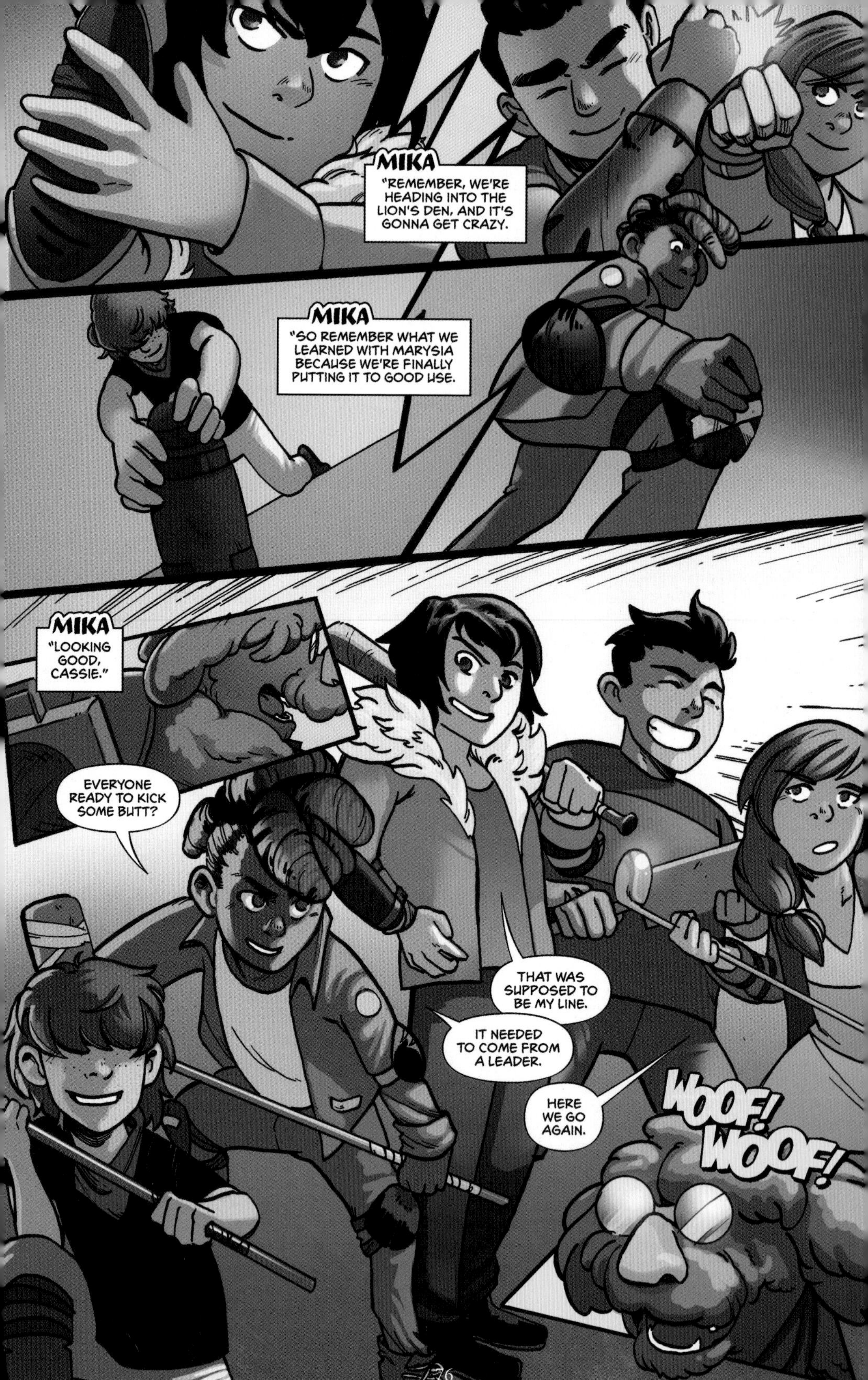
MIKA
"REMEMBER, WE'RE HEADING INTO THE LION'S DEN, AND IT'S GONNA GET CRAZY.
MIKA
"SO REMEMBER WHAT WE LEARNED WITH MARYSIA BECAUSE WE'RE FINALLY PUTTING IT TO GOOD USE.
MIKA
"LOOKING GOOD, CASSIE."
EVERYONE READY TO KICK SOME BUTT?
THAT WAS SUPPOSED TO BE MY LINE.
IT NEEDED TO COME FROM A LEADER.
HERE WE GO AGAIN.
WOOF! WOOF!

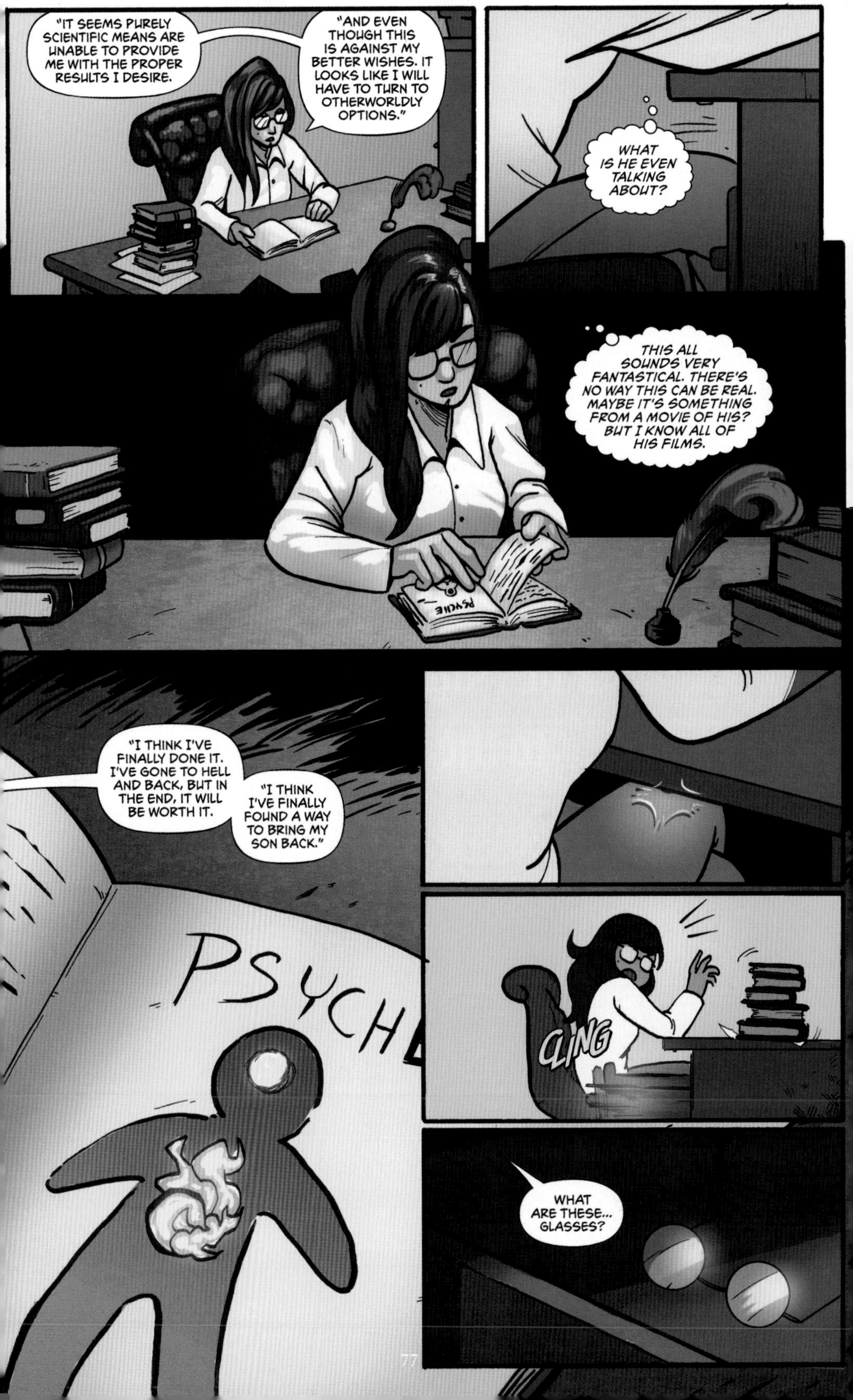
"IT SEEMS PURELY SCIENTIFIC MEANS ARE UNABLE TO PROVIDE ME WITH THE PROPER RESULTS I DESIRE.
"AND EVEN THOUGH THIS IS AGAINST MY BETTER WISHES. IT LOOKS LIKE I WILL HAVE TO TURN TO OTHERWORLDLY OPTIONS."
WHAT IS HE EVEN TALKING ABOUT?
THIS ALL SOUNDS VERY FANTASTICAL. THERE'S NO WAY THIS CAN BE REAL. MAYBE IT'S SOMETHING FROM A MOVIE OF HIS? BUT I KNOW ALL OF HIS FILMS.
PSYCHE
"I THINK I'VE FINALLY DONE IT. I'VE GONE TO HELL AND BACK, BUT IN THE END, IT WILL BE WORTH IT.
"I THINK I'VE FINALLY FOUND A WAY TO BRING MY SON BACK."
PSYCH
CLING
WHAT ARE THESE... GLASSES?

Chapter Four
The Nightcrawlers to the Rescue!

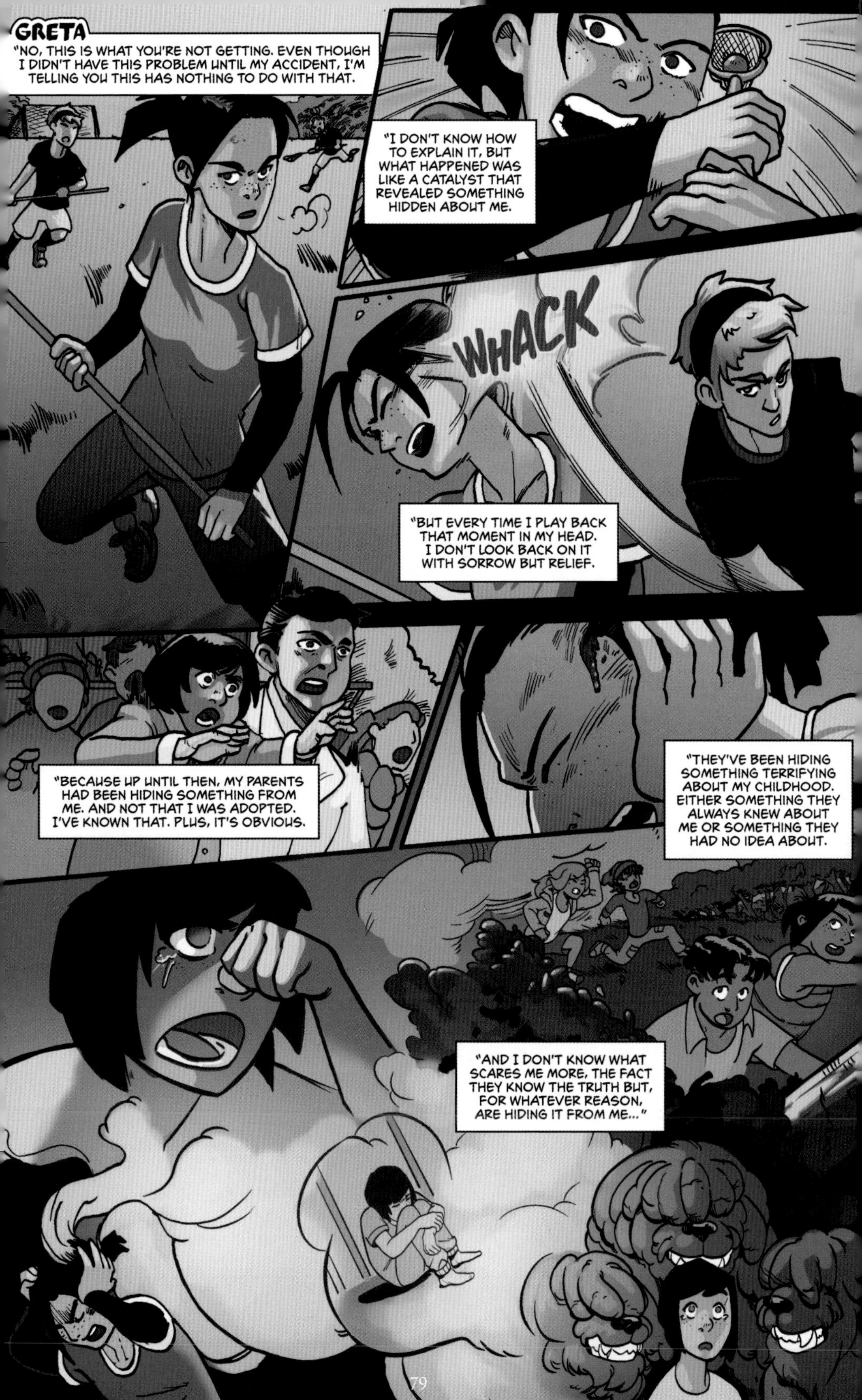
GRETA
"NO, THIS IS WHAT YOU'RE NOT GETTING. EVEN THOUGH I DIDN'T HAVE THIS PROBLEM UNTIL MY ACCIDENT, I'M TELLING YOU THIS HAS NOTHING TO DO WITH THAT.
"I DON'T KNOW HOW TO EXPLAIN IT, BUT WHAT HAPPENED WAS LIKE A CATALYST THAT REVEALED SOMETHING HIDDEN ABOUT ME.
WHACK
"BUT EVERY TIME I PLAY BACK THAT MOMENT IN MY HEAD. I DON'T LOOK BACK ON IT WITH SORROW BUT RELIEF.
"BECAUSE UP UNTIL THEN, MY PARENTS HAD BEEN HIDING SOMETHING FROM ME. AND NOT THAT I WAS ADOPTED. I'VE KNOWN THAT. PLUS, IT'S OBVIOUS.
"THEY'VE BEEN HIDING SOMETHING TERRIFYING ABOUT MY CHILDHOOD. EITHER SOMETHING THEY ALWAYS KNEW ABOUT ME OR SOMETHING THEY HAD NO IDEA ABOUT.
"AND I DON'T KNOW WHAT SCARES ME MORE, THE FACT THEY KNOW THE TRUTH BUT, FOR WHATEVER REASON, ARE HIDING IT FROM ME..."

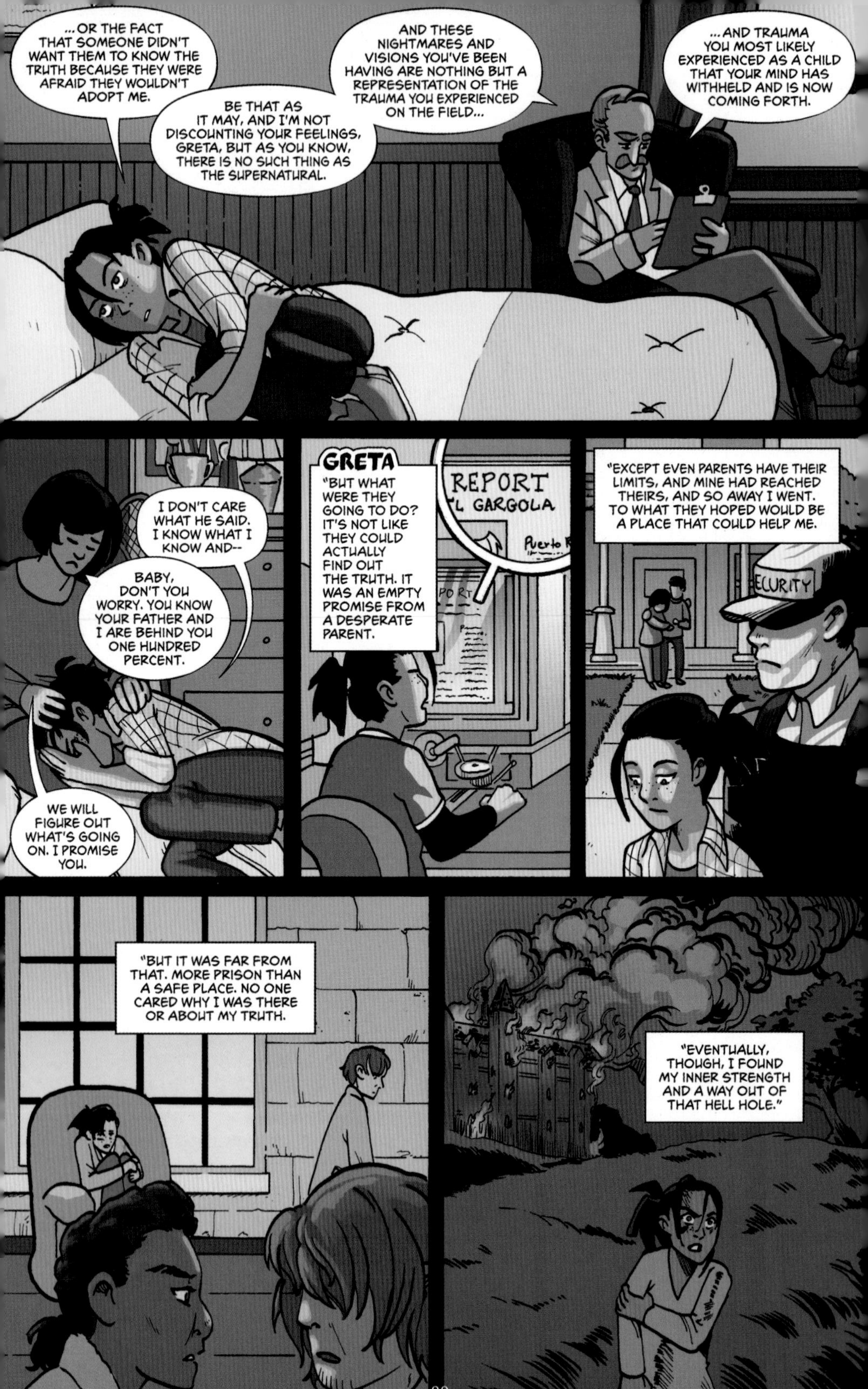

...OR THE FACT THAT SOMEONE DIDN'T WANT THEM TO KNOW THE TRUTH BECAUSE THEY WERE AFRAID THEY WOULDN'T ADOPT ME.
BE THAT AS IT MAY, AND I'M NOT DISCOUNTING YOUR FEELINGS, GRETA, BUT AS YOU KNOW, THERE IS NO SUCH THING AS THE SUPERNATURAL.
AND THESE NIGHTMARES AND VISIONS YOU'VE BEEN HAVING ARE NOTHING BUT A REPRESENTATION OF THE TRAUMA YOU EXPERIENCED ON THE FIELD...
...AND TRAUMA YOU MOST LIKELY EXPERIENCED AS A CHILD THAT YOUR MIND HAS WITHHELD AND IS NOW COMING FORTH.
I DON'T CARE WHAT HE SAID. I KNOW WHAT I KNOW AND--
BABY, DON'T YOU WORRY. YOU KNOW YOUR FATHER AND I ARE BEHIND YOU ONE HUNDRED PERCENT.
WE WILL FIGURE OUT WHAT'S GOING ON. I PROMISE YOU.
GRETA
"BUT WHAT WERE THEY GOING TO DO? IT'S NOT LIKE THEY COULD ACTUALLY FIND OUT THE TRUTH. IT WAS AN EMPTY PROMISE FROM A DESPERATE PARENT.
REPORT
L GARGOLA
Puerto R
"EXCEPT EVEN PARENTS HAVE THEIR LIMITS, AND MINE HAD REACHED THEIRS, AND SO AWAY I WENT. TO WHAT THEY HOPED WOULD BE A PLACE THAT COULD HELP ME.
ECURITY
"BUT IT WAS FAR FROM THAT. MORE PRISON THAN A SAFE PLACE. NO ONE CARED WHY I WAS THERE OR ABOUT MY TRUTH.
"EVENTUALLY, THOUGH, I FOUND MY INNER STRENGTH AND A WAY OUT OF THAT HELL HOLE."

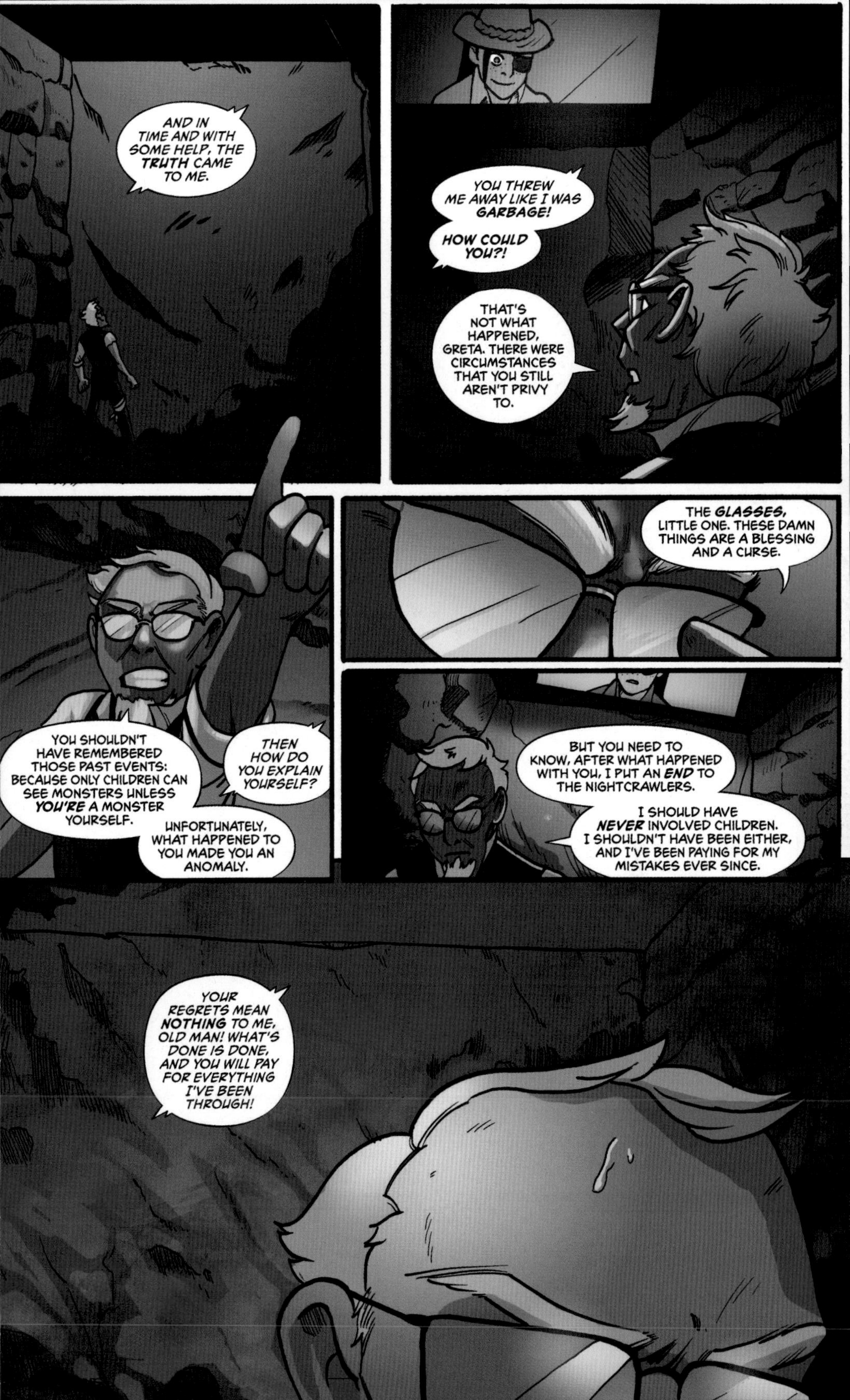
AND IN TIME AND WITH SOME HELP, THE TRUTH CAME TO ME.
YOU THREW ME AWAY LIKE I WAS GARBAGE!
HOW COULD YOU?!
THAT'S NOT WHAT HAPPENED, GRETA. THERE WERE CIRCUMSTANCES THAT YOU STILL AREN'T PRIVY TO.
YOU SHOULDN'T HAVE REMEMBERED THOSE PAST EVENTS: BECAUSE ONLY CHILDREN CAN SEE MONSTERS UNLESS YOU'RE A MONSTER YOURSELF.
THEN HOW DO YOU EXPLAIN YOURSELF?
UNFORTUNATELY, WHAT HAPPENED TO YOU MADE YOU AN ANOMALY.
THE GLASSES, LITTLE ONE. THESE DAMN THINGS ARE A BLESSING AND A CURSE.
BUT YOU NEED TO KNOW, AFTER WHAT HAPPENED WITH YOU, I PUT AN END TO THE NIGHTCRAWLERS.
I SHOULD HAVE NEVER INVOLVED CHILDREN. I SHOULDN'T HAVE BEEN EITHER, AND I'VE BEEN PAYING FOR MY MISTAKES EVER SINCE.
YOUR REGRETS MEAN NOTHING TO ME, OLD MAN! WHAT'S DONE IS DONE, AND YOU WILL PAY FOR EVERYTHING I'VE BEEN THROUGH!

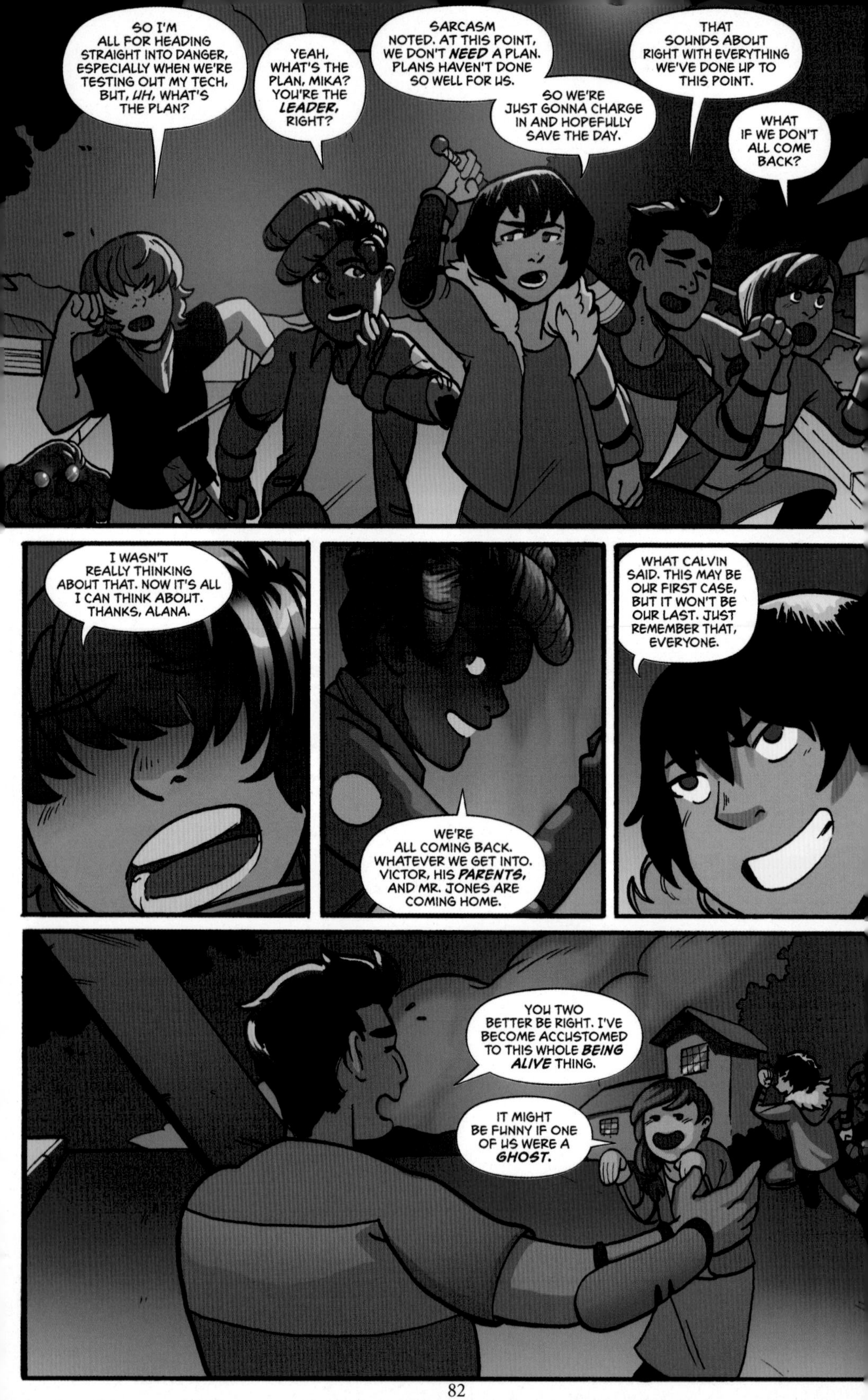
SO I'M ALL FOR HEADING STRAIGHT INTO DANGER, ESPECIALLY WHEN WE'RE TESTING OUT MY TECH, BUT, UH, WHAT'S THE PLAN?
YEAH, WHAT'S THE PLAN, MIKA? YOU'RE THE LEADER, RIGHT?
SARCASM NOTED. AT THIS POINT, WE DON'T NEED A PLAN. PLANS HAVEN'T DONE SO WELL FOR US.
SO WE'RE JUST GONNA CHARGE IN AND HOPEFULLY SAVE THE DAY.
THAT SOUNDS ABOUT RIGHT WITH EVERYTHING WE'VE DONE UP TO THIS POINT.
WHAT IF WE DON'T ALL COME BACK?
I WASN'T REALLY THINKING ABOUT THAT. NOW IT'S ALL I CAN THINK ABOUT. THANKS, ALANA.
WE'RE ALL COMING BACK. WHATEVER WE GET INTO. VICTOR, HIS PARENTS, AND MR. JONES ARE COMING HOME.
WHAT CALVIN SAID. THIS MAY BE OUR FIRST CASE, BUT IT WON'T BE OUR LAST. JUST REMEMBER THAT, EVERYONE.
YOU TWO BETTER BE RIGHT. I'VE BECOME ACCUSTOMED TO THIS WHOLE BEING ALIVE THING.
IT MIGHT BE FUNNY IF ONE OF US WERE A GHOST.

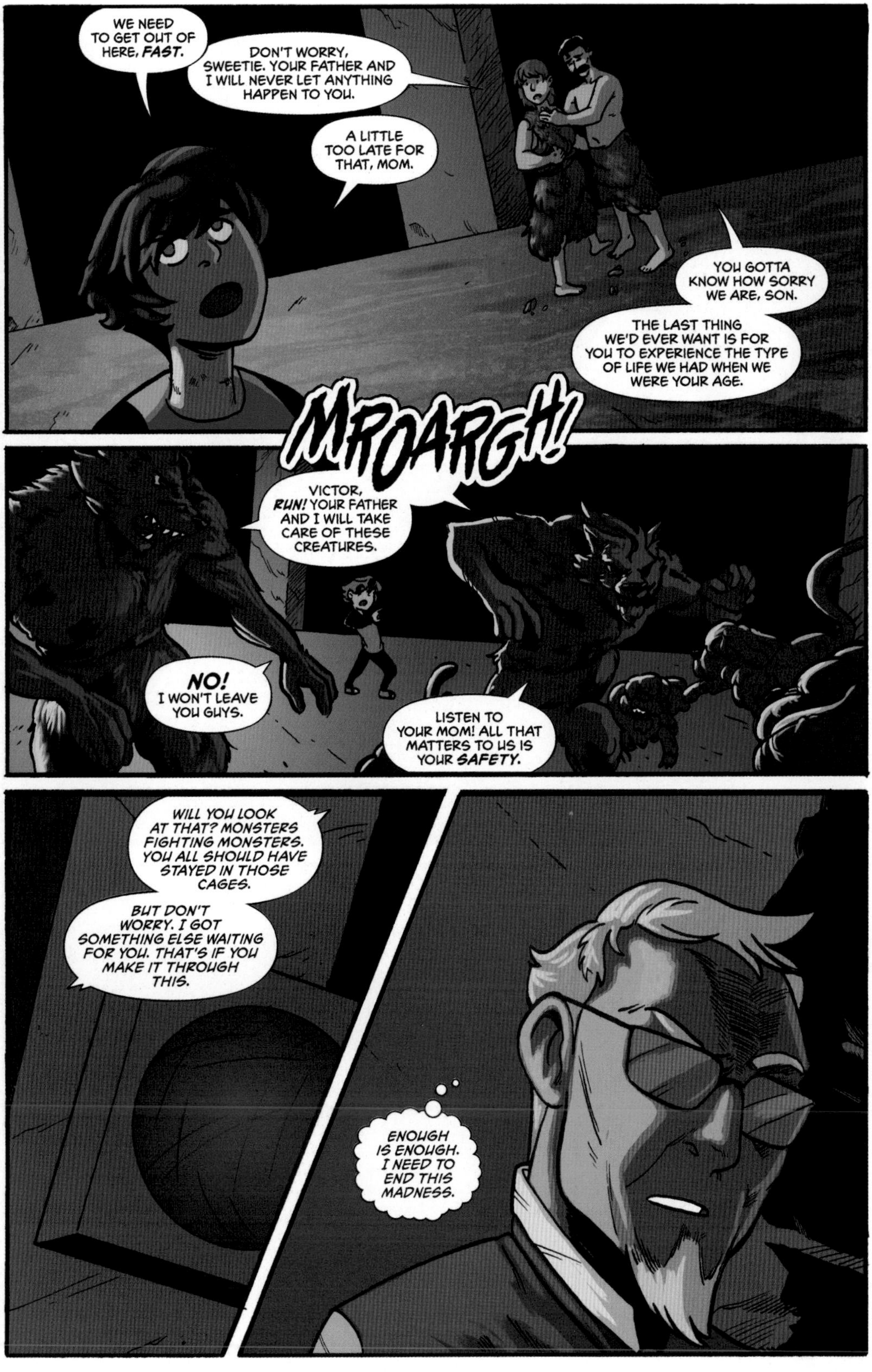
WE NEED TO GET OUT OF HERE, ***FAST.***
DON'T WORRY, SWEETIE. YOUR FATHER AND I WILL NEVER LET ANYTHING HAPPEN TO YOU.
A LITTLE TOO LATE FOR THAT, MOM.
YOU GOTTA KNOW HOW SORRY WE ARE, SON.
THE LAST THING WE'D EVER WANT IS FOR YOU TO EXPERIENCE THE TYPE OF LIFE WE HAD WHEN WE WERE YOUR AGE.
MROARGH!
VICTOR, ***RUN!*** YOUR FATHER AND I WILL TAKE CARE OF THESE CREATURES.
NO! I WON'T LEAVE YOU GUYS.
LISTEN TO YOUR MOM! ALL THAT MATTERS TO US IS YOUR ***SAFETY.***
WILL YOU LOOK AT THAT? MONSTERS FIGHTING MONSTERS. YOU ALL SHOULD HAVE STAYED IN THOSE CAGES.
BUT DON'T WORRY. I GOT SOMETHING ELSE WAITING FOR YOU. THAT'S IF YOU MAKE IT THROUGH THIS.
ENOUGH IS ENOUGH. I NEED TO END THIS MADNESS.

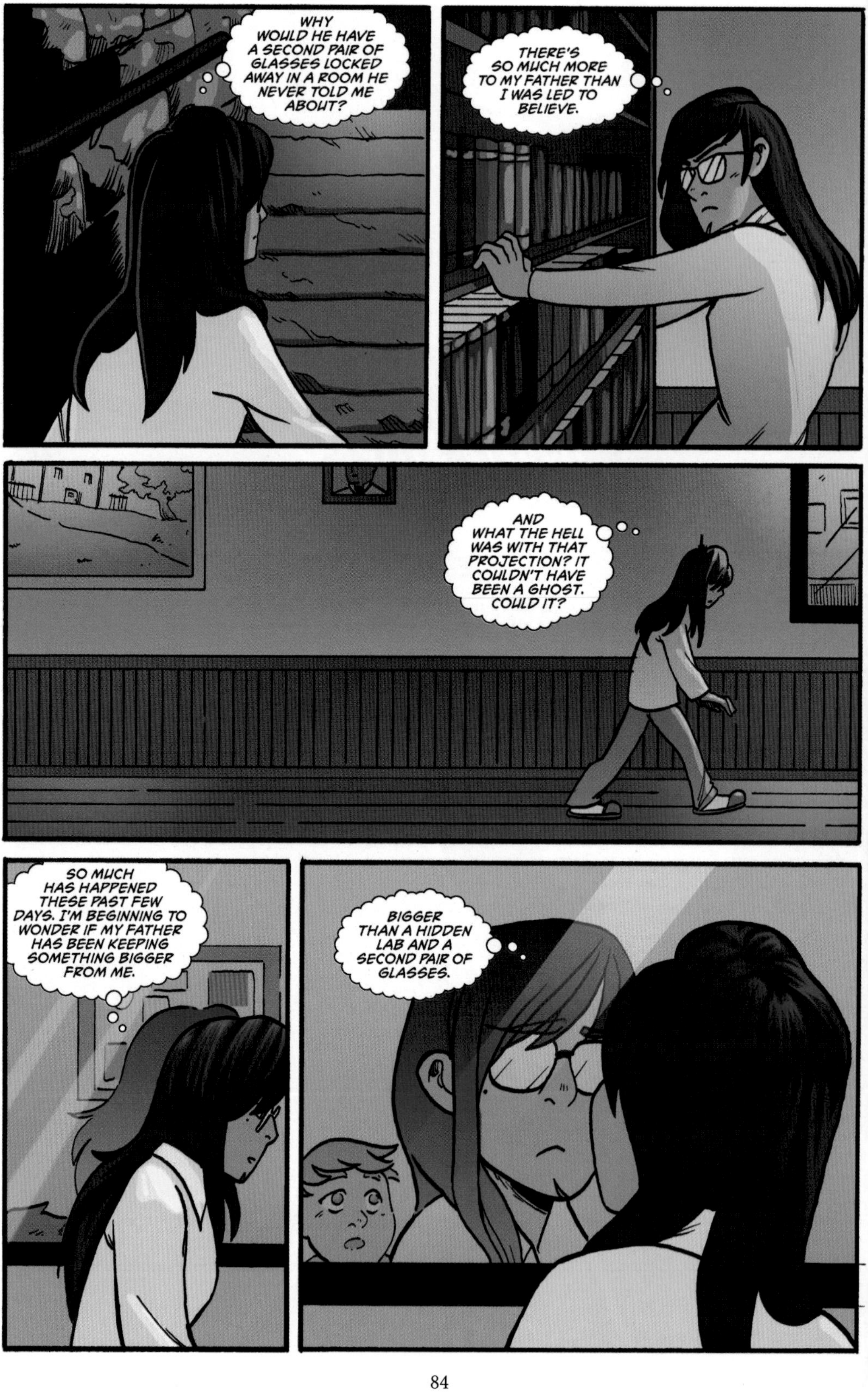
WHY WOULD HE HAVE A SECOND PAIR OF GLASSES LOCKED AWAY IN A ROOM HE NEVER TOLD ME ABOUT?
THERE'S SO MUCH MORE TO MY FATHER THAN I WAS LED TO BELIEVE.
AND WHAT THE HELL WAS WITH THAT PROJECTION? IT COULDN'T HAVE BEEN A GHOST. COULD IT?
SO MUCH HAS HAPPENED THESE PAST FEW DAYS. I'M BEGINNING TO WONDER IF MY FATHER HAS BEEN KEEPING SOMETHING BIGGER FROM ME.
BIGGER THAN A HIDDEN LAB AND A SECOND PAIR OF GLASSES.

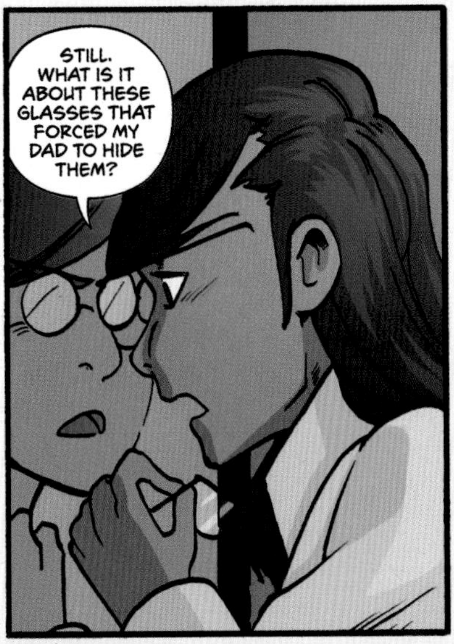
STILL.
WHAT IS IT ABOUT THESE GLASSES THAT FORCED MY DAD TO HIDE THEM?

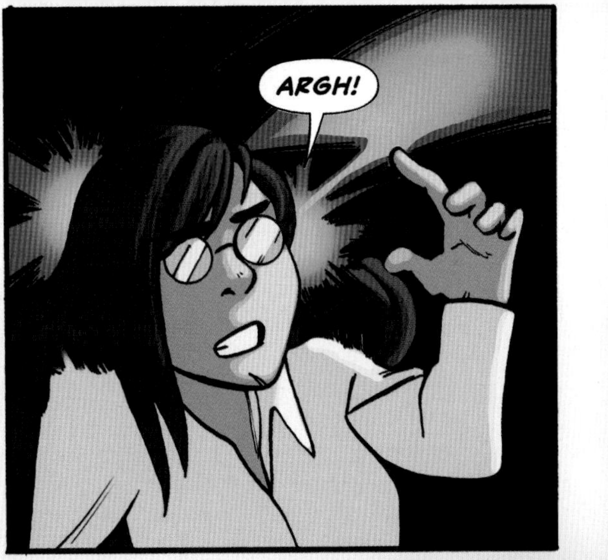
ARGH!

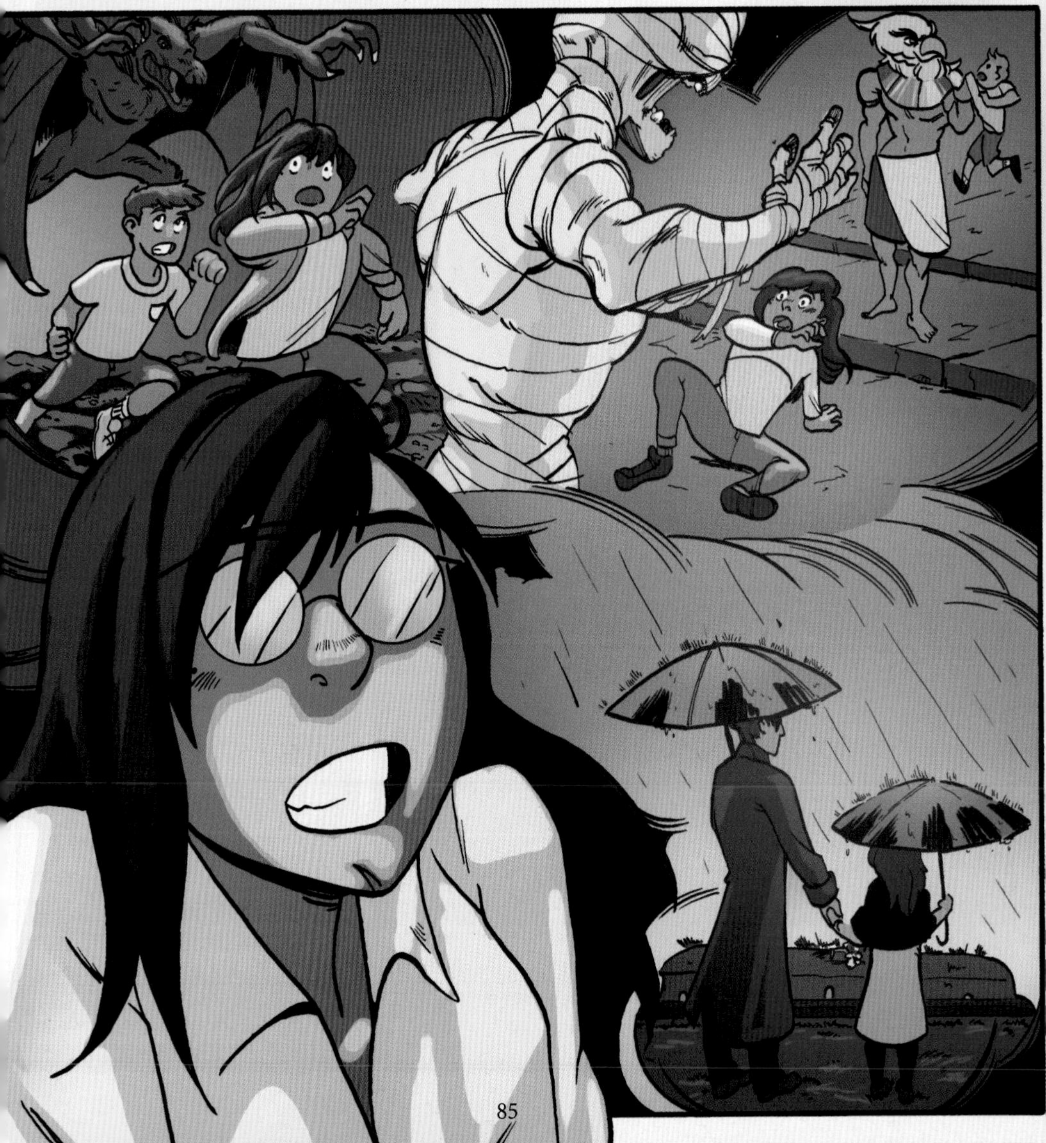

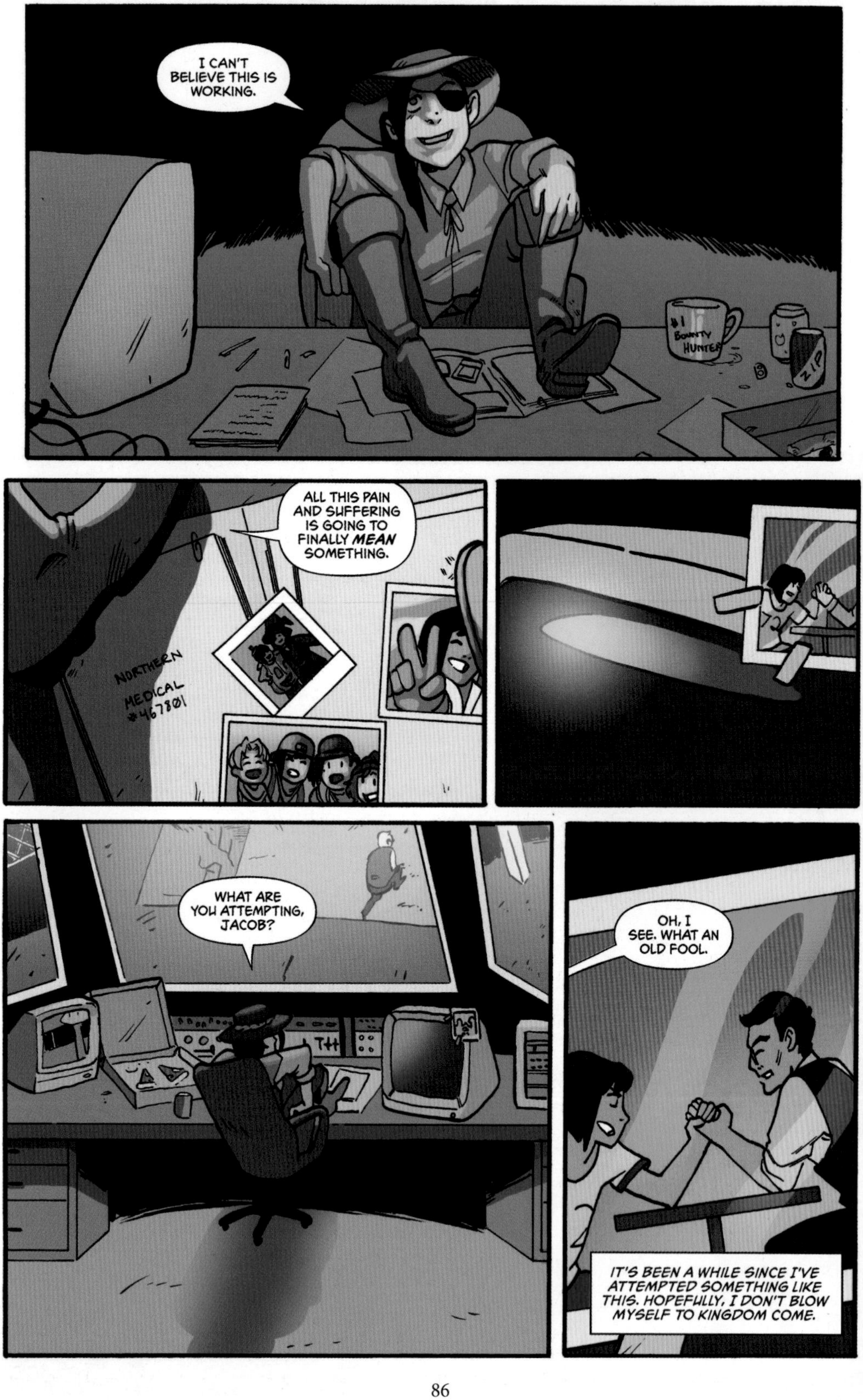
I CAN'T BELIEVE THIS IS WORKING.
#1 BOUNTY HUNTER
ZIP
ALL THIS PAIN AND SUFFERING IS GOING TO FINALLY *MEAN* SOMETHING.
NORTHERN MEDICAL #467801
WHAT ARE YOU ATTEMPTING, JACOB?
OH, I SEE. WHAT AN OLD FOOL.
IT'S BEEN A WHILE SINCE I'VE ATTEMPTED SOMETHING LIKE THIS. HOPEFULLY, I DON'T BLOW MYSELF TO KINGDOM COME.

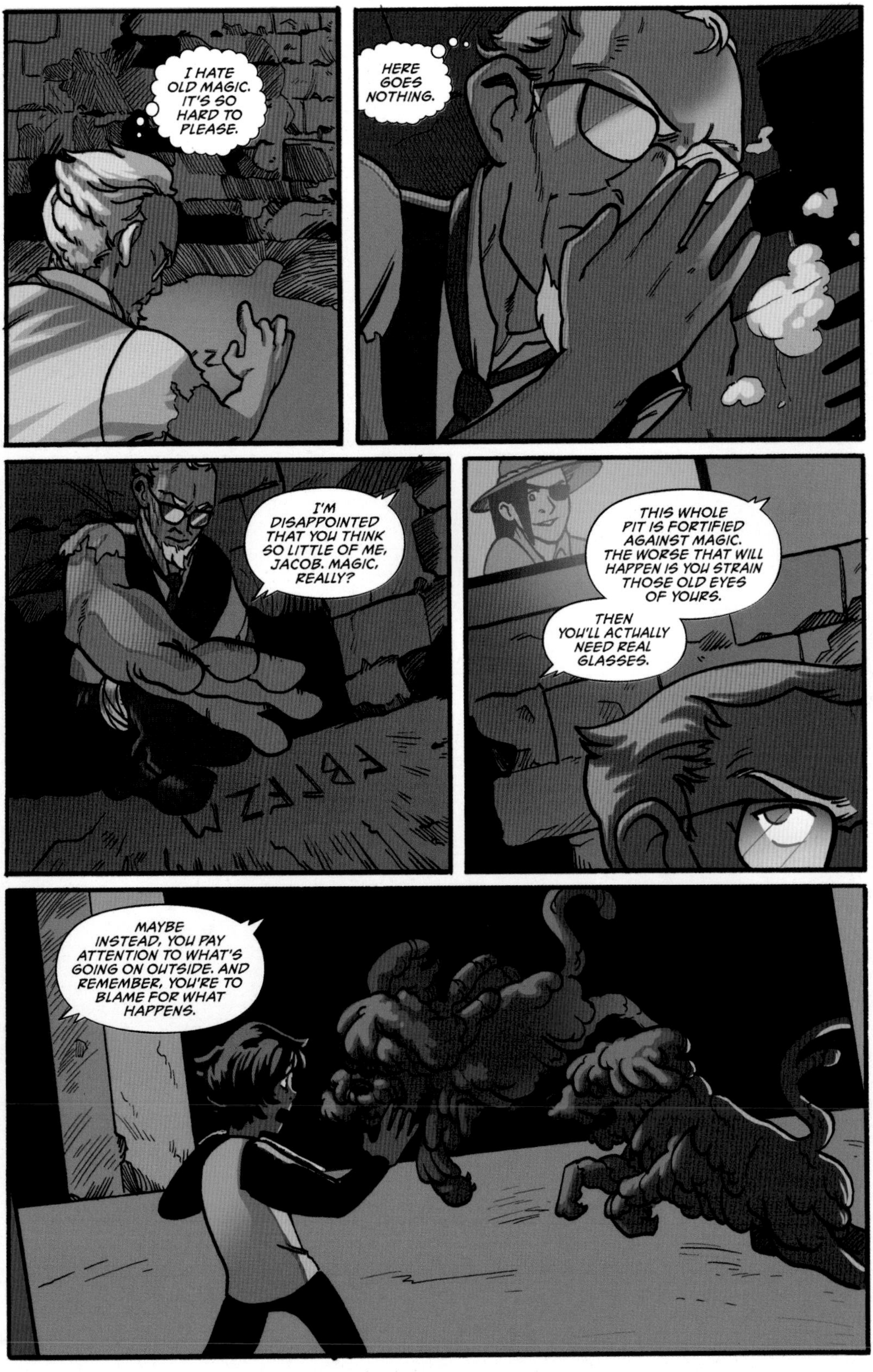
I HATE OLD MAGIC. IT'S SO HARD TO PLEASE.
HERE GOES NOTHING.
I'M DISAPPOINTED THAT YOU THINK SO LITTLE OF ME, JACOB. MAGIC, REALLY?
THIS WHOLE PIT IS FORTIFIED AGAINST MAGIC. THE WORSE THAT WILL HAPPEN IS YOU STRAIN THOSE OLD EYES OF YOURS.
THEN YOU'LL ACTUALLY NEED REAL GLASSES.
MAYBE INSTEAD, YOU PAY ATTENTION TO WHAT'S GOING ON OUTSIDE. AND REMEMBER, YOU'RE TO BLAME FOR WHAT HAPPENS.

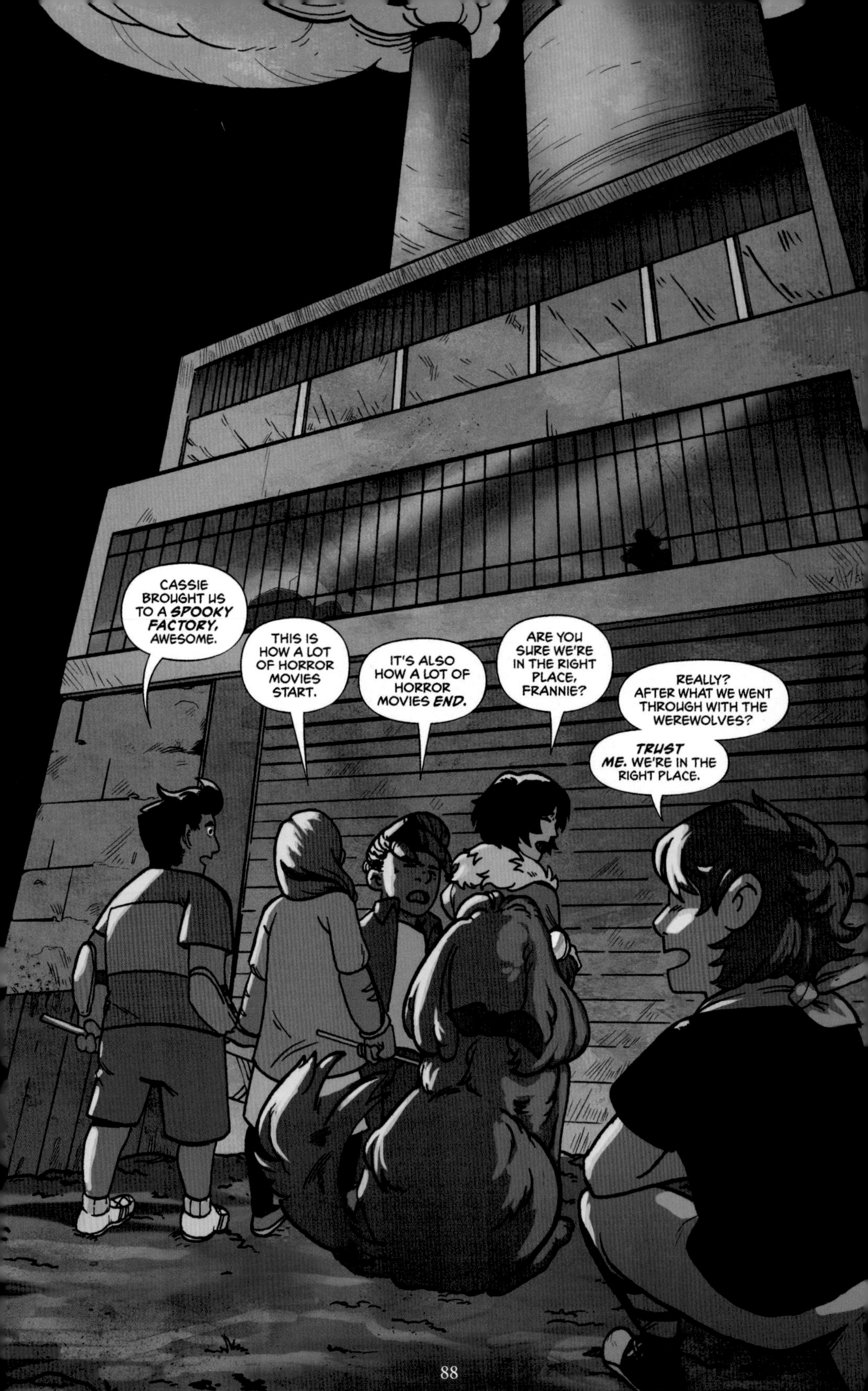
CASSIE BROUGHT US TO A **SPOOKY FACTORY.** AWESOME.
THIS IS HOW A LOT OF HORROR MOVIES START.
IT'S ALSO HOW A LOT OF HORROR MOVIES **END.**
ARE YOU SURE WE'RE IN THE RIGHT PLACE, FRANNIE?
REALLY? AFTER WHAT WE WENT THROUGH WITH THE WEREWOLVES?
TRUST ME. WE'RE IN THE RIGHT PLACE.

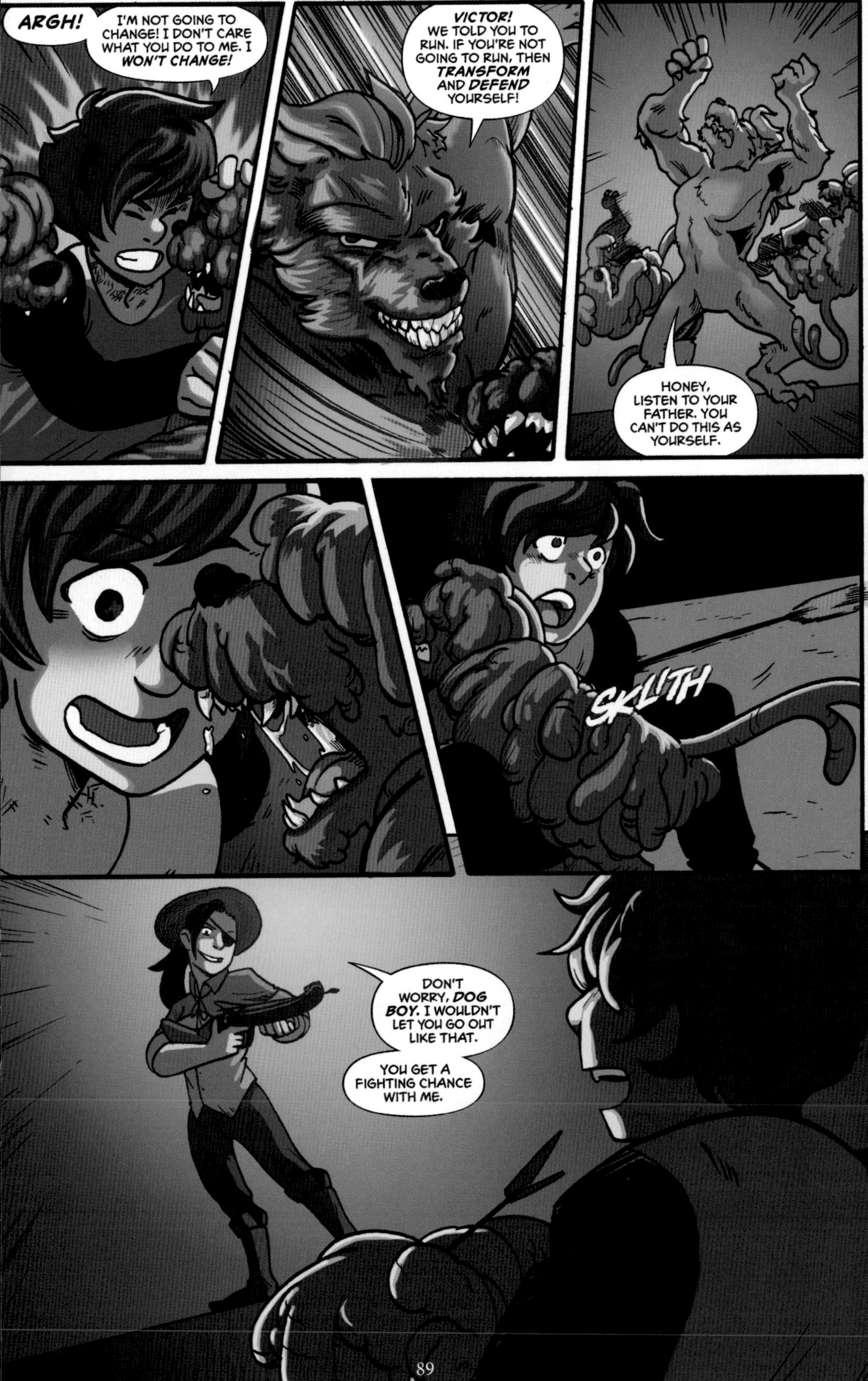
ARGH!
I'M NOT GOING TO CHANGE! I DON'T CARE WHAT YOU DO TO ME. I WON'T CHANGE!
VICTOR! WE TOLD YOU TO RUN. IF YOU'RE NOT GOING TO RUN, THEN TRANSFORM AND DEFEND YOURSELF!
HONEY, LISTEN TO YOUR FATHER. YOU CAN'T DO THIS AS YOURSELF.
SKLITH
DON'T WORRY, DOG BOY. I WOULDN'T LET YOU GO OUT LIKE THAT.
YOU GET A FIGHTING CHANCE WITH ME.

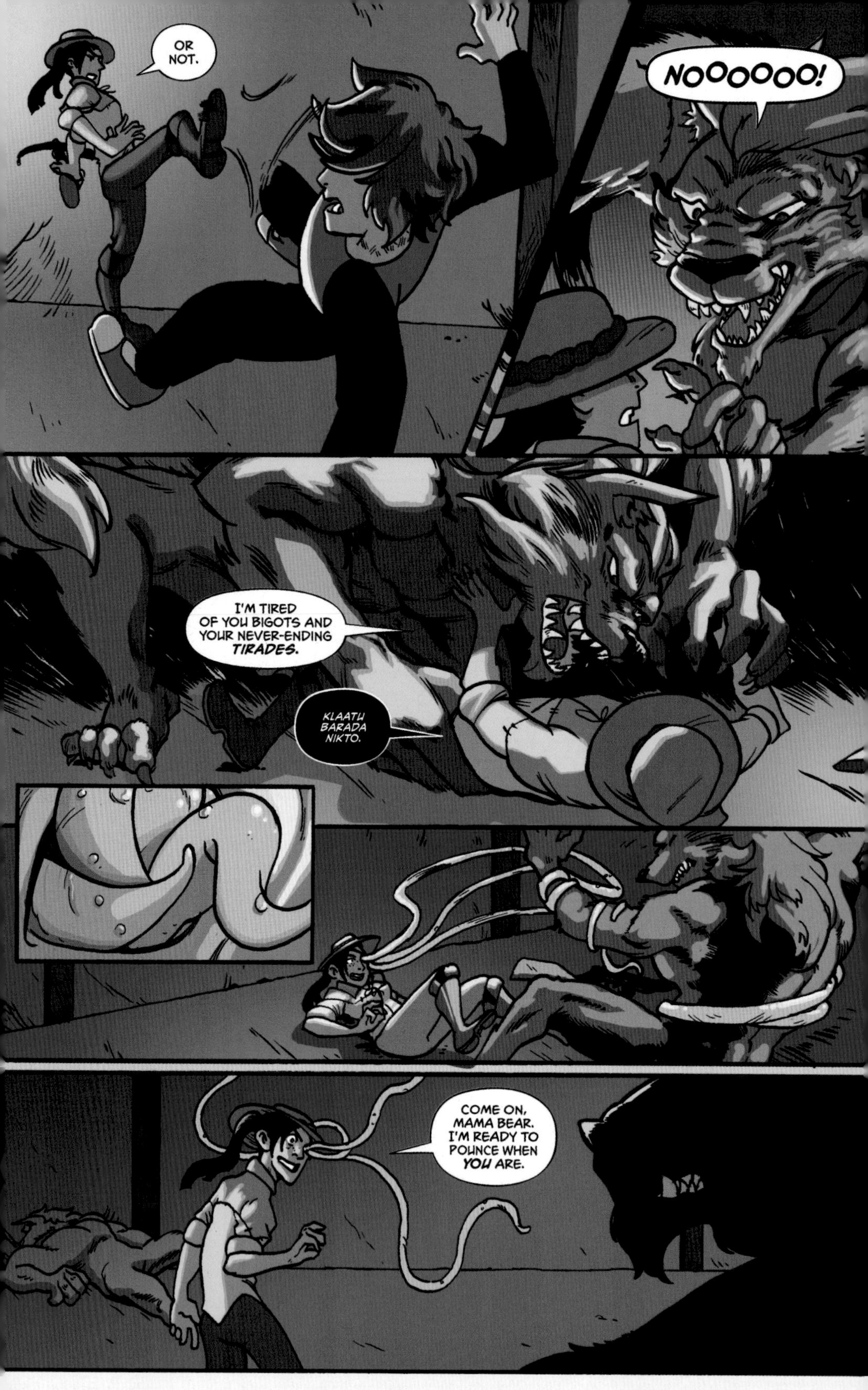
OR NOT.
NOOOOOO!
I'M TIRED OF YOU BIGOTS AND YOUR NEVER-ENDING *TIRADES.*
KLAATU BARADA NIKTO.
COME ON, MAMA BEAR. I'M READY TO POUNCE WHEN *YOU* ARE.

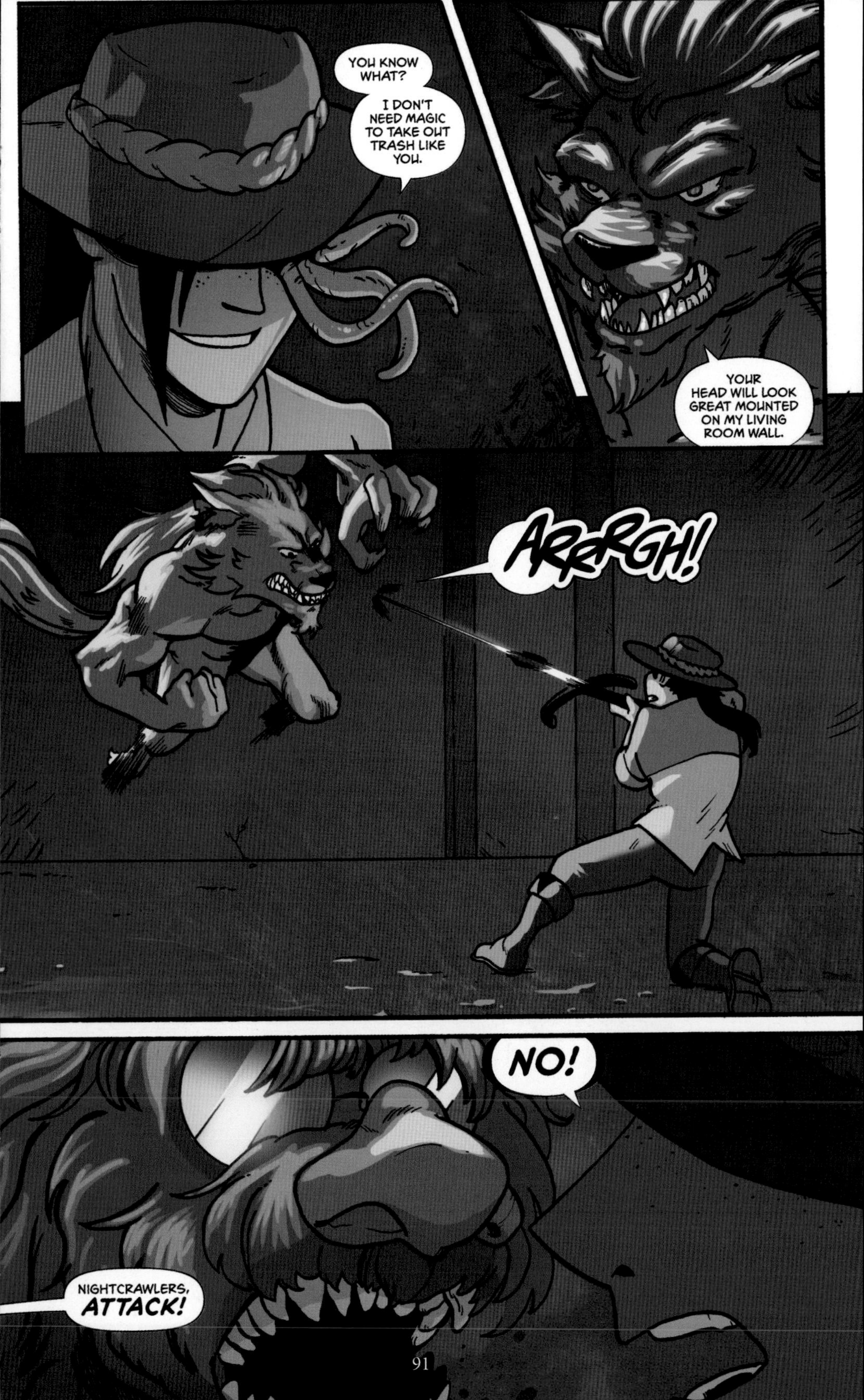
YOU KNOW WHAT?
I DON'T NEED MAGIC TO TAKE OUT TRASH LIKE YOU.
YOUR HEAD WILL LOOK GREAT MOUNTED ON MY LIVING ROOM WALL.
ARRRGH!
NO!
NIGHTCRAWLERS, ATTACK!

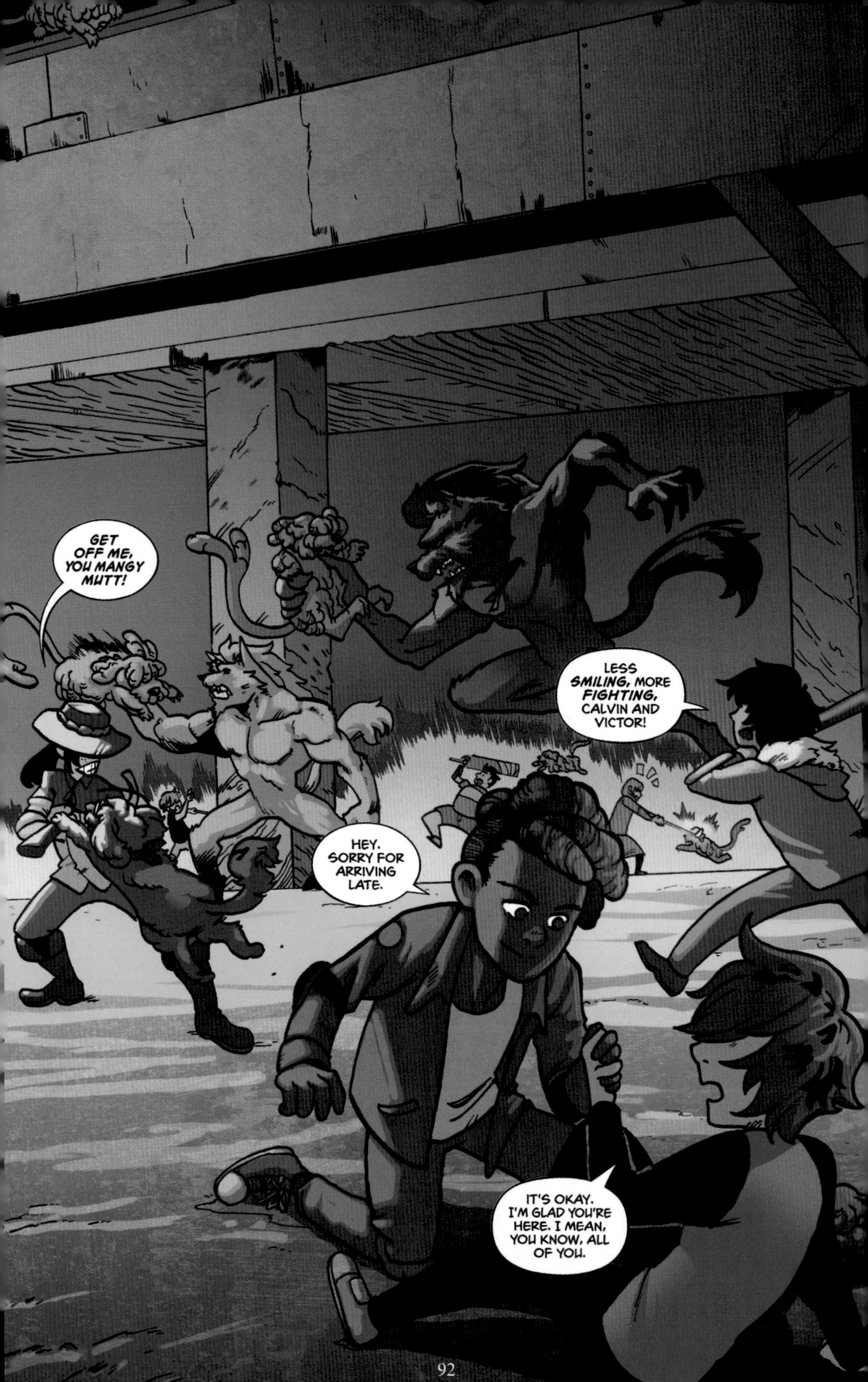
GET OFF ME, YOU MANGY MUTT!
LESS SMILING, MORE FIGHTING, CALVIN AND VICTOR!
HEY. SORRY FOR ARRIVING LATE.
IT'S OKAY. I'M GLAD YOU'RE HERE. I MEAN, YOU KNOW, ALL OF YOU.

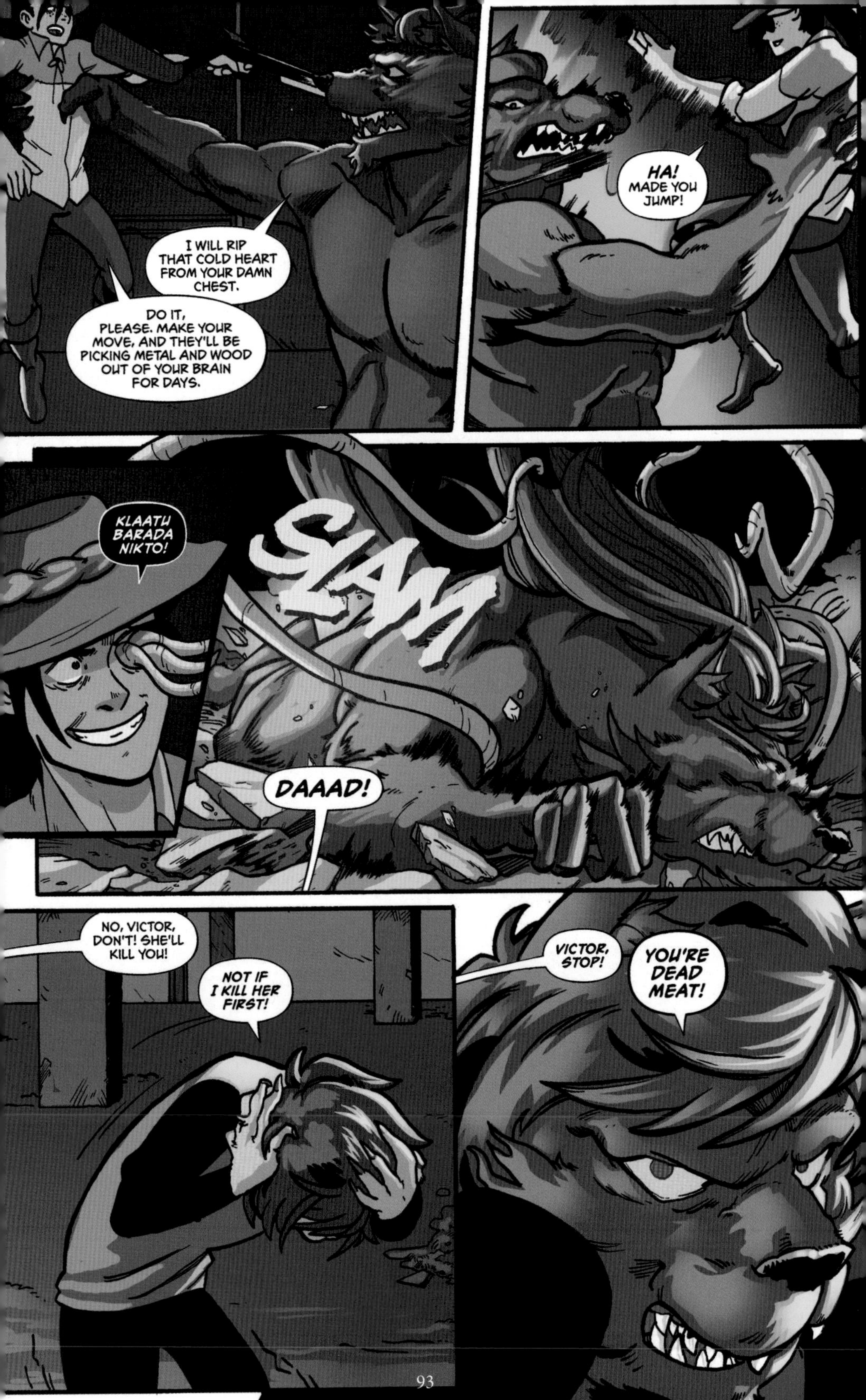
I WILL RIP THAT COLD HEART FROM YOUR DAMN CHEST.
DO IT, PLEASE. MAKE YOUR MOVE, AND THEY'LL BE PICKING METAL AND WOOD OUT OF YOUR BRAIN FOR DAYS.
HA! MADE YOU JUMP!
KLAATU BARADA NIKTO!
SLAM
DAAAD!
NO, VICTOR, DON'T! SHE'LL KILL YOU!
NOT IF I KILL HER FIRST!
VICTOR, STOP!
YOU'RE DEAD MEAT!

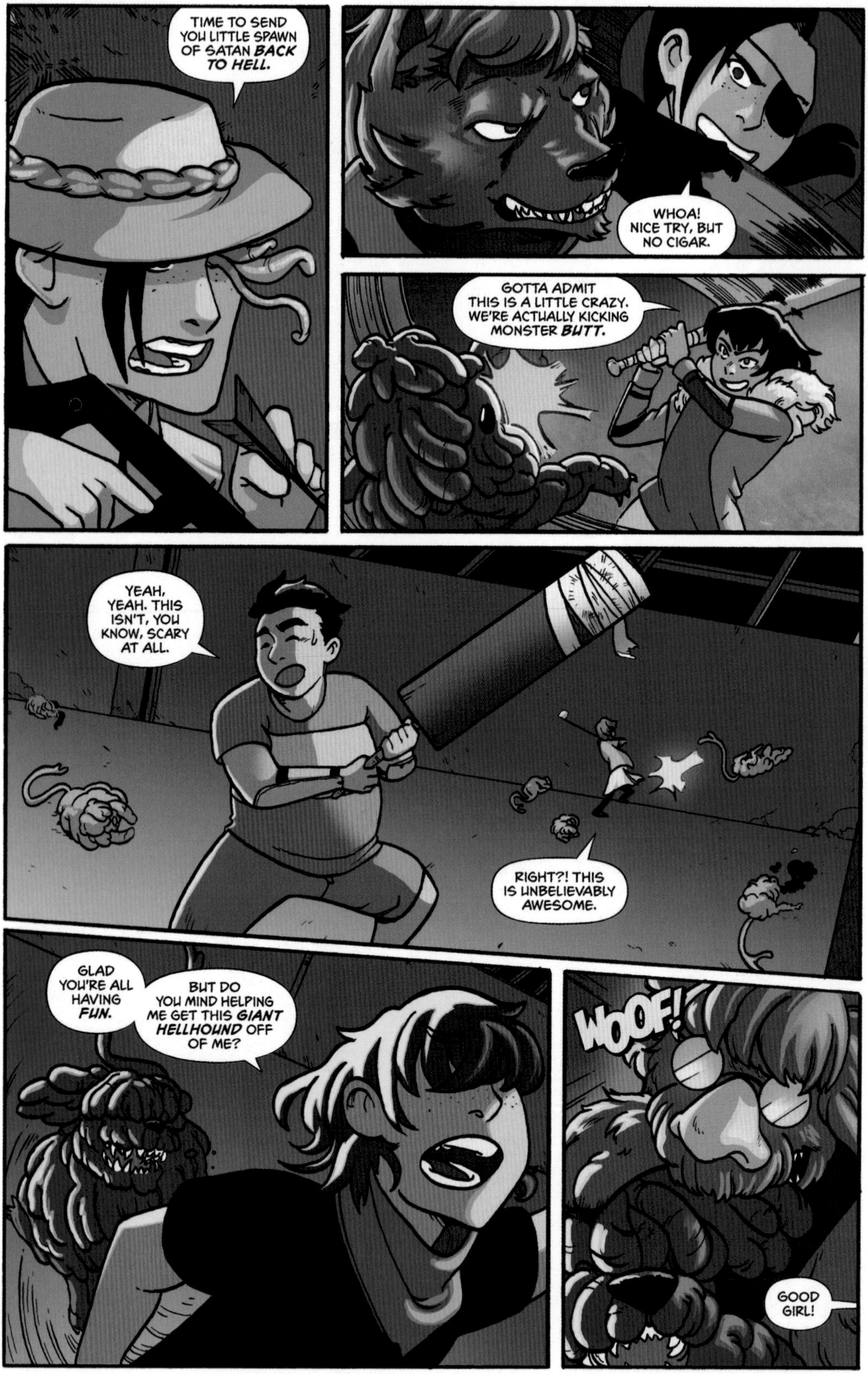
TIME TO SEND YOU LITTLE SPAWN OF SATAN BACK TO HELL.
WHOA! NICE TRY, BUT NO CIGAR.
GOTTA ADMIT THIS IS A LITTLE CRAZY. WE'RE ACTUALLY KICKING MONSTER BUTT.
YEAH, YEAH. THIS ISN'T, YOU KNOW, SCARY AT ALL.
RIGHT?! THIS IS UNBELIEVABLY AWESOME.
GLAD YOU'RE ALL HAVING FUN.
BUT DO YOU MIND HELPING ME GET THIS GIANT HELLHOUND OFF OF ME?
WOOF!
GOOD GIRL!

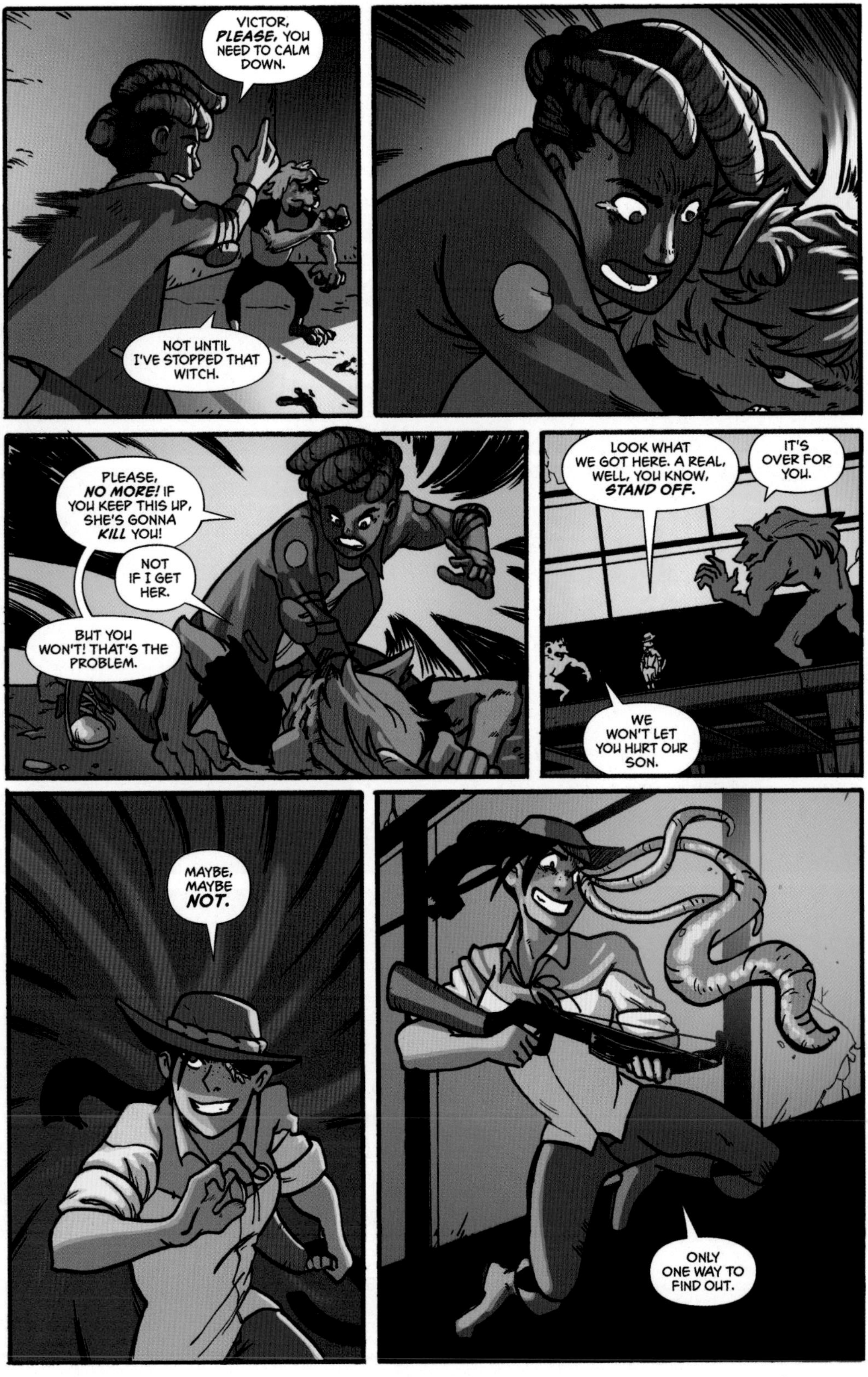

VICTOR, *PLEASE,* YOU NEED TO CALM DOWN.
NOT UNTIL I'VE STOPPED THAT WITCH.
PLEASE, *NO MORE!* IF YOU KEEP THIS UP, SHE'S GONNA *KILL* YOU!
NOT IF I GET HER.
BUT YOU WON'T! THAT'S THE PROBLEM.
LOOK WHAT WE GOT HERE. A REAL, WELL, YOU KNOW, *STAND OFF.*
IT'S OVER FOR YOU.
WE WON'T LET YOU HURT OUR SON.
MAYBE, MAYBE *NOT.*
ONLY ONE WAY TO FIND OUT.

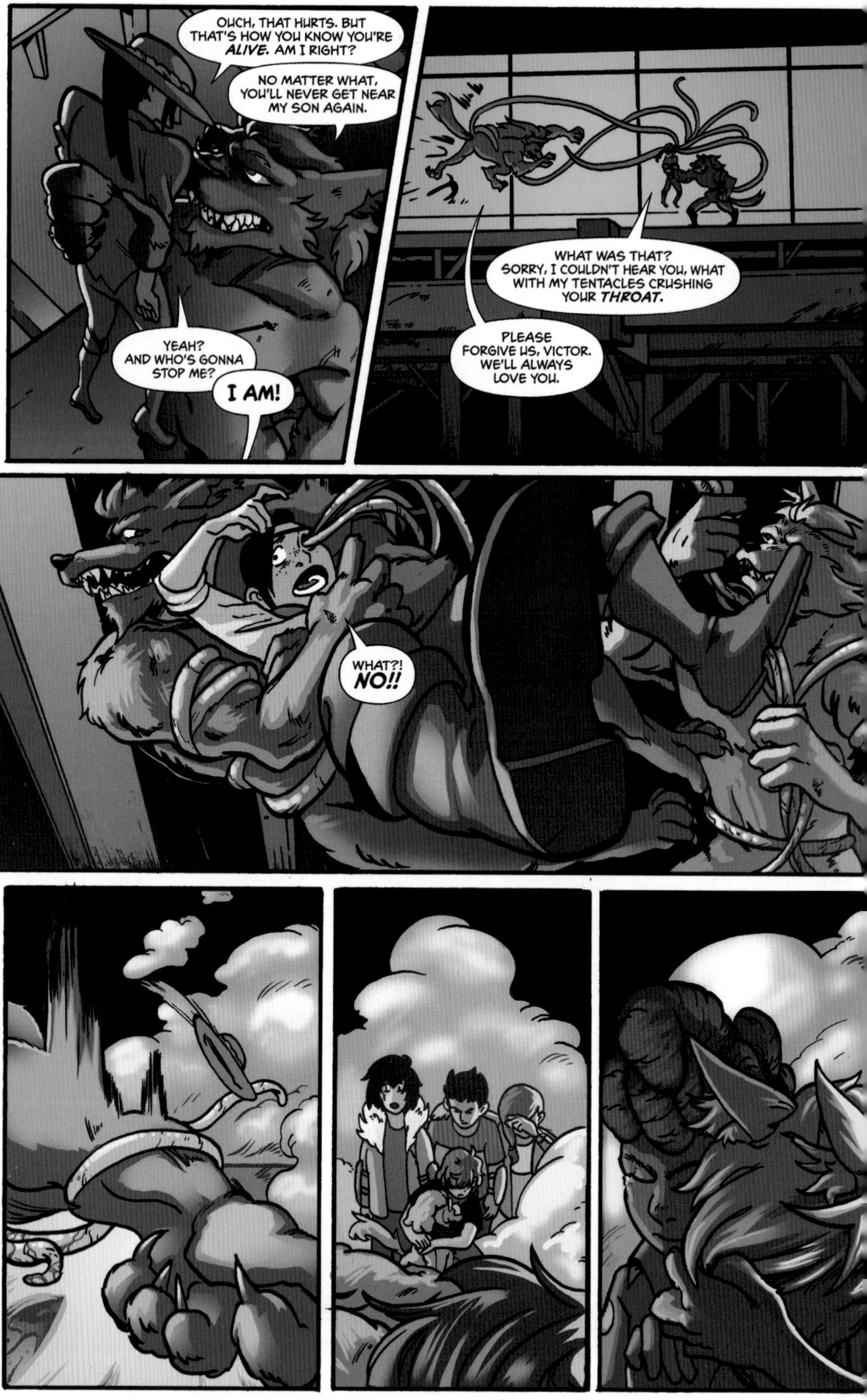
OUCH, THAT HURTS. BUT THAT'S HOW YOU KNOW YOU'RE *ALIVE.* AM I RIGHT?
NO MATTER WHAT, YOU'LL NEVER GET NEAR MY SON AGAIN.
YEAH? AND WHO'S GONNA STOP ME?
I AM!
WHAT WAS THAT? SORRY, I COULDN'T HEAR YOU, WHAT WITH MY TENTACLES CRUSHING YOUR *THROAT.*
PLEASE FORGIVE US, VICTOR. WE'LL ALWAYS LOVE YOU.
WHAT?! **NO!!**

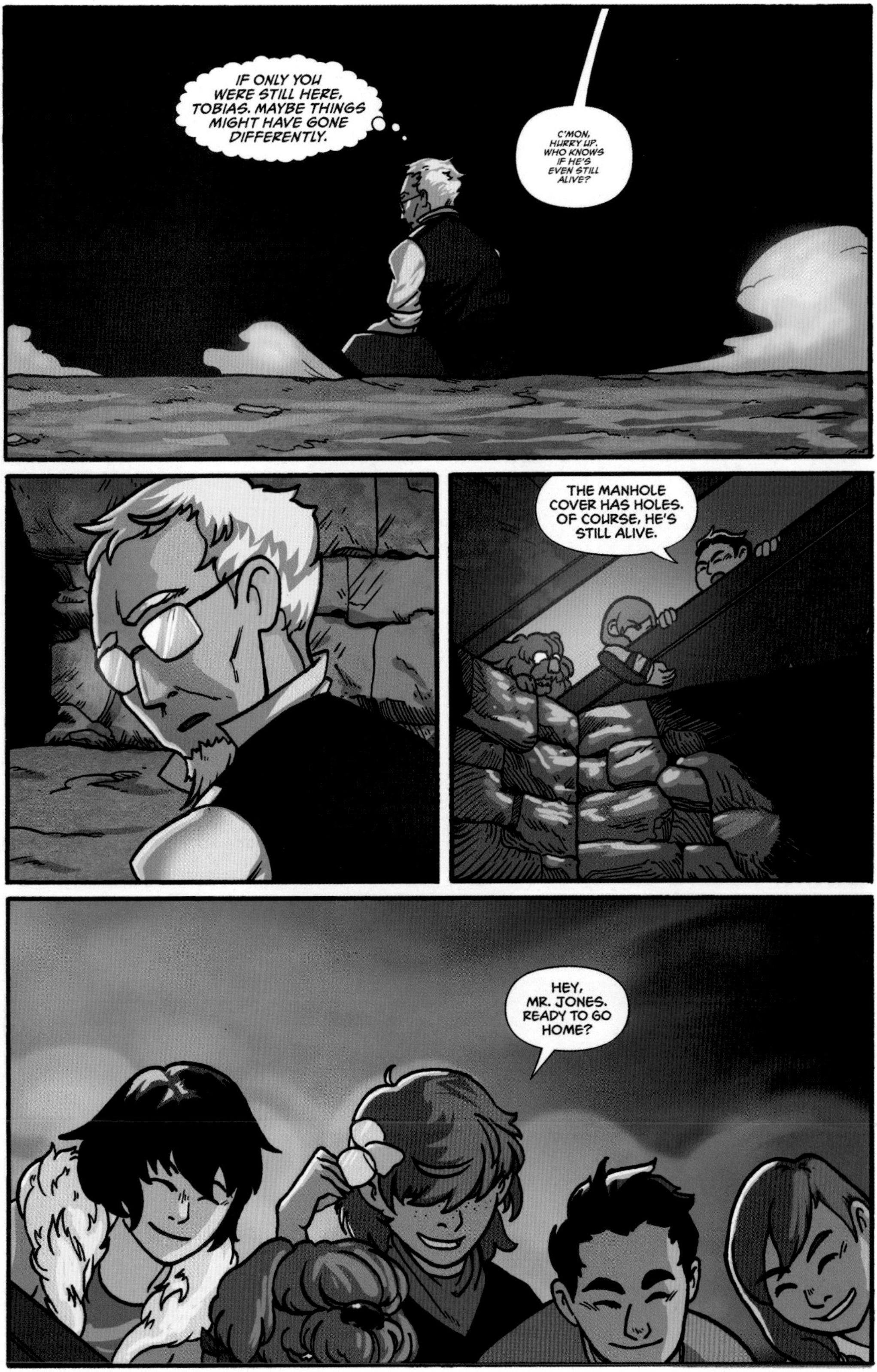

IF ONLY YOU WERE STILL HERE, TOBIAS. MAYBE THINGS MIGHT HAVE GONE DIFFERENTLY.
C'MON, HURRY UP. WHO KNOWS IF HE'S EVEN STILL ALIVE?
THE MANHOLE COVER HAS HOLES. OF COURSE, HE'S STILL ALIVE.
HEY, MR. JONES. READY TO GO HOME?

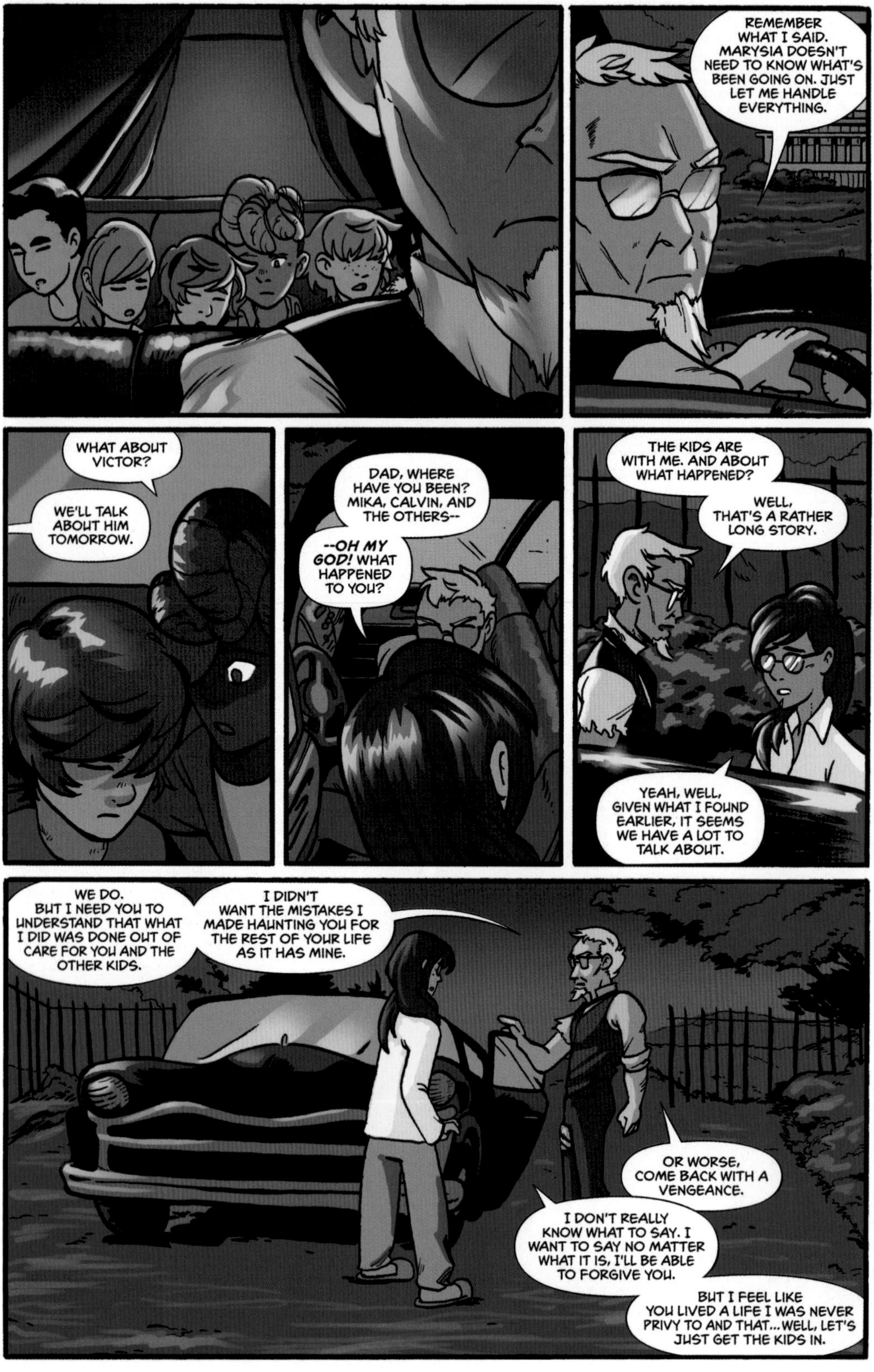
REMEMBER WHAT I SAID. MARYSIA DOESN'T NEED TO KNOW WHAT'S BEEN GOING ON. JUST LET ME HANDLE EVERYTHING.
WHAT ABOUT VICTOR?
WE'LL TALK ABOUT HIM TOMORROW.
DAD, WHERE HAVE YOU BEEN? MIKA, CALVIN, AND THE OTHERS--
--OH MY GOD! WHAT HAPPENED TO YOU?
THE KIDS ARE WITH ME. AND ABOUT WHAT HAPPENED?
WELL, THAT'S A RATHER LONG STORY.
YEAH, WELL, GIVEN WHAT I FOUND EARLIER, IT SEEMS WE HAVE A LOT TO TALK ABOUT.
WE DO. BUT I NEED YOU TO UNDERSTAND THAT WHAT I DID WAS DONE OUT OF CARE FOR YOU AND THE OTHER KIDS.
I DIDN'T WANT THE MISTAKES I MADE HAUNTING YOU FOR THE REST OF YOUR LIFE AS IT HAS MINE.
OR WORSE, COME BACK WITH A VENGEANCE.
I DON'T REALLY KNOW WHAT TO SAY. I WANT TO SAY NO MATTER WHAT IT IS, I'LL BE ABLE TO FORGIVE YOU.
BUT I FEEL LIKE YOU LIVED A LIFE I WAS NEVER PRIVY TO AND THAT...WELL, LET'S JUST GET THE KIDS IN.

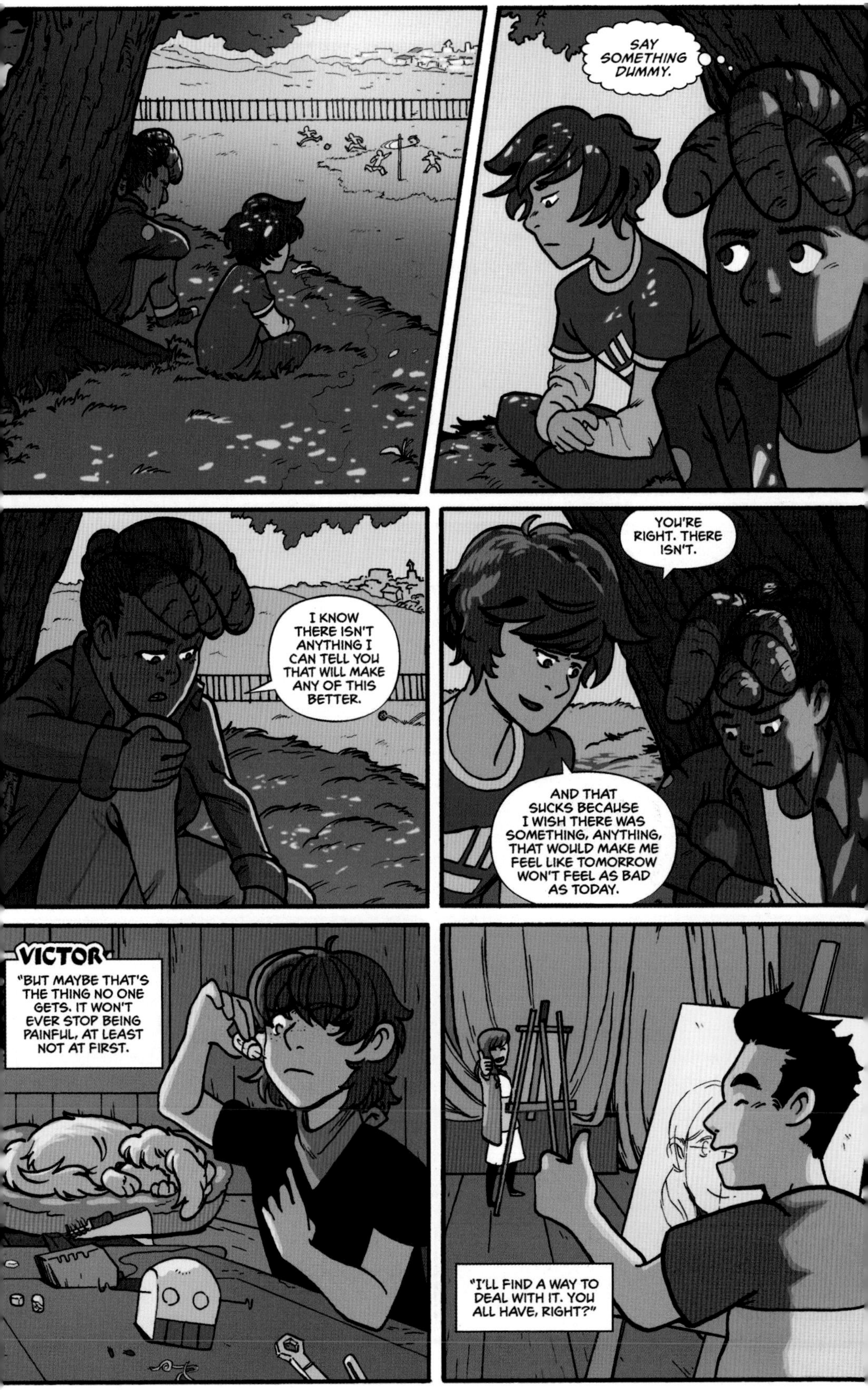
SAY SOMETHING DUMMY.
I KNOW THERE ISN'T ANYTHING I CAN TELL YOU THAT WILL MAKE ANY OF THIS BETTER.
YOU'RE RIGHT. THERE ISN'T.
AND THAT SUCKS BECAUSE I WISH THERE WAS SOMETHING, ANYTHING, THAT WOULD MAKE ME FEEL LIKE TOMORROW WON'T FEEL AS BAD AS TODAY.
VICTOR
"BUT MAYBE THAT'S THE THING NO ONE GETS. IT WON'T EVER STOP BEING PAINFUL, AT LEAST NOT AT FIRST.
"I'LL FIND A WAY TO DEAL WITH IT. YOU ALL HAVE, RIGHT?"

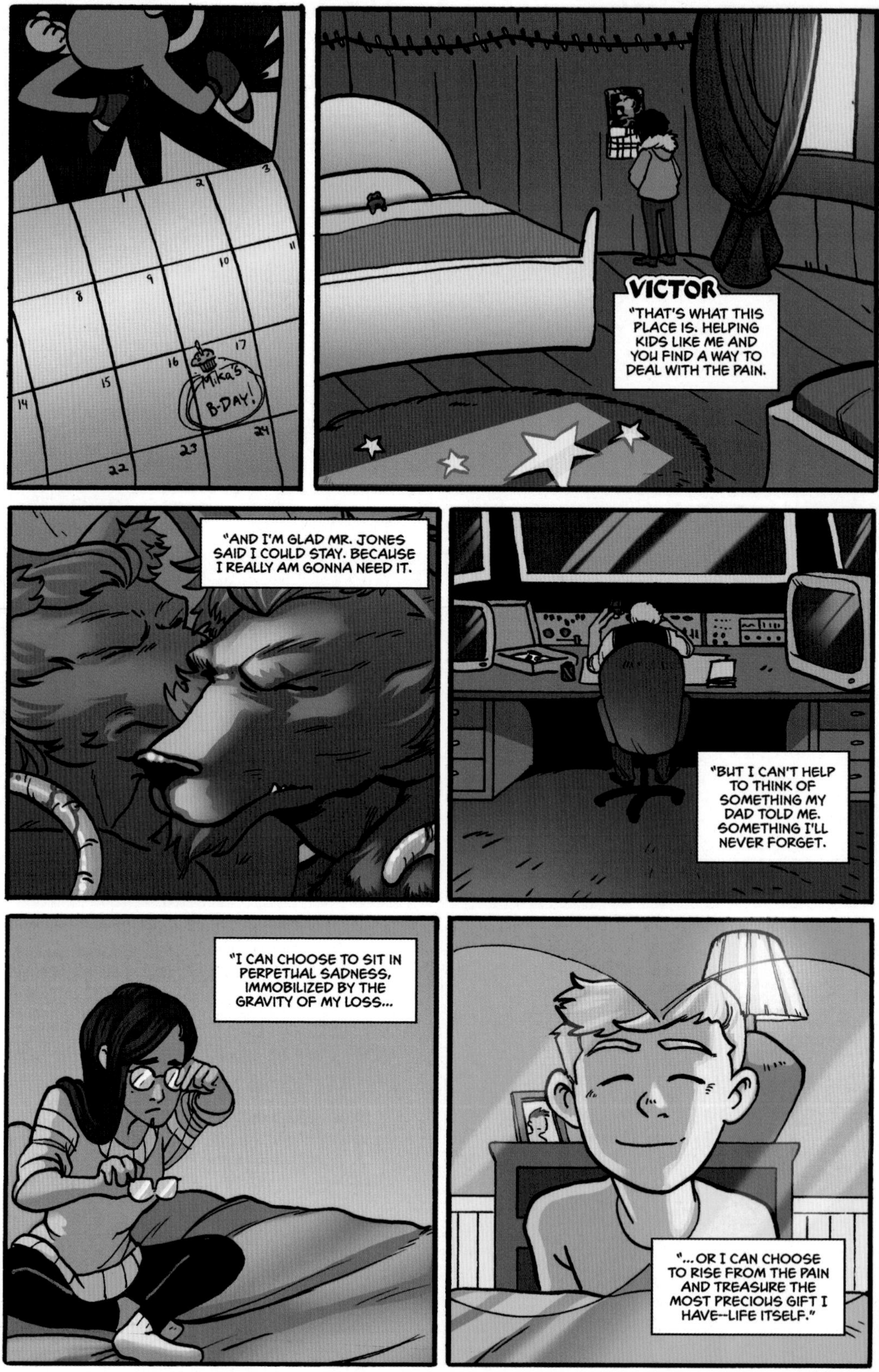
Mika's B-DAY!
VICTOR
"THAT'S WHAT THIS PLACE IS. HELPING KIDS LIKE ME AND YOU FIND A WAY TO DEAL WITH THE PAIN.
"AND I'M GLAD MR. JONES SAID I COULD STAY. BECAUSE I REALLY AM GONNA NEED IT.
"BUT I CAN'T HELP TO THINK OF SOMETHING MY DAD TOLD ME. SOMETHING I'LL NEVER FORGET.
"I CAN CHOOSE TO SIT IN PERPETUAL SADNESS, IMMOBILIZED BY THE GRAVITY OF MY LOSS...
"...OR I CAN CHOOSE TO RISE FROM THE PAIN AND TREASURE THE MOST PRECIOUS GIFT I HAVE--LIFE ITSELF."

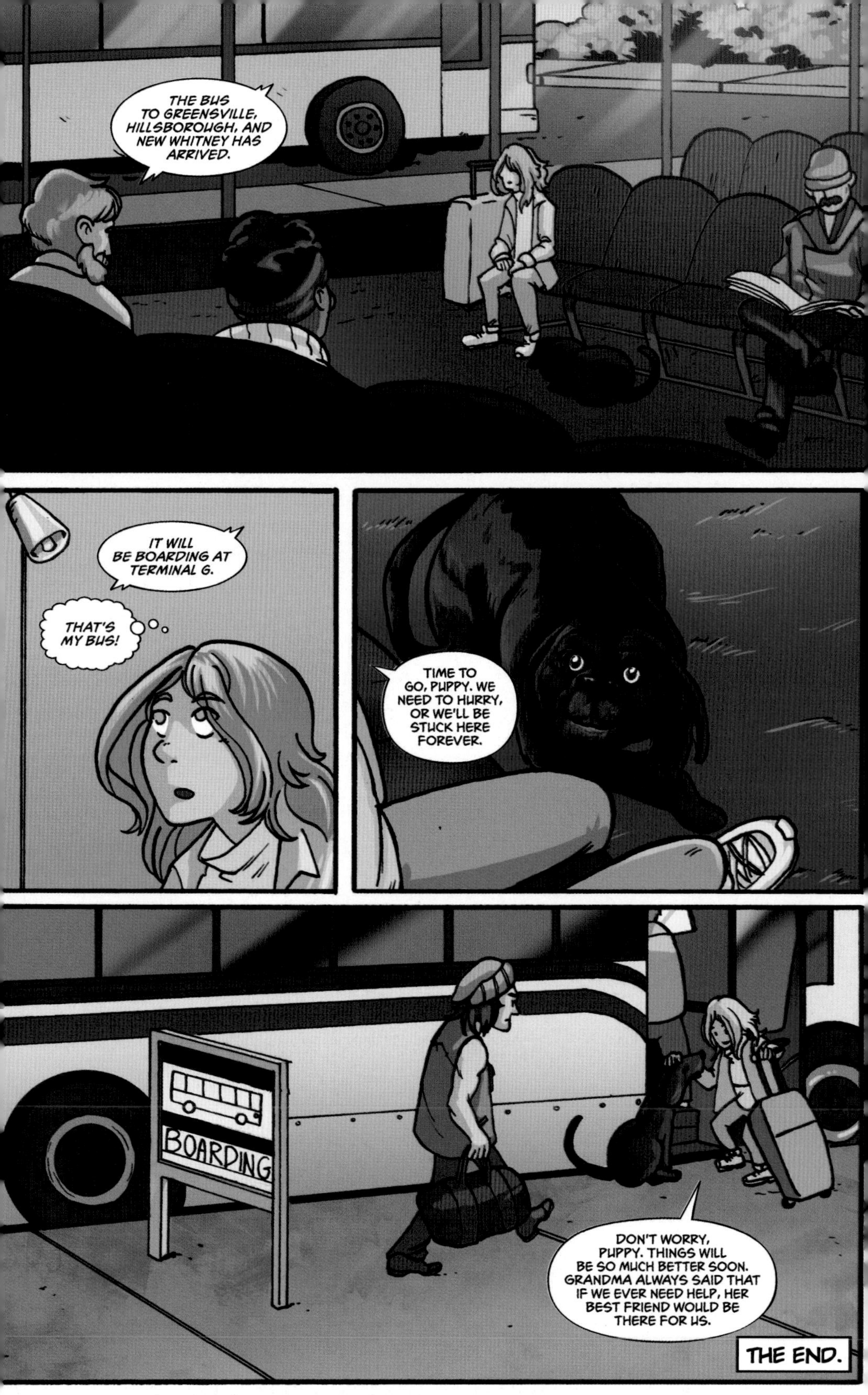
THE BUS TO GREENSVILLE, HILLSBOROUGH, AND NEW WHITNEY HAS ARRIVED.
IT WILL BE BOARDING AT TERMINAL G.
THAT'S MY BUS!
TIME TO GO, PUPPY. WE NEED TO HURRY, OR WE'LL BE STUCK HERE FOREVER.
BOARDING
DON'T WORRY, PUPPY. THINGS WILL BE SO MUCH BETTER SOON. GRANDMA ALWAYS SAID THAT IF WE EVER NEED HELP, HER BEST FRIEND WOULD BE THERE FOR US.
THE END.

AFTERWORD

Hey everyone! Thank you so much for reading The Nightcrawlers, and I hope it was as fun for you to read as it was for me to draw! Way back in 2016, I met Marco online, searching for an artist to collaborate on a script that went pretty differently, but always centered on our crew of Mika, Calvin, Frannie, Bruno, and Alana, and it came from a love of wanting to tell stories about mythology, urban legends, and the things that go bump in the night. Around that time, stuff like Five Nights at Freddie's, Bendy, and even a lot of ARGs were hitting new strides on the internet: people love horror! We've always been fascinated by what might lurk in the neighborhood.

The Nightcrawlers takes its inspiration from tales that go way back further, from movies around the mid-20th century to the 80s to ancient tales of the skinwalker, the Morrigan, fairies, things that have been passed down from generation to generation. While our first book gives just a taste of what's in store down the road (and there is a LOT of stuff), I hope that anyone who's read this got a thrill out of the mysteries laid out for what we could be planning down the road for our protagonists. What could the ghost of Marysia's brother be trying to tell her? What happened to Greta at such a young age, or the rest of the early Nightcrawlers, for that matter? What is Mr. William Jones hiding? And why is Mika looking so intently at her upcoming birthday?

One of my favorite things that I got to draw on this book was the friendships between the Nightcrawlers gang, from Mika and Calvin always butting heads on who is the real team leader, Bruno's thoughtfulness and supportiveness playing off of Alana's tendency to blurt out whatever is on her mind, and of course, Frannie, who is often off to her own devices (figuratively and literally). And now, with Victor the shapeshifter on the team, they're even more prepared to take on the strange occurrences in their world. I hope you support them all in the future!

Thank you, see you next book!

Rachel Distler

THE NIGHTCRAWLERS
BIOGRAPHIES

Francesca Cornblath (Irish/Jewish American): A heavy metal-loving eleven-year-old (nicknamed Franny), she arrives at the orphanage with her dog Cassiopeia (nickname Cassie), a German Shepard. Franny is the team's engineer who creates all their gear, gadgets, and chingamajigs. She's a cheerful, warm, and fun person but a homebody. She would rather spend her time with her computer, scrap metal, and junk parts listening to music and working on all her wild ideas.

Bruno Martinez (Puerto Rican): A stocky eleven-year-old obsessed with comic books that wants to be a comic book writer when he grows up. When not working on their next comic book project, he and his sister Alana discuss storytelling and how it applies to their lives, and always try to guess where things will go next. At first, it's funny to the group, but it gets old quickly. His disposition is like that of a bear. Bruno is cuddly and sweet, but if you make him mad, then all heck will break loose.

Calvin Reynolds (African American): Whenever the team is in a tight spot, he gets them out. Always prepared and three steps ahead with a backup plan. He's mature for his age, stoic, an amazing self-taught martial artist, and an amateur detective with a keen mind. He's a voracious reader, but he only reads non-fiction. He figures, "What's the point of reading fiction when my life is one giant tragic adventure?"

Mika Fukuyama (Japanese American): A twelve-year-old skateboarder and surfer with the worst tragic experience out of all the kids in the orphanage, Mika has a secret she's keeping from the group that could change everything. The clock is ticking for her, and she doesn't want to waste a minute. She's a thrill-seeker, risk-taker, and the de facto leader of the group, though that's mostly because of her age, as she butts heads sometimes with Calvin and Francesca over that topic.

Alana Martinez (Puerto Rican): Ten years old and the younger sister of Bruno, she loves comic books as much, if not more, than her brother. She's a fantastic artist, advanced for her age, and wants to become a comic book artist. She's the yin to her brother's yang and a sarcastic, sneaky little devil. Trust is hard to gain with Alana, and she'll do anything for those she loves, even if she won't admit that love to the group. She's also harboring a dark secret. Something that not even her brother remembers. She was responsible for the Chupacabra that destroyed her family and almost devoured her town. It's a pain that haunts her dreams every night.

William Jones (English): William has lived longer than any man has the right to and carries around too many secrets. Especially one that, if Marysia ever found out, would force her to leave him and the orphanage. And if the children ever found out, it could mean the end of the Nightcrawlers. Not much is known about his childhood except that he was born in London, England. He raised Marysia since she was a child and is the only person he talks to and confides in.

When William was twenty, he made his film debut in the horror production The Bride of the Count. It took the country by storm and frightened adults and children alike. It catapulted him to career stardom. It was a good distraction from the horrors of his past, the mistakes he made, and the lives he cost.

But now, as an old man hoping to enter retirement from a career, he kept up with more so out of guilt. He will find a second chance in life with the new Nightcrawlers if his past doesn't come back to haunt them.

Marysia Tatiana Lopez (Puerto Rican): Nickname Tati. Thirty-one years old. Marysia doesn't remember much of her life before the age of nine. Not even what her birth parents were like or what they looked like.

And anytime she's tried to remember anything about her past childhood, it's been nothing but fog. She tried various therapies and doctors growing up, but none have been able to help her. All that she knows is a tragedy struck her family and her parents were dear friends to William.

Whale's University in Somers Town, London, England.

After Marysia's graduation, William expected her to leave the nest and establish her own life. But she didn't want to leave the man she knew and loved as her father. She decided to stay and help him run his orphanage, and help other kids as he helped her. That was quite a shock to William as he had planned to retire and leave the orphanage and his estate to the town.

Along with a handsome endowment to ensure its prosperity well into the future.

William was reluctant, but seeing how happy the thought of working with him made Marysia, he gave in. The two could never fathom how soon their little family would fall apart and the dangers that would befall the new self-appointed Nightcrawlers.

SKETCHES

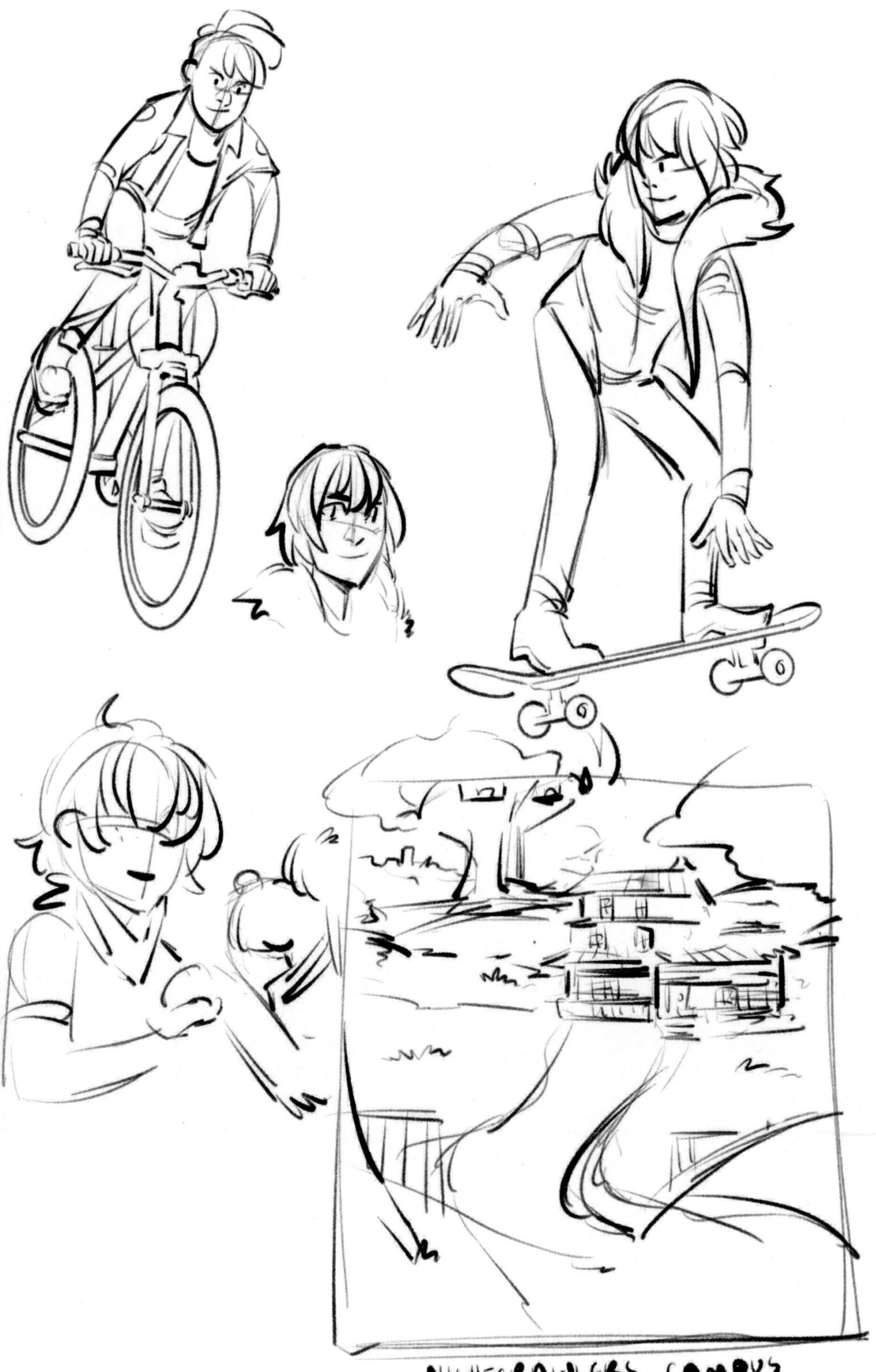
NIGHTCRAWLERS CAMPUS

THE NIGHTCRAWLERS

THE BOY WHO CRIED WOLF

Writer: Marco Lopez
Artist/Cover: Rachel Distler
Colorist: Francesco Montalbano
Letterer: DC Hopkins

For Ablaze
Managing Editor: Rich Young
Editor: Kevin Ketner
Associate Editor: Amy Jackson
Designers: Rodolfo Muraguchi & Julia Stezovsky

THE NIGHTCRAWLERS VOL 1: THE BOY WHO CRIED WOLF. Published by Ablaze Publishing, 11222 SE Main St. #22906 Portland, OR 97269. The Nightcrawlers © 2023 Marco Lopez and Rachel Distler. All rights reserved. Ablaze TM & © 2023 ABLAZE, LLC. All rights reserved. Ablaze and its logo TM & © 2023 Ablaze, LLC. All Rights Reserved. All names, characters, events, and locales in this publication are entirely fictional. Any resemblance to actual persons (living or dead), events or places, without satiric intent is coincidental. No portion of this book may be reproduced by any means (digital or print) without the written permission of Ablaze Publishing except for review purposes. Printed in China. For advertising and licensing email: HYPERLINK "mailto:info@ablazepublishing.com"info@ablazepublishing.com

Publisher's Cataloging-in-Publication data
Names: Lopez, Marco, author. | Distler, Rachel, artist.
Title: The nightcrawlers vol 1 : the boy who cried , wolf / [Marco Lopez; Rachel Distler].
Description: Portland, OR: Ablaze, 2022.
Identifiers: ISBN: 978-1-68497-058-2
Subjects: LCSH Werewolves--Comic books, strips, etc. | Child detectives--Comic books, strips, etc. | Mystery and detective stories. | Graphic novels.| BISAC JUVENILE FICTION / Comics & Graphic Novels / Paranormal | JUVENILE FICTION / Comics & Graphic Novels / Action & Adventure
Classification: LCC PZ7.7 .L67 Nig 2022 | DDC 741.5--dc23

 /ablazepub
 @AblazePub
 @AblazePub

www.ablaze.net

To find a comics shop in your area go to:
www.comicshoplocator.com

Contributors

4thWall Comics
Adam Kurzawa
Amanda Alnor
Andrew Taylor
Andrew Valdez
Andy Korty
Angela Wright
Art Zager
Austin Hough
Brent Fisher
Brent Schoonover
Brett Schenker
Brittany Matter
Byron O'Neal
Caleb Schoettlin
Carmen Lopez
Chad Stewart
Corinne Voith
Damien Becton
Dan Membiela
Dedren Snead
Ellora Carman-Boidock @
Pegasus Bookstore
Emily Aldridge
Emma Bierbaum
Eric Moss
Eric Palicki
Erik Carrasquillo
Evelynn Henry
Fell Hound
Gabe Martini
Gamer Bun
George Gant
George McRedmond
Greg AE
Gregory Milken
J L
James Emmett
James Ferguson
James Gaspero
Jared Lachmann
Jason Quinn
Jeff Trexler
Jenny Fleming
JOHN PEREZ
Jon Duckworth
Jordan Plosky
Jose Rodriguez
Joshua Harris
Kelsey deBorja
Kevin Joseph
KG Ming
Lauren Cramer

Leah Hooten
Leo Chan
lesly julien
Lisa Van Keuren
Liv Williams
Mark Poulton
Mark Roma
Martin Sexton
Mary Bierbaum
Mary Booth
Matt Lazorwitz
Matthew Murphy
Michael Calero
Michael Nimmo
Michael Parreno
Michael Perler
Michele Abounader
Mike Greene
Neil Schwartz
Ngeah! Comics
Nicholas Nace
Nicholas Poonamallee
Nicholette Stachowiak
Nina Kelechi
Noah Dominguez
Nydia Cardona
Pao Xyo
Patrick Coyle
Pearl Smith
Peggy Vera
Peter Crawford
PJ K
Randall Armstrong
rhea wolpoe
Rich Young
Richard Durante
Richard Hamilton
Richard Lafortune
Robert Jeffrey
Ronald Sioson
Roy Mitchell
Sarah Allen
Savannah Elise
Supriya Saxena
Terry Sala
Tom Lynott
Tony Cade @ Challenges
Games
Victoria Zukas
Wayne Hall
Wendy Schoettlin
William William
Zoe Tunnell

THE END?